STEAL A KISS

Julia Jarrett

CONTENTS

Chapter One

Evie

"Now, listen. Kai's a total softie, but he doesn't love animals the way I do, so you have to behave, alright? No barking, no chewing his shoes, or peeing on the carpet. We need him to like you so he lets you stay."

Great. I'm trying to negotiate with a homeless puppy.

Which is kind of ironic, seeing as the whole reason I'm currently standing outside my older brother's apartment building with a duffle bag over one shoulder is because I, too, am about to be homeless.

Thanks, campus housing staff, for giving me less than a week to get out of my university apartment after finishing my graduate degree in special education. Guess they don't realize the housing situation in Vancouver is absolutely insane.

As much as I don't want to admit to it, I'm grateful Kai basically insisted I crash on his couch until I can find a job with a local school district. His generosity makes it possible for me to focus on my job search without any distractions, like finding a place or coming up with rent money working a summer job.

Of course, that was before this morning, when I came across this dirty, sad bundle of fur on the side of the road.

Just when I thought I had a solid plan in place for finding my footing post grad school, an adorable set of puppy dog eyes goes and throws it off track. I can't explain it, the instant connection I felt. But something in me insisted I save her, and even more, keep her. I know I was meant to be the one to find her.

The puppy tilts her head to the side and gives a little yip, and I shake my own head to clear it.

"You're lucky I found you, girl. This might be the craziest thing I've ever done, but we're in it together now. You and me, against the world." I look up at Kai's building. "As long as big brother doesn't slam the door in your cute face."

I use the fob Kai gave me to buzz myself inside and move to the elevators. When the doors slide open, the puppy freezes with a little whine.

"Come on girl, it's okay. You're safe." I keep my voice soft, but it's clear she's not moving. "Fine, but don't get used to this. You're not going to be a small puppy for long." I heft her up in my arms, earning a very wet kiss to my cheek, and step into the elevator. It takes some shifting to free one hand to push the button for Kai's floor, because this puppy already isn't small. The shelter estimated she was only a few months old, but she has massive paws and a big block-shaped head that makes me think she's going to be huge.

I try to set her down, and she just wriggles and whines some more. "Oh my God, you big baby." I huff, but I can't hold back my smile. I love dogs. Always wanted one growing up, but my asthma was a lot worse back then than it is now, so my parents refused, saying the doctors advised no pets with fur.

The elevator doors open on Kai's floor and I step out. Finally, the puppy allows me to put her down. It takes some coaxing to get her to walk down the short hall to his apartment, but we make it, and I turn the handle to push the door open, still looking down at her as she snuffles the ground behind me.

"What the hell is that?"

My head shoots up at Kai's shocked voice, and I stumble over the puppy who has somehow managed to move in front of me. I'm about to meet the ground with my face when strong arms are grabbing me, saving me from crashing.

"Easy there, darlin'."

Oh crap.

That voice. That smooth, low southern voice. I know if I look, I'll see the short brown hair, warm eyes that I've gotten lost in more than once over the last six years, and deep dimples that voice belongs to. It takes a lot of self-control not to let myself melt into his arms the way I've always wanted to, but my pride wins out, giving me the strength to extricate myself from Rhett Darlington's hold.

But there are limits to my self-control. Especially when it comes to the man I've had a crush on since my embarrassing teenage years. And acknowledging his presence would push me past those limits right now, even if part of me hates being rude and not acknowledging his role in preventing me from hitting the ground.

Instead, I keep my gaze firmly on my brother who's standing to the side, his arms crossed as he tries to ignore the puppy dancing at his feet.

"It's a puppy, Kai, I know you're just an athlete, but don't play the dumb jock around me."

His dark gaze, so similar to mine, narrows into a glare that is the perfect combination of sibling love and sibling annoyance, as I hear a muffled sound of amusement come from next to me. But I continue to ignore Rhett. Had I known he would be here, I would've... Well, I probably would have tried to find a reason not to come.

"Why is there a puppy in my apartment, Gigi?"

"Don't call me that," I say, my automatic response every time he uses that awful nickname. Even if it does exist solely because I couldn't pronounce my own name as a toddler.

Then, taking a step farther into the apartment, I bend down to unclip the leash from the puppy's collar. It's just as frayed and old as the leash, but the best the shelter could offer. I was grateful they had even that since my alternative was carrying her everywhere.

She takes off toward Kai, and almost immediately trips over her own feet. Kai tries — and fails — to muffle a snort of laughter. "Pair of klutzes, both of you." He softens the teasing by pulling me in for a hug. "But seriously. Why do you have a puppy?"

I pull back from his hug, watching the puppy attack a pair of shoes. Until Rhett goes to gently remove them from her, and I swing my gaze elsewhere. "I found her this morning when I was out for a walk. I tried taking her to the shelter, but they were going to put her down. I couldn't let that happen. She's so sweet, and I'll do everything. You won't even know she's here, I promise." Turning to look up at Kai, I make a pleading gesture with my hands. I hate feeling like I'm begging him for this when he's already done so much for me. Things I can never repay him for, like helping with tuition, and now, pushing me to stop being stubborn and accept his offer of a place to stay. I couldn't argue that it made sense to crash on his couch instead of potentially having to move again when I find a job.

I watch his face soften as he crouches down to pet the dog. It's a promising sign from the guy who doesn't love dogs, made even more so when she immediately flops over onto her back. Then I hear him swear under his breath.

"Evie, I want to say yes, but she can't stay here."

I stoop down beside him, rubbing the puppy's belly. "Why not? I promise she won't get in the way." I don't ask my brother for much, hardly anything. But this...this I need from him.

"Because my building doesn't allow dogs." He looks over at me, regret on his face. "I'm sorry."

That's a complication I didn't expect. I slump down to sit on the floor, trying not to let myself get emotional over a puppy I just met this morning. A puppy whose future is now very uncertain.

Kai pulls me in to his side, rubbing his hand up and down my arm. "Sorry, sis."

Rhett, who's been a silent observer up until now, crouches down beside us, his close proximity making my stomach twist. He stretches out his hand for the puppy to sniff with a gentle smile. And my body rebels against my better sense as I look out of the corner of my eye at him. Dang it, so much for hoping he had somehow become less attractive in the time since I last saw him. Would it kill the guy to grow a pervy mustache or have a pimple?

But no, he's just as good looking as ever. It's a battle not to be too obvious as I drink in his tall, muscular body, the dusting of hair over his corded forearms, and the little dimple in his chin.

I suck in a sharp breath, my mouth goes dry, and my heart speeds up. All because he smells so darn good. It's unfair, really. That a man should be that handsome, that charming, *and* smell so delicious. Like a warm day at the lake in springtime. All fresh, and woodsy, and just...God. No. Snap out of this, Evangeline Yamaki. You're smarter than this.

Rhett Darlington is not an option. Not now, not ever.

Besides, I promised myself I'd stick to my priorities — find a job, find a place to live. No distractions, especially not six-foot-something baseball players.

"Listen. Why don't we call around to some other shelters? Someone's gotta have room for her, or a foster or something."

I'm already shaking my head before Kai finishes talking. "We did that when I took her to the first one. They called three others; every single one is full."

"Damn." Kai runs his hand through his hair, looking over at Rhett. "Got any ideas?"

Rhett makes a noise, like he's thinking, as he continues to pet the dog. "Friends? Anyone from your classes that might want a dog?" He's looking straight at me, but I can't make myself meet his stare. Can he tell my heart is still racing?

"I guess I could ask Lina," I say, mentioning one of my two closest friends. She's already got two kids and a bird, but maybe she wouldn't mind a temporary puppy? Until I remember something. "Wait, no, her son is terrified of dogs."

"Carlee?" Kai names my other friend and roommate throughout university.

"Nope, she's moving into a tiny studio apartment, and she's gone all day." I think through my former classmates, but no one stands out as a good option. Still, if it means this sweet girl has a home until I do, then I have to try. "I guess if I can't think of someone, I'll have to take her back to the shelter."

My disappointment fills the room, causing a somber silence to fall. Even the puppy has quieted down and is simply lying between us all, resting her head on her paws.

"Wait."

I lift my head to see Kai staring at Rhett.

"Dude. Your building allows dogs. You could —"

"Stop right there, Yami," Rhett interjects, his head shaking back and forth. "You know full well how much I'm gone, no way can I have a dog right now."

"How can you say no to that sweet face?" My brother gestures down to the puppy who has lifted her head, tilting it to the side.

I'm holding my breath, not sure how I feel about this conversation; the one I'm apparently not a part of.

"Yami, no. I'm not taking the dog."

"Not just the dog. Evie *and* the dog."

"Wait, what?" I interject, certain I heard wrong. "Kai, no."

He turns to me. "Hear me out. I hate that you were gonna be stuck on my couch. Rhett's got a spare bedroom at his place, *and* he can have dogs in his building. So why don't you both stay there?" Then, turning to Rhett, he says, "What do you think, bro? It's just for the summer, two months, tops. Just 'til she finds a job and a place of her own, right, Evie?"

Two sets of eyes turn back to me, looking for what, I don't know. Confirmation that this idea is crazy? My mind immediately starts trying to come up with a good reason why this is a terrible idea. Even if it is currently the *only* idea that lets me keep the dog.

Before I can come up with anything, Kai continues.

"Besides, Darling's like another brother to you anyway. It won't be all that different from staying here except you get a bed, not a couch, and the dog can stay."

My jaw clenches. There's so much wrong with what he just said, but there's also just enough right that I'm forced to consider my options.

Which amount to basically nothing.

I make myself turn my head to look at *him*, on purpose, for the first time since walking into Kai's apartment.

"Don't let Kai steamroll this, Rhett. It's your home. I don't want to invade your privacy."

Rhett gives me a gentle smile, that large hand of his still rhythmically stroking the dog's back. "I appreciate that, Evie, but my mama would slap me if she knew I turned away a friend who needed help. Especially one who's basically like family, as Kai said."

Ignoring the wince at his choice of words, I push on, needing to be certain he's truly fine with this. "Are you sure? You'd be okay with me and the puppy staying there? As soon as I get a job, I'll find an apartment of my own and be gone. And while you're traveling I can clean up, water your plants, whatever."

He just lifts his shoulder in an effortless shrug. "It's not a problem, darlin'. Like Yami said, I've got the space." He looks down at the dog, his smile deepening. "And this little lady deserves a second chance at life."

Well, crap. When he says stuff like that, I'm tempted to take the lid off my years-old crush and swoon all over him again.

"Okay. If you're sure, I guess I'll move my stuff into your place tomorrow, not here," I say quietly, still somewhat hoping he'll laugh and say he was joking and there's no way I can stay with him. Not that I have anywhere else to go, but still, the idea of living with Rhett is...slightly terrifying.

"Wait, where's the puppy going to stay tonight? Are you even allowed a dog in campus housing?" Kai asks, and I swear it's as if he's intentionally adding fuel to my panic fire.

"Um, n-no," I stammer out. "But I'll sneak her in, it's fine." After all, I'm technically finished with my master's degree, all that's missing from my graduation is the fancy piece of paper. What's the worst the university could do? Kick me out of housing? Too late, the deadline to move out is in two days.

"Or I can take her home with me tonight," Rhett says calmly.

"Oh no, I can't ask you to do that," I start to protest, my head shaking back and forth. "I have to go to the store and get her some food, and a bed, and well, everything. It's fine. I'll —"

"Let me take her." His soothing, deep voice interrupts me, and a warm hand lands on my arm. "I can cook up some rice and chicken for her tonight, and tomorrow we'll go together and get what she needs."

"Dude, we have practice and a game tomorrow."

Rhett looks at Kai and frowns. "Shit."

"I'll go to the store tomorrow and get what she needs. She's my dog," I interject, sharply pulling my arm away from Rhett.

Only to regret my tone. I do need his help for just tonight, and I don't want to seem ungrateful. I incline my head toward

Rhett. "But thank you, if you'll take her tonight, that would be great."

He smiles and nods, as if everything is settled and done.

Kai stands up and claps his hands together, making the puppy squirm to stand up and shake as well. "Great. Problem solved. Rhett takes the dog tonight, and tomorrow Evie moves her shit into his spare bedroom."

He reaches a hand out and pulls me up to stand before draping an arm around my neck and leading me into the kitchen. "Can we eat now? I'm fucking starving."

My brother might be ready to move on to dinner, but I'm still three steps behind, trying to figure out how I went from crashing by myself on his couch to staying with the object of many late-night fantasies, with a puppy in tow.

Chapter Two

Rhett

Can't say that I expected to spend my night having a standoff with a black and grey puppy with the floppiest ears you're ever gonna see, but here we are.

"Listen, little lady, there's no gettin' around it. You're gonna do your business before you come inside."

Her head cocks to the side, and I'm fighting a grin at how dang cute she is.

"C'mon now, let's get this over with," I cajole, crouching down to scratch her ears. All that earns me is a wet tongue along my forearm. I chuckle and straighten to stand before gently tugging the leash to get her walking.

"Fine, let's try somewhere else."

Swear on my mama's heart, if the guys saw me sweet-talking a puppy, they'd die laughing. I'm a charmer, I don't try to deny it. But normally my talents are best used on gorgeous women. Not dogs.

It takes a few more minutes, but finally, the little princess squats down and takes care of things.

"There you go, little lady," I murmur, scooping her up into my arms. "Now we can go inside and get you some grub in that belly of yours."

I carry the pup into my building. She whimpers at the elevator, but Evie had warned me she was nervous of them when we left Yami's.

Evie. Now there's a gorgeous woman. Long, cascading black hair, delicate features on a face that shows every emotion, a strong body, yet soft in the right places. She's short, I noticed that yet again when I was standing next to her earlier. She'd fit perfectly under my arm. And fuck, she smelled like jasmine floating in the breeze on a warm summer evening.

But none of that matters. She's my best friend's little sister. That alone makes her off-limits.

Which is what I have to remember, at all costs. Even if after six years of knowing her, she's no longer a teenager but rather a stunning young woman. One so full of compassion and fire, and one who has me struggling to stop imagining all the forbidden ways I want to get to know this grown-up version of her.

The ding of the elevator reaching my floor breaks me free from the dangerous direction my thoughts are headed. I stride down the hall, unlock my door, set the dog down, and close and lock it behind me before sinking to the floor.

The puppy immediately clambers back up into my lap, front paws landing on my chest. Her wet tongue is soft on my skin, but I don't push the dog away.

Until she licks my ear.

"Okay. That's enough of that." I set her down in my lap, gently guiding her to lie down so her head is on my knees, her belly stretched out in front of me. She wriggles from side to side as I tickle her belly, her adorable antics providing the distraction

I hoped she would.

Agreeing to take the dog was one thing. Agreeing to have Evie stay here? That might be the first sign I'm slipping into madness. What the hell was Yami thinking? The problem is, I know exactly what he was thinking. He figured his best friend was the perfect person to help his little sister out, because in his mind, she's like a sister to me, too.

Except the feelings toward Evie that I've been trying to ignore for years?

Definitely not brotherly.

My phone starts to vibrate in my pocket, and I twist to the side to pull it out, already knowing who it is.

"Hey Mama." I grin as her face fills the screen.

"Hey, baby, how's my favorite boy?"

"I'm fine. Had dinner with Yami and his sister." I lean back against the door, holding the puppy out of sight for now. I know exactly how she'll react, and I'd rather have a bit of conversation first.

"Oh, how nice. How are they doin'?" Mama's on her old couch, a cup of tea in her hand. It's late in Tennessee, but she calls me like clockwork every week at this time.

"Good. Evie just finished her degree." I debate telling her about my new roommate situation but decide not to. "Yami's the same as always. A pain in my ass."

Mama laughs. "You two always were trouble. But that Evie, she's one smart cookie." My mom's met Yami and Evie, and their parents, a couple of times over the years. It was inevitable with how long Yami and I have played ball together.

I nod. She is. Smartest woman I know, not that I'll say that to Mama. Of course, the puppy chooses that moment to decide she's done being ignored and digs her razor-sharp teeth into my finger.

"Ow, you little rascal, that ain't cool." I pull my finger free and examine it. There's puncture marks but no blood. Still, I scowl at the puppy who's got an innocent look on her furry face.

"Rhett? Who are you talking to?"

My head lifts to look at the phone. "Sorry, Mama." I lift the puppy in my arms, but she's not content to stay still, wriggling back and forth, slipperier than an eel. "Evie found this little lady on the road this mornin'. Since Kai can't have pets at his apartment, I'm the lucky one who gets to hang on to her for now."

As expected, my mother's squeal is high-pitched and beyond excited. She's retired now but was a veterinary assistant when I was younger, so we always had dogs running around. And chickens, cats, even a couple of goats at one point. My grandparents had some land outside Knoxville where Mama and I stayed for a couple of years after my father passed, and they had horses, along with all our other animals.

"Look at that gorgeous little face," Mama croons. "Hold the phone still, Rhett, I want a good look at my grandpuppy."

"Mama," I groan, rising to stand so I can prop the phone up against the basket of fruit on my kitchen counter. "She's not mine, don't go getting attached."

But even as I say that, I dutifully hold the puppy as still as I can manage, so Mama can get a good look at her.

"Oh, she's so sweet. What a good girl, yes, you are, you're the very best girl."

My smile is unavoidable. Making my mother happy is always my goal. Has been ever since Dad died, leaving the two of us alone. He told me to take care of her, and I have. Always will.

"Listen, I need to get this little one fed, and then figure out where she's gonna sleep. Evie's stopping by tomorrow with some supplies, but for now, it's just me and her."

"You've always got cooked chicken in that big ol' fridge of yours, heat some of that up with some sweet potato or rice. And make sure you give her a comfortable space of her own, maybe the bathroom. She'll be happier in a small room."

I smother my chuckle at how quickly she moved into animal welfare mode. "Yes, Mama. I know."

Her face melts back into one of pure adoration. "Of course, you do. You're a good boy, Rhett. You'll take good care of her."

I haven't been a boy for a long time, but I don't remind Mama of that. "Yes, ma'am." We say goodnight, and I set the puppy down as I move into the kitchen. Just as Mama predicted, there's containers of diced chicken breast and sweet potato already in my fridge, precooked and labeled, thanks to my obsession with meal prepping for the weeks when I'm at home.

Scooping some of each into a plastic container, I mash it together, add some warm water to make it easier for her puppy teeth, then set it on the ground. Seeing as all Kai had earlier that was safe for a puppy to eat was some eggs we scrambled up quickly, I'm not surprised when she devours the food quickly now.

"Hungry girl," I say softly, running my hand down her back. "No more or you'll make yourself sick. But we'll get some proper food tomorrow."

Now that she's fed, I turn my attention to figuring out sleeping arrangements. But once again, mother knows best. I grab some old towels and lay them out on the floor of my en suite bathroom before removing anything she could get into.

I go through my own nighttime routine quickly with the puppy pouncing on my toes the entire time. Guess she didn't get the memo that it's bedtime. Too bad, because I'm exhausted and tomorrow's a long day of practice and a game in the evening.

"Good night, little lady," I say when I'm done, turning the light down low and closing the door.

Her whimpers are audible through the door, same as the scratch of claws against the wood. I stay silent for a few minutes to see if she'll settle, and after a minute or two, it seems she does. Turning onto my side, I close my eyes.

I open them again, barely a handful of minutes later, when the whimpering starts again, this time escalating into a louder whine.

Tossing off the covers, I climb out of bed and open the door to see her sitting there, tail wagging back and forth.

"Listen up, it's bedtime," I say firmly. "That means no whining, just sleeping. You're safe, you're warm, you're fed. Now hush." Closing the door again, I wait with only the tiniest bit of hope that she'll listen.

This time, I manage to get back into bed, pull the covers up, close my eyes, and start to drift off before she starts up again.

With a growl, I get out of bed once more. When I open the door again, she darts through my legs and tries to jump onto my bed. Her attempts are cute, her little tail wagging as she looks over her shoulder at me.

"You're trouble, aren't you," I rumble, giving in to the inevitable. I know Mama would scold me for spoiling her, but damn it, I need sleep.

I lift her up onto the bed before climbing back in myself. She immediately makes herself at home, curling into a little ball next to me before letting out a big yawn.

"You pee in this bed and we're gonna have a problem," I mumble, but it's too late. Her little puppy eyes are already drifting closed.

Chapter Three

Rhett

Well, the puppy didn't pee in my bed.

Instead, I was woken up by a tongue on my face and some loud whimpers no less than four times last night.

Which could've been the start of some good times if that tongue and those whimpers belonged to a woman and not a damn dog.

But thanks to Evie's damn bleeding heart, I'm on my second cup of coffee by 8 am, having given up on sleep somewhere around five thirty. The puppy, or Jack, as I've decided to call her, is racing around my apartment like she's chasing a gopher.

I'm scowling at the little scamp, even if she is fucking cute as hell, when there's a knock on my door. Not a lot of people have access to my apartment. Yami and Mama have a set of keys, and Monty, too, since he lives in the same building.

I'll blame the lack of sleep for the fact that I don't remember giving Evie a set of building keys last night until I yank open the door and see her startled face. A large bin is in her arms, and a backpack is on her back.

"H-hi," she stammers, her eyes darting all over except at me. "Is this an okay time? I know we said eight, but I can come by later when you're gone."

I hold up a hand to stop her rambling and step to the side, only then realizing I'm still shirtless, wearing nothing but my pajama pants. I guess that explains her awkwardness. I'd apologize, but I'm too exhausted.

"It's fine," I say, my voice still rough from sleep. "I've been up for a while. Jack thinks sleep is for the weak."

Evie's already down on her knees loving on the damn terror, but she lifts her head to look at me. And I can't help but notice her cheeks turning pink when her gaze goes over my bare chest. "Jack?"

I sink back down onto one of the stools lining my kitchen counter. "Short for Jackass. Trust me, you'll understand when you're the one waking up every couple of hours."

I see her fighting a laugh as she presses a kiss to the puppy's head. "Sorry, Rhett."

"It's fine." I stand up, setting down my coffee and stretching my arms overhead. Once again, Evie's eyes dart over to me, then back to the puppy, then back again, bouncing back and forth like a tennis ball. A part of me is intrigued by her reaction. But I tamp that down quickly.

Clearing my throat, I move toward my bedroom. "I'll just get dressed and then we can get the rest of your stuff moved in."

She nods, giving the puppy one last kiss before standing up. "Okay, I don't have much."

A few minutes and one awkwardly silent elevator ride later, I follow her out to the front of my building where a bright blue hatchback is parked in the loading zone. Evie opens the trunk and reaches for a bin.

"We can leave it here for a few minutes, but once your stuff is inside you can move it into the underground." I give her my spare key fob for getting into the parking garage before lifting out the suitcase and duffle bag sitting in the back seat.

When I turn back to Evie, she's setting another bin on top of the first one waiting on the sidewalk and she closes the trunk.

"Is that it?" I ask, and Evie shrugs.

"Yep. Don't need much when you live in campus housing, it's fully furnished."

We take the last of Evie's belongings upstairs, where we're enthusiastically greeted by the puppy, who also left behind a puddle of dog piss as a gift.

"Crap, sorry." Evie springs into action, grabbing paper towels off the counter and wiping it up. She pauses and looks at me. "Um. Where's the garbage can?"

"Under the sink."

She moves to dispose of the paper towel, coming back with a bottle of spray cleaner she must've found.

Soon, the mess is gone, and Evie's clipping a leash onto the old collar around the puppy's neck. "I'll take her out, then move my car."

She's gone before I can respond, and it's only as the door closes behind the two of them that I exhale. I never expected things to feel so fucking awkward between us without Yami around.

And I've got up to two more months with her living here, showering here, eating here, hell, sleeping just down the hall from me night after night?

Fuck.

The Vancouver Tridents' facility is probably the best I've ever played in. State-of-the-art training and treatment centers, a field that dreams are made of, and a team of players and staff that make my job easy. All I gotta do is walk out on that field, catch some balls, hit some balls, and run some bases.

In the locker room, I drop down on the bench next to Yami.

"Hey man, did Evie get her stuff to your place?"

I nod. "She didn't bring over much." I cast a glance his way, but he doesn't seem surprised.

"Yeah, she doesn't like having a lot of shit, and her campus apartment was tiny and fully furnished." He finishes pulling on a compression shirt and turns to me. "I'm glad she's with you, bro. Keep an eye on her, okay? And if she gets sick, call me right away." His expression sobers as he pulls off his ball cap and flips it around in his hand. "You probably didn't know this, because by the time we met she was a lot better. But she had really bad asthma as a kid."

I let out a low whistle. "Damn."

"Yeah. It was scary shit. In and out of hospitals, on puffers and nebulizers. Mom and Dad always told my sisters and me that we had to look out for her at school and stuff. Make sure she was okay and not overexerting herself. Which was fine, whatever. But when she got older, Evie started getting kinda mad that we kept babying her." He grimaces. "It's a hard habit to break. Looking after her, I mean. Getting her to accept help with tuition was a fucking battle; she only gave in when I pointed out that her only other option was staying at home with our parents."

I exhale slowly. I had no idea Evie was sick as a kid. But some of her words and actions from earlier make sense now. She's someone who desperately wants to prove that she's okay. That she doesn't need looking after.

"Is she okay now?"

"Yeah, she still has asthma, but it's not as bad. Only comes out if she gets sick. I know it's not likely, being summer, but seriously. She gets a sniffle, call me. She's old enough to manage it herself, but that doesn't stop me from worrying about her."

His worry seems a bit much to me, but what do I know? I don't have siblings.

A bunch of the other guys walk in then, ending our conversation. The locker room quickly fills with the noise and chaos of all of us getting ready for our quick warm-up practice before we get some rest, then come back for the game tonight.

Yami starts talking with our starting catcher Monty, leaving me alone. I finish getting my gear on and head to the field, nodding my head at Lark, Monty's girlfriend, who's rubbing her pregnant belly as she walks toward her office in the trainer area.

"How ya feelin', baby mama?" I ask, slowing to walk beside her.

Lark grimaces but turns it into a smile. "Good, even if this baby is choosing to do somersaults on my bladder right now."

I cringe and sling my arm over her shoulder. "Y'know, my mama always said she knew I was gonna be a big boy because I had big feet even in her belly. She could feel 'em kickin' her all night. Said she figured I'd be a football player. Maybe your girl's got a future in gymnastics."

She laughs, shaking her head. "We'll see, I guess. Have a good practice, Rhett."

I give her a wave as we part ways, and I head to the field. It's good to see Monty and Lark together at last. It's even better not to have to see Monty pining over his best girl friend like he has for the last few years. But it also drives home the truth that my buddies on the team are all pairing up. Falling in love. It used to be fun, going out with the guys, sweet-talking the ladies. Now it just leaves me feeling kinda empty. Like I'm missing something great.

Maybe someday I'll know what it's like to have a partner in life. Someone to love, who loves me in return.

Someday. Not today.

Chapter Four

Evie

The second the door closes behind Rhett, my body relaxes, my shoulders drop away from my ears, and my pulse slows to a normal rhythm.

If I thought I had a handle on the annoying crush I've harboured for far too long, all it took was him opening the door with no shirt on, and deliciously rumpled hair, to tell me I was very wrong.

"I am in so much trouble," I mumble under my breath. The puppy wanders over and sits down at my feet after abandoning the mess she was making drinking water from a clear plastic container Rhett must have put out for her.

I smile down at her and bend over to ruffle her floppy ears. If I had to guess, she's at least part Great Dane, but definitely not purebred. There's a few other things mixed in, giving her the sweetest face, floppy ears, and big gangly body. She looks like her parts don't quite fit together, yet they do, and wow, do I ever empathize with that feeling. The difference is, she's got a good chance of growing into herself. Whereas I'm meant to be fully grown, if you will, and still don't feel like I fit.

I missed a lot of school as a kid, thanks to frequent hospital admissions. Not that I struggled to catch up, school came easy to me. But being absent so much made it hard to form friendships. To say nothing of the years when mean, ignorant kids thought asthma was contagious, so I was often avoided altogether.

But it's all over now. I'm finished with school, master's degree in hand. There's nothing between me and the real world.

And that real world is already knocking me sideways with my current housing and employment situation. While special education is a field with a desperate need for qualified teachers, finding a job that lets me stay near the city, near Kai, doesn't seem to be as simple as I hoped it would be. And over the last two years, I've come to love it here, the combination of mountains on one side and ocean on the other, the vibrancy of the city, and the easy access to quieter areas to explore outside the city limits. Everything is here, including my brother and my friends. And I don't want to leave.

Scooping up the puppy, I move to the pile of my belongings Rhett helped me move in this morning. I hate clutter, and a quick look around Rhett's apartment makes it clear he's a tidy person as well. Which means I need to get all of this moved into the bedroom he pointed out before he left.

It doesn't take long, a benefit to not having a lot of stuff, and I've got my clothes put away, my stack of books I want to read on the nightstand, and my few photos set up on the dresser. One is of my grandmother and me, one of my entire family, Kai in his college baseball uniform the year he got scouted to his first major league team, and one of Lina, Carlee, and me from three years ago when I let them drag me out to celebrate my twenty-first birthday. I smile at the photo, remembering how I tried to argue that with the legal drinking age being nineteen in Canada, turning twenty-one was no big deal. But they teamed up against me, and treated me to a lovely dinner, then dancing at a salsa club. We had an amazing time, and our happiness is captured perfectly in the photo the dance instructor at the club took of the three of us.

That was also the night I lost my virginity, to a man I had been dancing with at the club. That part was less than amazing. Fine, I guess, but not enough to make me desperate to do it again. The next couple of times were just as lackluster.

Carlee likes to tease me that I've got everything in my life figured out except my social life. And she's not wrong, it just hasn't been a priority for me.

And it won't be until I have a job and am out of Rhett's apartment. That's for certain.

I wander back out into the main living area, now free of my boxes and bags, and take another look around.

Rhett's apartment is immaculate. Everything is tasteful, yet simple, clean lines and sparse decorations. There's something missing, but I can't quite put my finger on it as I move slowly around the room, pausing at the fireplace mantle lined with photos. Most are of him and his mom, but there's a few of him with Kai and some other Tridents players. One, in the largest frame, front and center, is a much older photograph of a young Rhett with who I'm guessing is his father. Rhett's in a baseball uniform, his dad beaming with pride, as they stand side by side with their arms slung across each other's shoulders.

Kai's mentioned before that Rhett's father is no longer around, but it's clear that at some point, he was an important person in his life. My heart aches for his loss. I can't imagine what it would feel like to lose a parent so young.

I move on from the photographs, my gaze landing on a pair of headphones on a side table. Then it hits me. What's missing are books.

There's not a single book in the apartment. No bookshelf filled half with knickknacks and half with books, no coffee-table books, nothing. Odd, because I swear I can remember Kai saying something to my dad the last time our parents were out visiting about a book he read that Rhett recommended. It stayed in my mind because the book, a historical science fiction, sounded fascinating and I wanted to check the university library for a copy.

But if Rhett's a reader, then where are the books? Or an e-reader or tablet? Anything?

It's hardly a question I need an answer for, but my curiosity gets the better of me, and before I know it, I find myself standing outside his bedroom, my hand on the doorknob.

It would be rude of me to snoop in his bedroom. I know this. Still... My hand turns the knob, and I push the door open just a little. Just enough to look around, taking in the large bed, covered in a deep forest green blanket. The walls are a deep grey, so dark they almost look black. The only thing that seems out of place is a pair of pajama pants — the very ones he answered the door in earlier — dropped on the end of the bed.

And not a book in sight.

I close the door quietly, which is stupid, seeing as there's no one here except me and the puppy.

Crap, the puppy. Hurrying back to the living room, I find her sprawled out on the floor, eyes closed, her little belly lifting up and down slowly.

I look around but don't see any messes I need to clean up. Good. As soon as she wakes, we'll go outside for a potty break, then I had better get to the pet store and grab a few supplies.

Which means she'll need a name, I suppose. I sit sideways in a comfortable-looking chair, draping my legs over the arm so I can watch her sleep.

"What should I call you? Something elegant, I think. Classy, ladylike," I murmur quietly over the light sounds of puppy snores. "Hmm, how about Maeve? No, that's too fussy. Jasmine? Nope, definitely not right." I study her for a few more seconds before it comes to me. "Ruth. Your name is Ruth. Or maybe Ruthie."

As if she hears me, she yawns, stretches, and her little eyes slowly blink open. I get off the chair and pick up the leash from the kitchen counter. "Come on, Ruthie girl. Let's go shopping."

I'm on the floor, Ruth in front of me, as we attempt to work on some obedience commands when the front door opens. Instantly breaking the sit I finally got her into, Ruth bounds over to Rhett.

There's no denying how appealing it is to watch a big handsome baseball player squat down and kiss the top of a puppy's head. And when he straightens with her in his arms, smiling at her excited wriggles, something in my chest flip-flops.

No matter how much I want to pretend I'm not attracted to him, no matter how much I want to insist that my focus is on my future career and not on men, being this close to Rhett without the buffer of my brother or my family around is challenging my self-control.

But I won't break. I won't give in to temptation and put myself out there again. One round of mortification at the hands of Rhett Darlington is enough, thank you very much.

"Aw, c'mon, little lady, did you have to do that?" Rhett grumbles, holding Ruth away from his chest with a frown. A wet spot is evident on his shirt, and I jump up to stand and go to take her from him.

"Sorry, I swear I took her out for a potty break not that long ago." I'm clipping on her leash to take her out again when Rhett puts his hand out and ruffles Ruth's ears.

"It's fine, Evangeline. She's a puppy, they often lose control of things when they get excited. No harm, no foul."

He flashes us a quick grin before pulling off his baseball hat, and then his shirt. My mouth goes dry as all of those muscles covered in golden, tan skin come into view, far closer to me than is comfortable. Gah, it's not fair he looks like that and makes me shiver when he says my full name.

"Right. Yeah. Well, I'll take her out again anyway before bed. And I got some pee pads for overnight so we should be good." I whirl around, shove my feet into the sandals I left at the front door, and leave before I do something stupid, like drool.

Ruth yips excitedly in my arms, and I turn a half-hearted scowl down at her as we wait for the elevator. "Really, Ruthie? Peeing on the man nice enough to give us somewhere to stay for the next couple of months? Not cool. Not at all. He thinks you're cute now, but if you pee on him, or eat his shoes, or whatever other things puppies do that they shouldn't, we're going to be out on our butts."

My lecture only earns me another yip, and I sigh. Stepping into the elevator, I slowly lower her to the floor once the doors close. When she doesn't whine, just plops her cute butt down, I praise her and pull out one of the little treats I have stashed in my pockets with a smile.

We're making progress on conquering her elevator fear. Now to conquer my fear of Rhett somehow discovering my crush is alive and well.

When Ruthie and I get back upstairs after a quick walk, Rhett's changed into a black shirt and his pajama pants. He's in the kitchen, pouring a glass of water.

"I see you went shoppin' for the pup. Does she have a name yet?" he asks, his tone perfectly friendly and nothing more.

I nod, moving to one of the kitchen stools. "Ruth. Or Ruthie. I haven't decided which I like better."

He flashes me an approving smile. "Good name. It suits her."

"Thanks."

An awkward silence settles over us, and even Ruthie's quiet for once.

"I'll be —"

"I wanted —"

My cheeks heat. "Sorry. You go first."

"Ladies first." Rhett inclines his head, taking a sip of water.

I try not to lick my lips as I watch his throat as he swallows. It shouldn't be sexy, but on him, it is. And I'm in so much trouble.

"All I wanted to say was thank you again for letting me stay. And Ruthie. I know it might seem crazy taking in a dog when I don't even have a job, but I couldn't leave her in the shelter. I never thought that Kai's building might not allow her. So I guess I also want to apologize for putting you in this position of having to let us stay. I'd like to help out anyway I can, when you're traveling or whatever," I finish lamely, realizing I've just said way more than necessary. Where's the strong, smart, independent version of myself that defended her master's thesis with confidence just a week ago?

Not here, that's for sure.

"Evie, it's all good. I love dogs, so havin' Miss Ruthie is no problem at all. And I'm always happy to help Yami. And you. Make yourself comfortable while you're here. But speaking of travel, you know we leave for a few days tomorrow. I wanted to make sure you have everything you need while me and Yami are gone."

I nod quickly. "I'll be fine, thank you. I can take care of myself." Wait, that sounded rude. "And the apartment, of course. While you're gone," I hurry to add.

He nods again, and my head bobs up and down.

"Alright then, I guess I'll head to bed. Early start tomorrow. See ya in a few days."

I watch him crouch down to love on Ruthie again, *lucky dog*, then straighten and saunter down the hall to his bedroom.

I wait a few minutes, even after hearing his door snick shut, before scooping up Ruth and making my way to my own room. I set her inside, then duck across the hall to the bathroom, making quick work of my nighttime routine.

Back in my room, Ruthie's sniffing the dog bed I bought for her. I lift her into it, and she circles a few times before collapsing into a pile. Based on what Rhett said about his night with her, I have very low expectations for how much sleep I might get tonight.

But while she's calm, I might as well try to rest. Climbing into the soft, luxurious bed covered in a beautiful grey and white floral duvet, I lie down and let out a slow breath.

One day down, sixty or so more to go.

Chapter Five

Rhett

My eyes close as I lean against the wall of my elevator. It's almost midnight and I'm tired. More tired than a porch swing after a tornado. Six days, two cities, eight games. Those doubleheaders were early on, thank fuck, but my body is still hurting. I know there'll be hell to pay tomorrow when I head to the stadium to see the trainers, but right now, all I want is a hot shower and my bed.

I stagger off the elevator and down the hall to my apartment, trying to be as quiet as possible when I unlock the door. Who knows whether Ruthie is sleeping better than she did those first couple nights, but either way, I don't want to wake up the dog or Evie.

Just thinking about seeing her has some of the tension melting from my shoulders, then tightening right back up again as my conscience kicks my own ass.

I push the door open and stop. She left a light on for me in the kitchen. It's dimmed, but the warm glow is something I haven't had welcoming me home in years. In the low light, I look around, expecting to see signs of puppy mayhem, but the apartment is clean. I wouldn't know I had a temporary roommate or a dog living here if it weren't for a few subtle signs, like her much smaller shoes at the door, a dog leash hanging off the handle of the coat closet, and two mugs set out by the coffee maker instead of one. That last thing makes a smile rise, unbidden. She's thoughtful. The light, the mug, those are things no one has ever done for me.

Hell, my own mama never set out a mug for me, although she did wait up more than once when I'd been out late.

Setting my bag down, I move farther into the apartment, and my gaze lands on a piece of paper on the kitchen counter. I pick it up and curse.

The flowy handwriting must be Evie's.

But my eyes are dry and bleary from travel, and my brain is not functioning anywhere near as well as it could if I wasn't so damn exhausted.

Yeah. That's what I try to tell myself when the letters dance around on the page, the lines and loops making no sense to me. It's got nothing to do with me having wires crossed the wrong way in my brain, and everything to do with me being tired.

I've used that line before.

Still holding that damn note, I pick up my bag again and make my way to my bedroom. Inside, I drop everything, including the note, to the floor. Then I strip off my clothes, for once not caring that I'm leaving a messy trail behind me, and move to the bathroom. I need a fucking shower and a solid eight hours of sleep.

I shower quickly, then pull on a pair of boxers before crawling beneath my clean sheets. Fuck yeah, there's nothing better than the first night in your own bed after a set of away games. Hotels ain't got nothing on my thread count.

But the sleep I desperately need won't come. Instead, I find myself tossing and turning, ears tuned for any sound from the apartment.

This is ridiculous.

I've slept in the same house as Evie before, many times, in fact. Yami and I were instant friends when we were first signed to the same team back East in Buffalo. And with his family living relatively close by, just across the border in the Toronto area, we'd go there for a visit when we could. I've never once struggled to fall asleep simply from knowing that Evie's in the same building as me.

Then again, I haven't spent the night in the same house as her for a few years. Four, to be exact. Not since the time I went back to Yami's parents' house with him and she tried to kiss me.

Fuck, I wanted that kiss. Even then, just barely out of her teen years, she was a stunning young woman. And there was something about her that drew me in. But my conscience wouldn't let me. She was still in university, still living at home, and I was in the early years of my career, freshly traded to the Tridents, a team across the country. To say nothing of her being my best friend's baby sister.

I had to push her away then. Would I do the same now?

I should. For Yami's sake, I should.

Stifling a groan of frustration, I roll out of bed and drop to the floor, working my way through a set of push-ups and sit-ups to try and remind my body of just how goddamn tired we are.

I freeze when I hear a door open and then soft footsteps. Guess I'm not the only one having a hard time sleeping.

Several minutes pass before I hear them return. There's no chance in all of creation that I'll fall asleep knowing they're outside, so I don't even try. But when the quiet click of the guest room door shutting eventually reaches my ears, I let myself fall back against my pillow, my eyes finally falling shut.

We get a rest day after traveling like we did yesterday, so my usual early alarm is turned off. Not that I would have needed it, seeing as my clock registers it's not even 8 am when excited puppy barks rouse me from sleep.

I hear the front door open and close. Guess I might as well get up myself. Throwing off the covers, I grab a pair of shorts and tidy up the mess of my clothes and travel bag that I left last night when I was too tired to do anything.

A piece of paper flutters out from under the sweats I was wearing last night.

Damn. The note.

I snatch it up and flatten it out on my bed, squinting down to see if I can read it. But dyslexia isn't magically fixed by a few hours of sleep.

With a curse, I pick up my phone and open the app that will hopefully be able to convert Evie's handwriting into speech. It works better with printing, but it's my only chance. I never was able to make my brain understand cursive.

Thank fuck, the app works, and I can make out the note.

Welcome home, Rhett.

I went to the store and grabbed a few things, please help yourself if you come in hungry tonight. If I remember correctly, you should have tomorrow morning free. I'd like to make you some breakfast as a thank you for letting me stay.

Oh, and Ruthie has a trick to show you.

Sleep well,

Evie

Damn. Why does she have to be so sweet, so considerate, so...off-limits. The second the electronic voice of my phone finishes reading Evie's note, there's the chime of an incoming message.

A different voice, the one I have programmed to read my messages aloud automatically starts talking, reading Yami's text. Guilt floods me, as if he can somehow sense that I was thinking about his sister just now.

> **YAMI: Hey bro, you better be awake. I'm on my way over. Evie said she's making our grandmother's recipe for tamagoyaki and I'll eat them all if you're not up.**

I pull on a shirt, brush my teeth, and jam a Tridents hat on my head backward before going out into the living room just as the front door opens and Ruthie comes bounding across the floor. Her paws lose traction and she slides into my legs, tumbling over herself, making both Evie and I burst out laughing.

"Well now, little lady, I see we gotta work on some coordination," I say, reaching down to pet the gangly rascal. "Those legs are too darn big for you, aren't they."

"She'll grow into them. I think she's got a lot of Great Dane in her," Evie offers up, still standing by the door.

I smile up at her. "I think you're right. My mama had a dog that looked like Miss Ruthie here, and she was half Great Dane, half hound. Those big ears and long legs are a dead giveaway."

Evie walks in and goes to the kitchen, flipping on the coffee maker and busying herself with something or other. "Coffee will be ready soon, and I hope it's okay that I invited Kai over for breakfast. Well, he sort of invited himself. As soon as he heard I was making tamagoyaki."

I move to the kitchen counter and lean against it, folding my arms over my chest. "Evie, it's fine. This is your home for now. Of course you can invite people over. Besides, even if you weren't making those little rolled omelets he's obsessed with, Yami shows up here most off days, no matter what. He says my sauna is better than the stadium one."

"You have a sauna?" She turns, eyes wide. "Wait. Is there a pool?"

I nod, tamping down my grin at her excitement. Fuck, she's cute. "The same key fob that opens the front door will open the door to the fitness facilities. Use it whenever you want."

She beams, and it's like staring into the sun. All that, over a pool.

"Thank you, I definitely will." Some of her happiness fades as she glances over at the laptop I now see sitting on the coffee table. "I'll use it as my reward for putting in some time on the job hunt."

The coffee machine beeps that it's ready, and I move over to it and start to pour. She's next to me, not so close that we're touching, but close enough.

I slide one mug over to her before dumping in the spoonful

of sugar I add to mine, then I make my way out of the kitchen to a safer distance.

"What kinda job are you lookin' for?"

Some of that smile returns as she doctors up her own coffee, then moves to lean against the counter opposite me.

"My degree is in special education, with a focus on early literacy. I spent a lot of time in hospitals as a kid." She looks at me, indecision over how much to say clear in her expression, so I decide to tell her what I know.

"Your brother mentioned you have asthma." I take a sip of coffee, and she continues.

"Yeah. I'm basically fine now, but it was really bad when I was younger. I had plenty of time to read when I couldn't go to school. It was an escape for me. A way to forget about all the treatments and tests. Plus, I really enjoy working with young kids, and after spending a few years volunteering at my local library, I knew I wanted to combine those two things. Did you know that even today, many schools use an outdated literacy program that doesn't take into account different learning styles and abilities? There are so many kids out there who struggle in school for no reason other than the fact that the way teachers have to teach doesn't meet their needs."

Ah, fuck.

Hearing Evie speak about her passion, her goals, and what she wants to do for kids that are struggling the way *I* struggled?

Fuck if it doesn't make her even more attractive than before.

If there had been someone like Evangeline Yamaki around in Tennessee when I was growing up, maybe I wouldn't have had to do whatever was necessary just to scrape by and get my diploma. Maybe I wouldn't be a twenty-eight-year-old man who still can barely read. Maybe I wouldn't feel like a fucking dumbass any time Yami has to lean over and whisper whatever shit Coach scrawls onto the whiteboard at strategy sessions.

Maybe I wouldn't feel like the only thing I could ever hope to offer a woman like Evie is a charming smile and a good time.

When she deserves so much more.

Chapter Six

Evie

"What did you do?" I cry out as I close the door to Rhett's apartment behind me. Ruthie doesn't move a muscle from where she's passed out on top of the cushion on his couch. Obviously, she tired herself out plenty, destroying what looks like both of the cute toys I bought her yesterday, along with one of Rhett's socks. To say nothing of the pillows and blankets she must have tugged all over the floor.

"How did you even get out?" I murmur with dismay, looking at the mess. I could have sworn the door to the bathroom was closed before I left for Aikido class, but that door is wide open now.

I'm tired, both from a lack of sleep and from a grueling class where we focused on sparring, but I get to work tidying up the mess. Who knows when Rhett will be home, but I'm sure he won't be pleased by my screwup.

If I can at least get all the things that are ruined put into the garbage, and the blankets into the laundry, then maybe he won't be too upset.

Of course, any hope of having everything cleaned up is out the window — or rather, the door — when he comes in just as

I'm bent over, my ass in the air, as I try to pull out a piece of fabric Ruthie somehow managed to get under the couch.

"Ah-ha!" I say, waving the fabric triumphantly.

"Am I interrupting somethin'?" Rhett's amused voice has me turning, my hand dropping to my side. He's smirking at me, and his eyebrows raise as he pointedly looks down at my hand.

"Shit," I swear, a rare occurrence, but warranted this time as I realize the fabric I was waving around a second ago is a pair of red lace panties. I stuff them in my pocket and move to stand, knocking my knee on the corner of the table. "Ow." I grimace, and Rhett moves swiftly to my side.

"You okay there?"

I nod and step away. "Yep, totally fine," I say, probably sounding far too chipper, but I'm mortified. "Sorry about the mess. I'll have it all cleaned up super fast, I promise. And I'll replace anything she wrecked. I think a pillow and some socks might have fallen victim, but other than that, it was just her toys and a couple of my towels I put in the bathroom for her. I guess I didn't close the door, and...yeah. Sorry."

"Evie, it's alright."

That delicious drawl of his stretches out the words, the sound a soothing, warm wave covering me. But I take another step back, glancing down at the innocent-looking puppy still snoring away on the couch.

"It's not. You're being so kind to me, and then I do something stupid like not close the bathroom door properly and now your property is getting destroyed."

Rhett closes the distance between us in just a few strides, and one hand cups my chin, lifting it from where I was staring at the floor.

I can't help but gasp at his touch. Has he ever touched me like this?

"It's a pillow and some socks, Evangeline, not a prized possession. And she's just a lil bit. She's gonna make messes."

I open my mouth to protest some more, but he fixes me with a look that has me staying silent.

"But we can get her set up with a few things so that leaving her won't result in warfare against my pillows." His hand drops away and he smiles. "You said you've never had a pet before, so I'm guessing you didn't know all the things a young pup needs. I'll help you make a list if you want. My mama was a vet assistant, so I grew up with all kinds of animals around."

My grateful nod comes automatically. "Please, that would be wonderful."

Then he starts listing things off, and with every item, my eyes grow wider.

"A crate is the most important thing so she can have a safe space to go. That's where we'll keep her when we have to leave. We'll need lots of toys and treats to entice her into likin' the crate. A soft bed that fits in the space, and we can use one of my sheets or a towel to cover it and create a dark place. Some pee pads for when she has accidents. Speaking of accidents, we better make sure we have some appropriate cleaning supplies that aren't toxic. A good stain remover, too. Have you thought about training methods? Gettin' her into a puppy class would be good for socializing and making sure she stays a good girl." He gives me a small smile before glancing down at the puppy, clearly unaware just how out of depth I feel.

"Right. Yeah, that all makes sense," I eventually manage to say, even though my head is spinning, not only with all the things I apparently didn't know I needed for the puppy that I didn't plan on getting, but also with how much all of this will cost.

"And of course we'll need to register her with the city. Get a license and all that." Rhett strokes her soft nose before looking up at me, a surprisingly bashful expression on his face. "Sorry, darlin'. I keep saying *we*, as if I have any claim over Miss Ruthie. Guess I just got caught up in havin' a dog around again."

I blow out a slow breath, some of my tension and worry leaving me. He means every word he says, I can tell.

"Okay. Well, thank you. Um, do you think you could text me that list right now? So I have it when I go to the store?"

Something crosses his face. Panic? No, that doesn't make sense. But Rhett moves away, almost stumbling over himself. "Naw, no need. I'll come with you."

My brows furrow in confusion. "You don't have to do that."

He glances back at me briefly, his brows pulled together in almost a frown. It's clear something's still off. "It's fine, Evie. We'll take Ruthie with us and go together. That way I can help if you have questions."

I stare at him for a moment, but he's not facing me. I don't have a clue what I said, or what happened to make him react the way he did. Even though he's offering to come with me to the store to help, there's a stiffness to his movements, a nervous energy that wasn't there before.

"Alright," I reply softly, moving to pick up the leash. I clip it on Ruthie's collar, and she finally stirs from her nap. Her little yawn makes me smile, despite the tension that's still buzzing between Rhett and me. But when he glances over and sees her, I see those brows relax with a small upturn of his lips.

The power of puppy love, I guess. Even if I do wish I could be the one to bring a smile back to his face. Or at the very least, not somehow be the reason for that tension in his shoulders.

The drive to the pet store is quiet. Well, between the two humans it is. Ruthie keeps up a steady stream of noises, from excited barks to lower whines. I try to keep her down at my feet, but she keeps trying to climb up until finally, I cave and put her in my lap.

Rhett glances over, one hand holding the steering wheel while the other spins his cap around to face backward. "Looks like we also need a restraint for her so she's safe in the back seat."

I kiss the top of her head and get a lick in return. "She'd whine the entire time."

"Better whining than havin' her fly through the windshield if I have to stop suddenly."

That makes my throat tighten. "Good point," I manage to say.

I hear Rhett's exhale, my gaze on the bundle of fur I'm now holding a little bit tighter.

"I'm sorry, Evie, I didn't mean to scare you like that."

"It's fine, you're right. About all of it. You know way more than I do about caring for an animal, obviously. I just hate the idea of anything happening to her."

He darts a quick look over at me before reaching his free hand over to stroke the top of her head. His hand comes dangerously close to my chest with how she's resting in my lap.

"You know she deserves to be loved. That's the most important thing about havin' a pet. The rest you can figure out as you go."

I'm saved from having to say anything in reply to that sweet statement by our arrival at the pet store.

The same store clerk that helped me yesterday recognizes me and Ruthie and comes over with a big smile that turns into a look of disbelief when she realizes who's with us.

"H-hi again," she stammers, her gaze bouncing between me and Rhett, obviously trying to figure out why we're here together.

But if Rhett is annoyed by the obviously starstruck clerk, he doesn't let it show, giving her a wide, charming smile. "Hey there. I'm hoping you can help my friend and me find a couple of things for this little lady."

He gestures down to Ruthie before flashing the now-blushing girl a wink. I shouldn't be jealous of a pet store clerk. Really, I shouldn't. But that smile, that wink, I've never once seen it turned my way. And a part of me really wants to.

"Of course, whatever you need. It's so cool you're here, like, in our store. My boyfriend is gonna go nuts when I tell him, he's a huge fan. Of the team. And you, of course. Oh my God."

I watch the interaction curiously. I've seen Kai get fawned over by fans before, but he's my brother, so it's easier to roll my eyes and move on. Besides, his cocky swagger makes me want to vomit sometimes.

But Rhett... It's easy to see why he's known as the southern charmer on the team. He's friendly, polite, and yes — hopelessly charming.

"Well now, if you help us find all that we need, maybe we could give your man a quick call and say hi." Another wink, another smile, and the girl, even though she has a boyfriend, almost melts into the floor.

"Ohmygosh, that would be so amazing! What do you need?"

Rhett rattles off the list, and with how easily he remembers it, I can't help but wonder why he wouldn't just text it to me like I suggested. It might be a lot for me to take in, but for someone like him who knows animals, it would be simple.

There's no time to ponder that too much before I'm trailing after the two of them, the clerk now pushing a cart as she and Rhett both add things — far more than I remember being on the list, but what do I know.

When we come across a young boy and his mom in one aisle, the boy's face lights up. Not at Rhett, to my surprise, but at Ruthie. He starts tugging on his mom's sleeve, and I watch her crouch down and start to move her hands, forming letters and words in sign language. His noises of excitement are obvious, and I squat down to his level as well. My hands are too full to use the rudimentary amount of sign language I know, but I try to keep my speech clear in case he can read lips at all.

"Would you like to say hi to the dog?" I keep my face pointed toward the boy, but my eyes glance over at his mom.

Mom smiles, and quickly signs to the boy, saying to me at the same time, "Thank you, that's so kind. He loves dogs, but we can't have one right now. We're here to look at fish, but he's not so excited about that."

I chuckle at that just as the little boy makes another sound and stretches out his hand. I tuck Ruthie's leash under my foot, secure enough that she can't jump on him, but freeing my hands so I can sign, "Her name is Ruth."

This time, both the boy and his mom look at me with happy surprise. "You can sign?" his mom asks as we both watch the little boy laugh as Ruthie covers him in kisses.

"A little. I took some courses during my master's degree. I'm going into special education, and it seemed like a very useful skill to have," I admit.

Her hand reaches out and clutches my arm. "Thank you. Thank you for caring enough to learn, and for this. You've made his whole week."

We sit there for a few more minutes, the boy loving on my puppy, and my puppy loving him right back before the mom gets to her feet. "We'd better go," she says, tapping her son on the shoulder. She signs and talks at the same time. "It's time to leave, Ryan. Say thank you to the nice lady and goodbye to the puppy."

Ryan looks like he's going to protest, so I quickly try to cobble together some signs of my own, still speaking clearly since I noticed his gaze going to my lips often. "Thank you for petting Ruthie, but I have to go, too. She needs her dinner."

Ryan's mom gives me a grateful smile as Ryan reluctantly stands, then looks at me and signs *thank you* before bending down to give Ruthie one more hug.

I give them a wave before realizing I have no clue where Rhett and the salesclerk have ended up. Making my way to the front of the store, I see him leaning against a wall, his hat facing forward now and tucked down lower. If he thinks that makes him any less noticeable, he's wrong.

Then I see the bags at his feet.

"Rhett, you shouldn't have paid for that," I protest as he scoops up the bags and leads me outside. We reach his truck and he puts the bags in the back behind his seat before moving to the front. I still haven't opened my door as he looks at me over the hood.

"You were busy, darlin'. I wasn't gonna interrupt you. Not when it was clear that little boy was in heaven."

He opens his door and gets in, as if that's the end of that. Eventually, I do the same, lifting Ruthie into my lap and securing my seat belt. But when I go to open my mouth to insist on paying him back, it becomes clear that Rhett's not done.

"You're a good person, Evie. Real good. You're smart, and kind, and you know how to take care of yourself. I see that, I swear. But you gotta realize it's not a bad thing to let other people do good things for *you* sometimes. It doesn't make you any less smart and kind and capable."

It's still hard for me to accept that people might do nice things for me, not because they think I need to be taken care of, but simply because they might want to. A lifetime of being the baby of the family and feeling like I had to prove my ability to take care of myself isn't easy to forget.

But with Rhett's words, warmth steals over me. I look out the window so he doesn't see my blush. What the heck am I meant to say? Thank you?

That seems silly, so I say nothing.

"By the way, I got the little lady somethin' special. Open up that small bag, would you?"

My head turns to face him, but he's staring straight ahead at the road, a soft smile curving his lips.

I twist in my seat and locate the smaller bag he must be talking about. It feels like there's nothing in it, but then I open it up, and a small dark green piece of metal shaped like a heart falls out.

"It's the closest to Tridents green I could find. Hope that's okay."

His words register as I flip it over and see *Ruthie* engraved in gold letters.

"I thought Ruthie suited her best. But if you prefer Ruth, we can go back and get it redone."

Somehow, I find my voice. "I love it. Thank you, Rhett." I clear my throat and bend down to take off her collar so I can attach the tag. "And Ruthie is perfect."

I chance a quick look in his direction, and his gaze flashes to mine at the same second. Something burns between us, quiet and subtle, but it's there, nonetheless.

Chapter Seven

Rhett

If I had known just how much of a struggle it would be to ignore my attraction to Evie being around her so much, I might have protested the whole temporary roommate situation a little more.

Because over the last few days that I've been home, we've fallen into a morning routine that feels a little too comfortable.

And uncomfortable, all at the same time.

I'm waking up thinking about her, knowing she's just down the hall, wondering if she's awake or still sleeping. I'm getting in my shower, fully aware that I'm naked and she's in my apartment. To say nothing of when I hear her shower turn on and have to stop myself from picturing *her* naked.

It's just basic biology. Put an attractive woman in front of any red-blooded man for long enough and he'll feel something. Especially when that woman is smart as a whip, kind, and funny.

Biology doesn't give a fuck that she's your best friend's little sister, that you've known her for years, or that you're only meant to be looking out for her and giving her a place to stay.

I'm an early riser, thanks to spending so much time at my grandparents' place. Horses and cows don't wait for nobody, and I was the one responsible for the morning feed. I'd come in from farm chores around six every morning to my mom and Nana already sipping coffee, talking about the latest romance novel they'd finished reading. Even now, years after moving away from the ranch, I'm still used to being the first one up.

But Evie's been up even earlier, thanks to Ruthie. Which means by the time I make it to the kitchen, she's usually got the coffee going.

It's just good manners for me to pour two cups instead of one and fix them both up the way we each like it.

Not that I'll let anyone in on the fact that I know just how much sugar and milk to add to Evie's mug. But the grateful smile I get when I slide it across the counter to her is worth it.

Ruthie bounds over to me and tries to jump up and climb my leg. She's gonna be too big to pick up soon, but that doesn't stop me from scooping her up for a snuggle. She's too dang cute to ignore.

"Mmm. I needed this, thanks. I hope we didn't wake you last night," Evie says, her voice still a little raspy with sleep.

I shake my head and set the pup back on the floor before moving to where we've been keeping Ruthie's food, getting her breakfast dished up. "Nah, I slept like the dead."

That's a lie.

My body seems attuned to my new roommates. Both times she got up with the dog, I was awake in an instant, and didn't fall back asleep until I heard them come back in. "She should be able to go all night soon; I think because she was a stray she's a bit delayed. But normally, by four or five months they can hold it."

"Oh, thank God for that." Evie slumps into one of the stools, setting down her coffee and resting her head on her hand. "I'm exhausted."

I hide my grin as I put down Ruthie's food dish. "Yeah, a puppy is a full-time job at first. You're doin' great."

She gives me a tired smile as the dog noisily starts devouring her food. "Thanks, Rhett. I really appreciate that. You've been a big help."

I tip an imaginary hat her way and wink. "No problem, darlin'. Happy to help." I meant it to be casual, my usual flirting that doesn't mean a damn thing. But Evie's blush has me feeling kinda weird about it.

Grabbing my coffee cup, I move out of the kitchen and sit down on the couch. I'm about to ask what she wants me to add to the grocery order when her phone rings. She glances down at it, and curses under her breath. "It's my mom, I have to answer this." She looks back up at me, her eyes widening. "She doesn't know I'm staying with you. Can you, um, hide or something?"

My eyebrows raise. "Hide? In my own apartment?"

Evie nods vigorously. "Yes! It's a video call. Hurry up. Please? I'll just stand by the window so she can't tell where I am." She gestures at me in a shooing motion and I'll be damned if I don't do as I'm told, going back down the hall to my room.

Even so, I can hear their voices.

"Hi Mom," comes her chipper greeting, and then her mother Helen's reply.

"Hello, sweetie. How are you doing? All moved off campus?"

"Yeah, it was pretty easy. I didn't have a lot of stuff, you know that."

I peek my head out the door, angling so I can try to see Evie. Her voice sounds nervous, and sure enough, when I see her by the window, she's wrapping a long strand of black hair around her finger, twirling it.

"Your dad and I want to come out and visit, watch a game or two, but I'm not sure when we'll be able to. Oba-chan has some appointments coming up."

Evie stops twirling her hair. "Is she okay?"

"Yes, yes, just getting some tests. She's been feeling tired, that's all. Have you been taking care of yourself? Are your prescriptions all filled?"

"Yes, Mom, I got new inhalers just last month. I'm fine."

The exasperation in Evie's voice is evident, and I get the feeling this is a common question from her parents. But Helen doesn't seem to mind, carrying straight on.

"Good. Now, tell me about your job search. Have you applied for anything yet?"

I'm also curious to hear this, even though I know I should just ask Evie myself. It's a perfectly appropriate conversation topic, after all.

"No, I haven't seen anything worth applying for yet. I'm looking every couple of days, though."

"Something will come up," is her mother's confident reply.

"Hope so." Evie turns slightly, and I duck back into my room before she can see me.

"Evangeline, where are you? That doesn't look like Kai's apartment."

"Ahhh," Evie stammers.

Without another thought, I hustle out of my room and walk

over to her side, smiling at the phone. "Hey, Helen, how're you doin' this fine day? Evie was just dropping something off I left at Kai's last night." It's an outright lie, and I can only hope she hasn't talked to Yami recently.

Evie and Yami's mom beams at me. "Rhett. Lovely to see you." But then she tilts her head to the side, and her smile fades. "Why is Evie dropping it off, won't you see Kai at the stadium later?"

A foot kicks my shin, and I glance over to see Evie shooting daggers my way. Okay, so maybe I didn't think my plan through that well.

"Sure, but I was needing this particular thing before we have practice and Evie was goin' past my place." The lie rolls off my tongue way too easily. I give her a smile. "Your daughter was nice enough to make the stop so I could have my, ah, shoes, for my run this morning. You know how it goes, gotta have the right shoes." I finish with a wink, and thank fuck, Helen seems to buy it.

"I see. Well, I hope you enjoy your run. Evie, text me later? We'll catch up when you aren't running errands."

Evie turns the phone toward herself and plasters a big smile on her face. "Okay, Mom, say hi to everyone for me. Love you, bye."

She ends the call and smacks my chest. "I had to drop something off?" she says, her voice incredulous. "What the heck, Rhett!"

I hold up my hands. "It sounded like you needed a save."

Evie just huffs, letting her head fall back as her eyes roll up to the ceiling. "I'm a grown woman, Rhett, I didn't need a save."

The position pushes her tits against her shirt, and it becomes abundantly clear she's not wearing a bra.

She lowers her head back down, and I see the second she registers just how close we are, and what I might be able to see. Her cheeks go red as she folds her arms over her chest. "I...I should get dressed."

"Not on my account," I say in a low voice, then wince. "Sorry. That wasn't... Shit." I grab the back of my neck, feeling my own face heat up. "Sorry." There I go opening my damn mouth and being all flirty again.

She'd have every right to smack me across the face, but instead, when my traitorous eyes dip back down, I see those nipples are even stiffer against the fabric holding them back.

Fuck me.

Ruthie barks, and we both startle as if coming out of a trance. "Okay. I'm gonna go now." She slips around me and is gone, her bedroom door shutting seconds later.

Leaving me wondering how the hell I'm going to deal with the fact that I am *more than aware* that Evie Yamaki is one hundred percent grown woman.

Chapter Eight

Evie

> **KAI: I'm outside**

I pocket my phone, bend down to scratch Ruthie under the chin, then grab my purse before heading out the door.

At least once a month, Kai and I go out for dinner. We've always been close, for all that he's my brother, and therefore, an expert at driving me nuts. I love the weirdo, and being close to him was such a huge reason behind me choosing British Columbia for my graduate program.

Outside, the sun is beating down on the pavement. The city is full of sounds, sights, and smells, and I can't help but smile at the vibrancy of it all.

"Gigi! Let's go!"

That smile turns into a scowl at Kai's shout through the open passenger window. I fold myself into his ridiculously low sports car. "Calm down, it's not like we're going to be late."

He peels away from the curb before answering. "Did you just spend four hours doing grueling training drills? Hmm? Didn't think so. Don't get between me and my food."

I roll my eyes at his griping, even though he's got a valid point. Kai, and Rhett, too, it seems, are perpetually hungry. It's like every time I see Rhett, he's grabbing another protein shake or eating another meal of chicken and veggies. I know from being around Kai that the players eat relatively well, but every now and then, they indulge.

And for Kai, there's no better indulgence than all-you-can-eat sushi and Korean barbecue. A strange choice for someone with Japanese heritage who's used to top-quality Japanese food made by our grandmother, but whatever. Even I can't resist the allure of endless short ribs.

A short drive later, we're walking into our favourite restaurant and being shown to a small booth.

As soon as we're seated, Kai leans forward and fixes me with a stare. "Alright, spill. What's the tea on living with Darling."

I've just taken a sip of water when he asks, and it goes down the wrong pipe, making me cough and sputter.

"You okay?" he asks, his face full of concern. Once my eyes stop watering and I stop choking, I manage to nod.

"Yeah, fine, just went down the wrong way," I rasp. Then, clearing my throat, I ask nervously, "What do you mean, tea?"

Kai settles back and waves his hand. "You know, gossip. Dirt that I can use to give him shit in the locker room. I haven't lived with the guy in years. For all I know, he clips his toenails in the bathroom sink or leaves dirty clothes everywhere."

"Right, because you were the picture of cleanliness when we lived together," I respond drily. "Pretty sure I recall coming across stinky sports uniforms and worn jocks more than once in our shared bathroom."

"Whatever, I was a kid. That's different."

I shake my head in disbelief. "Still gross. But for what it's worth, Rhett's been a great roommate." *And he basically saw my boobs yesterday.*

I keep that last bit to myself, obviously. And then I'm saved from saying anything more by the arrival of a server. Kai rattles off our usual order, and before he can grill me anymore on living with his best friend, I change the subject.

"Mom called yesterday. When did you last talk to her?"

Ah, there it is, the flash of guilt I always manage to get out of Kai when I mention talking to our parents. It's the easiest, foolproof way to get the heat off me when he's giving me a hard time.

"We were just on an away series," he mumbles, and I arch my brow at him.

"Mm-hmm, and does your phone stop working when you leave Vancouver?"

He lifts his straw to his lips, with half the paper wrapper still on, and blows it in my direction. I bat the paper away with a scowl. "Grow up, Kai."

His shoulders lift in a carefree shrug.

"So how many times did Mom ask about your inhalers?"

Great, somehow he's managed to shift the conversation back to me.

"Only once, thank you very much," I say primly. "She trusts me to be a grown-up and manage my own health."

"Did you tell her about the cold you had over spring break?" he asks pointedly, and I wince.

"There was nothing to tell."

"Oh, so I wasn't at your place dropping off an emergency Ventolin refill? Huh, must have dreamed that."

"I could've had the pharmacy deliver it," I grumble back. At his sound of consternation, I make myself look up. "You know I'm grateful you were home. Especially with Carlee out of town."

The truth is, that was one time I *did* need my big brother. A simple cold virus can turn ugly for me. It doesn't happen often, but when it does, I need my inhalers and medications quickly. And with my roommate away, discovering I had somehow forgotten to refill my prescription and was out of one of my inhalers was an added level of stress I didn't need when I was already feeling gross. The last thing I wanted was to spend spring break in the hospital.

"Either way, there's no need for Mom and Dad to know. They'd just worry, and I'm *fine*. You know perfectly well that's the only time I've ever run out of my prescription."

Kai's face softens in understanding. "I know, Gigi. You're good at managing your asthma now. But it's not so easy to forget the little girl that I used to visit in the hospital with fucking oxygen tubes in her nose."

I muster a small smile. "I get it."

Our food arrives and serves as the perfect reason to move on from the rather depressing subject of my health history. I know my brother loves me and means well when he hovers or worries. That doesn't mean I don't wish he — and the rest of my family — would dial it back a bit.

Eventually, we're pulling up outside of Rhett's apartment.

"Are you coming up?" I ask as I unbuckle my seat belt. Kai

looks at the clock on his dashboard and turns his lips down in a pout.

"Nah, I should go home. We're heading out early tomorrow for the next series. But you're coming to our next home game, right?"

"Of course." I smile, then lean over to give him a hug. "Thanks for dinner. Next time, you let me pay."

Kai just rolls his eyes, the same way he does every time I try to pay the bill for our dinner. "Yeah, whatever. Night, sis."

I enter the apartment quietly, in case Rhett has already turned in for the night. But he's not only awake, he's once again shirtless.

"Oh. Hi," I say, coming to a stop just inside the door. Because not only is he shirtless, but his lower body is covered only in a towel, and droplets of water are running down from his wet hair.

"Shit, sorry," he says, apparently just as surprised to see me as I am to see him like this. "I didn't think you'd be home already."

Don't look down, Evie. Don't look down.

"Kai wanted to get to bed early, travel day tomorrow," I say, then cringe. "But you know that, of course."

"Uh, yeah. I was just grabbing some water, then I'm headin' to bed myself." Rhett nods his head toward the kitchen. "Sorry about this." He gestures at himself, and dang it.

I look down.

Then immediately back up, hoping my cheeks are not flaming red. Because while he might be holding that towel tightly so it doesn't fall down, the side effect is that it's tight enough around his hips to make a certain bulge *very* noticeable.

"No problem, it's your apartment you should be allowed to wear whatever you want. Or not wear." I say.

Oh God, kill me now.

"Have a good trip." I fly down the hall, into my bedroom, sinking to the floor as soon as the door closes. It's only then I realize something's missing.

Taking a deep breath, I crack open my door, keeping my eyes cast down to the floor. "Hey Rhett, where's Ruthie?"

"Ah, about that."

Why does he sound guilty...

He walks past, still wearing that damn towel, and I'm treated to a view of his backside. And what a view it is.

Stopping at the door to his room, he gestures for me to come over. Swallowing down my whimper at moving any closer to his half-naked body, I step just close enough to be able to peek around the corner of his door.

And spy my puppy sprawled out across his bed, her head on one of his pillows, fast asleep.

"Oh."

He chuckles. "She snuck in during my shower and passed out, I guess. I don't mind keeping her tonight."

"You can't do that," I protest. "You've got to be up early tomorrow. You need to sleep."

Rhett shrugs and looks surprisingly bashful. "It's okay, I always wake up when you get up with her anyway."

"You do?"

He lifts his gaze to meet mine. "I do. It's the middle of the night; I just want to know you make it back inside okay."

Do not melt into a puddle of goo. Do not melt into a puddle of goo.

"That's...sweet of you. Thank you."

We share a smile, then Rhett moves farther into his room. "Anyway. She can stay here if you don't want to wake sleeping beauty. Maybe you'll get a good night sleep."

"Alright. I mean, I guess that's fine, if you're sure." I twist my hands together. I should take his offer and go back to my room for a night of hopefully uninterrupted rest. But I'm also reluctant to walk away from the peaceful, almost intimate moment we just shared.

Rhett looking out for me when I take Ruthie out at night doesn't feel the same as when my siblings or my parents pull that sort of protective nonsense. No, this makes me feel safe, and in a small way, cherished.

Which is probably not a great way to feel about a man who's doing nothing more than being considerate and polite. Heck, for all I know, he's just doing what he thinks Kai would want him to do, acting like a big brother again.

That ruins the moment.

"Okay. Good night. And good luck on your trip." I turn on my feet and go quickly back to my room, closing the door and flopping face-first down on the bed.

I'm jealous.

Of my puppy.

Chapter Nine

Rhett

"Let's go, boys!" Yami lets out a whoop as he claps his hands, and the team responds with a cheer. We make our way down the hall that leads to the dugout and out onto the field to warm-up for tonight's game.

As soon as my cleats hit the grass, everything else fades away. All that exists is me, my teammates, and the next nine innings.

Mav and I team up to throw the ball back and forth for a while, warming up our arms. Then it's on to some stretches as the seats fill with Tridents fans. I glance up at the stands now and then, seeing the flood of green and gold and letting it infuse me with pride, excitement, and motivation.

We're gonna win.

Our opponents are from the Midwest, and they're a solid team, but we've got a history of beating them every game for the last two seasons. That doesn't mean we get to be cocky, as rumour has it they've had a massive shake-up and have some new guys on the team that could change things up.

Half an hour later, Coach calls us back to the dugout for a last-minute pep talk before we go out for the national anthem.

"Alright, boys. You know what to do. Trust yourselves, trust each other, and make the goddamn play. This is just one game out of one hundred and sixty-two, but that doesn't mean it matters any less than the rest of 'em. Go get 'em, Tridents."

Short and sweet. Just the way I like it. We all jog back out and take our places in a row on the first baseline, hats off for the singing of the anthems. Then it's time to play some fucking ball.

Two innings later and we're up by three. Mattias, the head trainer, is checking out Mav's shoulder as Yami and I get ready to bat.

"Evie's here," he says casually, leaning against the railing next to me.

Thank fuck I've got a good poker face, because there's no way I'm letting him know how that makes me stand up a little taller and want to hit a little harder.

"Yeah? Nice. She in the box?" I keep my tone neutral. Just making conversation. And definitely not letting my eyes skip over the rows of bleachers to the box where all the wives and girlfriends of the players often watch the game.

"Yeah. Willow came to get her earlier. Guess she's off duty today and watching the game with Sin's mom and the kids."

Mention of Ronan Sinclair's family, which includes his wife – our head of media relations, and kids has small grin breaking free on my face. Their daughter Peyton's a riot, and we all love her. And their baby boy Jett? Too fucking cute.

Yami slaps my shoulder just before he jogs up the steps to the on-deck circle. "See ya at home plate, dude."

I exhale as he leaves, my fists clenching and unclenching.

I don't know exactly when or how things changed, but the attraction to Evie I've been fighting has become harder to ignore. On this latest stretch of away games, I found myself missing our early morning conversations. Missing laughing over Ruthie's antics. Missing the simple reality of sharing space with someone.

She's under my skin, that's for sure. And that's a dangerous truth to hold on to.

Just then, Yami hits the ball, hard and fast to the outfield. He takes off running as Wilson heads up to the plate and I move into the on-deck circle. Yami reaches second base easily, and Sin jogs into home, bringing our lead up to four runs.

I blow out a slow exhale, clearing my mind as best I can, to try and bring back that single-minded focus I had when I hit the field for warm up. The focus that normally comes and doesn't leave until the game's over. But today, one gorgeous woman up in the players' box is messing with me. And she doesn't even know it.

Wilson's bat connects, but it's a pop fly easily caught by the pitcher. He comes off the field scowling without a second glance my way. That's fine, my attention is on the man standing sixty feet away from me.

I take a couple swings outside the box, then step in. The ball flies at me, and I swing. And fucking miss.

Cursing under my breath, I take a step back and breathe in and out slowly. Baseball is my life. I can't let anything get in my way. Not even Evangeline Yamaki.

Stepping back up to home plate, I get ready for the next pitch.

It's a slider, and it's headed for the outside of the plate. I adjust slightly, swing, and connect. I'm off running without a second thought. I make it to first, Yami to third, and that's all it takes to get me back in the game.

The next hour and a half flies by. I'm kept busy in left field, with a hell of a lot of hits coming my way. More than one of which I fumble, which pisses me right off. By the end of it, I'm exhausted, and more than happy to spend the last inning on the bench when Coach puts Martinez out instead of me.

We pull off a solid win and the energy in the locker room postgame is high. Monty, our catcher, is in charge of the music pumping through the speakers and today it's some weird remix that sounds like a country song got stuck in a blender with EDM. Somehow it works. But his dance moves definitely don't.

"Monty, I swear on my mama's head, if you don't stop shakin' that ass around, I'm gonna get Lark in here to slap it." I whip my towel in his direction to emphasize my point, but the fucker just turns and grins.

"Joke's on you, Darling, because that sounds like a good time."

The guys laugh, and so do I, because that's exactly what I expected he'd say. "Oh yeah? Well, maybe I'll call Mattias in here instead."

Monty's look of mock horror has us all laughing even harder. These men, they're my family. I don't have siblings, but I have these shitheads, and I wouldn't want it any other way.

"Hey bro, you coming out with me and Evie to get some food?"

I want to say yes. I want to see her, talk to her, and spend time with her. But not with Yami there. "Nah," I say, pulling on a pair of shorts under my towel before unwrapping it from my hips. "You two go, I'll head home and check on the pup."

Yami shakes his head with a grin. "Can't believe she still has that thing. But I'm guessing you're enjoying it, aren't you? Fucking animal lover." He's teasing, but he's also not wrong, so I just shrug and give him a smirk.

"I get all the benefits of having a dog without any of the work. Sounds like a good deal to me." We head out of the locker room together, Yami peeling off to head to Evie's side.

Roddy, one of the new rookies, comes up next to me and elbows me. "Damn, is that Yami's sister? She's fucking hot. Wonder how she feels about shortstops."

I not-so-lightly shove him away, fixing him with a glare. "Shut the fuck up, rookie. That's no way to talk about any woman, but especially not a teammate's sister."

Roddy has the good sense to hold his hands up, his face apologetic. He's young, wet behind the ears, and caught up in the excitement of his first season in the big leagues. That's the only reason I'm not doing more than shoving.

"Sorry, man. Didn't mean no disrespect like that."

I arch my brow, folding my arms across my chest. I've got several inches of height over him, which lets me look down and emphasize my disapproval. "Just don't let me hear you talking like that again. It's one thing to flirt with the ladies when you're out, but you damn well better be respectful, and you sure as shit better respect the women that are part of this family."

Roddy nods rapidly and turns to walk away. I glower after him, taking several slow breaths.

"Well, damn, Darling, didn't know you had that in you."

I turn at Monty's voice. "Had what in me?"

"That big dog, take-no-shit, badass energy." He's holding

Lark's hand as they come up beside me. "You're always so nice to everyone. Good to see you can give 'em shit when they need it."

"Come on, Dan, Rhett's a southern gentleman. He'd never put up with someone being disrespectful," Lark chimes in, leaning against Monty's side. His arm comes around to cup her pregnant belly protectively. "Although, I have to admit, I've never heard you sound quite so growly before."

"Yeah, that was something else. Anything to share?" Monty waggles his eyebrows, but I just narrow my eyes at him.

"Not a thing. Now, if you'll excuse me, I need to be getting home." I nod at them both and move quickly down the hall to the parking lot. I don't stop until I'm in my truck.

Fuck. Now she's not only messing with my game but causing me to act differently enough that my friends are noticing. I don't regret giving the rookie shit, but if I don't want anyone knowing that I'm dangerously attracted to my roommate, I gotta pull myself together.

Besides, we might have won tonight, but that's in no part thanks to me. Which means I need to find a way to cut the shit and find my focus.

The game is a hell of a lot more important than some annoying attraction to my best friend's little sister. It has to be.

CHAPTER TEN

Evie

Living with Rhett when he's on a home game stretch is exceptionally different from when he's away.

I mean, obviously. When he was away, I could almost make myself forget that I was living with him at all. I could do what I wanted, not having to worry about anything except myself and Ruthie. I also felt lonely, having all those quiet mornings to myself.

But with him home, everything's different. The apartment feels smaller, somehow. Maybe it's just because he's so big, taking up so much physical space, but I think it's more than that. It's the energy crackling between us.

The last thing I want to do is read too much into it, but the smiles he gives me each morning over our cups of coffee feel different from the ones he so easily flashes to everyone else. They're more...authentic, in a way. Like I'm seeing the real Rhett, not the flashy, charming baseball player he shows everyone else.

This latest stretch, he was gone for over a week. And then he kept busy for a couple of days with games and practices. We haven't had a lot of time when we're both at the apartment, aside from those moments in the morning.

But tonight, we're both home. When I get back from Aikido, he's already returned from an afternoon game. I find him stretched out on the couch, Ruthie on his chest, both of them snoring lightly. It's such a sweet scene, I whip out my phone and take a picture. By the time I've changed out of my Gi and returned to the living room to find something to drink, he's awake and clipping Ruthie's leash on.

"Hey," he rumbles. "Didn't hear ya come in. I'm just gonna take the little lady out for a quick walk." He stretches his arms overhead, causing his shirt to ride up just enough to show me a sliver of tanned skin covered in a dusting of hair. "Oh, and thanks for switchin' over the laundry." He gives me an almost bashful smile. "I tend to forget shit in the washer a lot."

"No problem," I say, unable to formulate anything more eloquent, my brain on the fritz from the peek of bare skin, even though, by now, I've seen much more. He leaves with Ruthie, thankfully unaware of my reaction.

He's so kind, so generous, so...perfect. Who could blame me for being drawn to him? But what used to be a physical infatuation alone is now becoming something more. Something risky.

Late at night, I definitely spend too much time imagining what it could be like to feel all that hard muscle bare beneath my hands. To have him in charge of bringing me pleasure instead of a battery-operated toy.

Thankfully, I manage to get my libido — and thoughts — under control by the time he returns with Ruthie. He's carrying her and kissing the top of her head when they walk in. I lean against the counter with my arms folded across my chest in an attempt to look unaffected, when the truth is, it's also to cover my pert nipples that had an instant reaction to his adorable affection toward my puppy.

"She's never going to get used to elevators if you keep carrying her," I say, arching my brow.

Rhett gives me a sheepish grin. "I know, but I can't stand the sound of her crying. And when she looks up at me all scared, well, there's no stopping it. I'm a sucker for a damsel in distress."

And apparently, I'm a sucker for a southern charmer.

A smile creeps across my own face. "You're the one who said training her right away was important. And pretty soon, she'll be too big to be picked up."

He lets out a throaty chuckle as he sets Ruthie down and unclips her collar, hanging it on the hook next to his keys.

"That's for sure. With paws like that, she's gonna be a big girl." He moves into the kitchen and opens the fridge, pulling out some ingredients and setting them on the counter. "How do you feel about fajitas for dinner?" he asks over his shoulder.

"You don't have to cook for me," I protest.

"Why wouldn't I? I'm not cooking for just myself and letting you starve." He actually sounds insulted, and I look at him, wavering between annoyance and wanting to swoon.

"I'm not a damsel in distress, Rhett. I can make my own meals. You're already doing so much just by letting Ruthie and me stay here." In the back of my mind, I know how ridiculous I sound. I should just be grateful, not annoyed.

Rhett sets down the red pepper he pulled out and turns to face me, leaning forward and resting his hands on the counter. The position makes his biceps bulge under the grey T-shirt he's wearing, and I fight not to let my gaze bounce to them.

"Listen, Evie. I know you're no damsel in distress. I know you're more than capable of doing just about anything you decide to do. But you're here, I'm here, and there's no sense in us avoiding each other. So if I want to make two plates of food instead of one and sit them across from each other on the table, then I'm gonna do just that. And whatever happens to that second one, happens." He raises his eyebrows. "Besides. You can't tell me you wouldn't do the same for me, or am I wrong in remembering the breakfast you made for both of us yesterday mornin'?"

He's got me there, and he knows it, judging by the smirk he gives me.

"Now, if you're done being difficult, you could get in here and help me."

My own smile cracks my face as I move into the kitchen. "Fine. What can I do to help?"

He inclines his head to the fridge. "First up, mind grabbing me one of those beers on the door? They're nonalcoholic. I don't drink much at all during the season, but it still gives the idea of an ice-cold beer. There might be some coolers in there as well if you want one, I try to have a few on hand for guests."

I open the fridge and pull one out for him, opening the can as I answer. "I don't drink at all."

He raises his eyebrows at that. "Never?"

I shake my head. "Nope."

"Any particular reason?"

"I can't stand the taste of most alcohol, and I hate how it makes me feel."

"Fair enough."

I'm grateful Rhett doesn't push. I've had too many people — mostly men on the few dates I've been on — try to convince me to just try a beer or wine, and I truly don't enjoy the flavour. Simple as that.

Instead, we continue cooking dinner together. And every time he brushes past me to get something or lifts a spoonful of filling for me to taste, I try not to get too caught up in the fantasy.

This is nothing more than two friends enjoying preparing and eating a meal together. Even if it does feel intimate and comfortable. Even if I could easily picture him leaning in for a kiss following the sampling of food or wrapping his arms around me as I grate the cheese.

None of that happens. None of that will happen. And the sooner I get my whole heart and mind to believe that and let go of the fantasies, the better.

The next day, the team is playing a doubleheader. I go to the early game and sit in the stands wearing Kai's jersey. I'm close to the dugout, so a lot of the players acknowledge me with a wave. Kai takes it one step further, climbing the steps and opening the gate to the stands to give me a quick hug.

"Hey lil sis, here to watch me make our family proud?"

I scoff, but he's not wrong. I am incredibly proud of him. "Maybe I'm here to check out the other team. Their pitcher's pretty cute."

The look of horror on his face is priceless. "Shut your mouth, Gigi, or I'll tell Mom you're the one who broke her Kutani vase."

His coach hollers at him at that moment, and Kai disappears back through the gate and into the dugout. He's lucky, or I would've smacked the hat off his head for calling me Gigi.

I'm pretty sure the stadium staff monitoring the gate want to murder him for the excitement his crazy antics causes, and I'll be next in line, because for the rest of the game, I'm all too aware of the whispers and looks I get.

When the first game ends with the Tridents down by one, I duck out of the stadium with the crowds, sending Kai a quick text telling him I'm heading home.

Then, before I can talk myself out of it, I send one to Rhett as well.

> **EVIE: Hey, good game. Sorry it didn't end better. I'm heading home, hope the evening game goes better, Ruthie and I will be cheering for you!**

I'm halfway home on the bus before I get a reply.

> **RHETT: Thanks can't win them all see you in the morning sleep well.**

His message is short, but I'm guessing he's busy with the team, so it's sweet that he even bothered to reply.

Back at Rhett's apartment, Ruthie greets me from her crate with an eager whine. "Let's go, girl," I say, letting her out and clipping on her leash. We head out for a long walk, and by the time we get back, the poor pup is exhausted. She crashes hard, right in the middle of the living room rug, even though her bed is just down the hall in my room.

Part of me wishes I could take a nap as well since she's still not quite making it through the night without a potty break. But job searching won't happen on its own, so instead, I pour a cup of herbal tea and crack open my computer once again.

I've already got my highlighted priority list in terms of what I want in a job next to me. My top choice school districts are open and bookmarked on my web browser, along with a generic job posting site that was recommended to me by my advisor at university.

But all the organization in the world can't make a job appear out of thin air. An hour later, I've applied to two jobs, neither one that enticing. One is up in northern British Columbia, and the other is a part-time position about an hour outside the city. It's hard not to feel discouraged by the lack of prospects. Maybe I was a fool, but I thought it would be a breeze to find my perfect job. Turns out, all the good special education positions are filled, I suppose.

When Ruthie wakes up, I distract myself by working on some obedience training. She's smart, but her attention is easily swayed by everything. A siren outside, the sunlight on the glass coffee table, her own tail. After about twenty minutes, I give up and flop down on the floor. She immediately climbs on top of me and starts licking my face.

In no time, I'm laughing and pushing her away. "Oh my God, not the nose, Ruthie." She barks and lunges forward again. I manage to sit up, and she tumbles to the floor. Recovering in an instant, she starts zooming around the apartment. "If I could have a fraction of your energy," I say with a smile as she circles around me again and again.

I drag myself up to stand and try to think of what to do for dinner. In the end, girl dinner wins out and I find myself on the couch with a glass of sparkling water and a mini charcuterie board on my lap.

Turning on the television, the Tridents game pops up on screen. Of course, the sports channel is on. Looks like the game is almost over with the Tridents in the lead. I watch the last inning and a half, my breath catching in my throat when I see Rhett dive to make a catch. But he pops up and whips the ball across to Maverick King at third base, making the play and tagging the other player out.

I'm not a sports fan, other than baseball. And I much prefer to watch live than on TV, so after that play, I switch the channel, finding a cooking show that I used to have on in the background when I'd study late at night. Curling my legs underneath me, I finish my dinner to the sounds of the show's host waxing poetically about turmeric.

I don't remember falling asleep, but the next thing I know, I'm startled awake by a pair of strong arms lifting me off the couch.

"Wh-what are you doing?" I sleepily protest, even as my arms wrap around Rhett's neck. "The dog?"

"Shh. It's okay. You were fast asleep when I came in. I took Ruthie out already, she's waitin' for you in your room," he murmurs into the top of my head.

Maybe I'm lucid dreaming because I swear I hear him inhale deeply as if he's smelling my hair. My body relaxes into his arms, sleep winning out over common sense. I'll probably feel all sorts of embarrassed about this in the morning, but right now, I'm going to let myself enjoy the feel of being held by Rhett Darlington.

And when he gently lowers me to the bed and draws a blanket over me, I know I must be dreaming. Because this time, I don't miss the warmth of his breath on my skin when he leans down and whispers in my ear.

"Sleep well, honey."

Chapter Eleven

Evie

"Let me get this straight. You turned down my offer to take over my kid's bedroom this summer, not for your brother's couch, but for his best friend's bougie apartment?" My friend Lina says as she and Carlee check out Rhett's apartment. "I don't blame you one fucking bit, girlfriend. This is way nicer than putting up with my gremlins." She bends down to pet Ruthie, who has been bouncing between the two of them for attention ever since they walked in the door.

"I happen to enjoy spending time with those gremlins," I object, but there's a smile on my face. "But yeah, it's not exactly a hardship being here." We move into the living room and sit down on the couch. Ruthie, of course, is hopping up between us, putting her paws on Lina's lap for more cuddles.

Lina's two kids are adorable, and she's one of my closest friends despite being almost fifteen years older than me. But we connected at Aikido when I first moved out here, and when she heard about my post-graduation housing dilemma, she was quick to offer her assistance. I turned her down, not wanting to impose — and not wanting to subject myself to the chaos of her household.

"Mm-hmm, and I'm guessing the scenery is a lot better." Carlee, my former roommate and other best friend, waggles her blonde eyebrows as she comes to sit down, setting two glasses of colourful liquid on the coffee table. She points to the one in front of Lina. "Full strength Blue Bomber for you" — she gestures to the one in front of me — "and non-alcoholic for you."

Carlee goes back to the kitchen and gets her own drink before rejoining us. "Like I was saying. The scenery. Baseball players and their butts, know what I'm talking about?"

I blush as Lina cackles. "Amen to that." She picks up her glass and raises it in our direction. "To your graduation, ladies, congrats. You've both got bigger brains than me, but we knew that already. Just don't forget, I can still kick your butts."

Seeing as Lina is a third-degree black belt in Aikido, compared to my first degree, she's not exaggerating. I got lucky that my two friends get along so well. The first time they met was when Carlee joined me for a trial Aikido class. She quickly figured out it wasn't for her, but the three of us went for coffee afterward, and they immediately hit it off.

I don't know what I'd do without the two of them. They're a big part of why I want to stay in British Columbia. The idea of moving far away from them makes my heart twinge.

I lift my own glass along with Carlee, and we clink them together. "Thanks, Lina. If only a big brain was the sole requirement for a job."

"Still no luck?" Carlee asks sympathetically. She had no trouble at all finding a job as an engineer and an apartment to rent. Unfortunately, that apartment is a tiny studio, which was why we couldn't continue being roommates after graduation.

I shake my head. "Nothing worth pursuing at least. I really thought all the districts would have their postings for next year up by now."

"The school year hasn't ended yet for kids, there's time. Your perfect job is out there waiting for you," Lina says confidently, and I shoot her a grateful smile.

"I know. I'm not giving up hope. It just would be nice to know where I'm working so I can figure out an apartment sooner rather than later."

"Oh? So living with the hot baseball player isn't as magical as we imagine it to be?" Carlee says, and there's mischief colouring her tone. "Trouble in paradise?"

Heat suffuses my face. "Stop. Get your mind out of the gutter. It's not paradise, it's a temporary roommate situation. Nothing more."

"But you wouldn't mind if it became more. Or am I wrong in remembering Rhett Darlington is the same teammate of your brother's that you kissed four years ago?"

"I'm sorry, what?" Lina cries, sitting forward. She puts her drink down and props her head in her hands, looking at me way too eagerly. "Tell me everything."

I, on the other hand, slump back against the couch, my hand dropping to Ruthie's back, petting her absently. "It's not that great of a story, Lina. Don't get so excited."

"Okay, but you kissed him? That actually happened?"

I nod, but without any enthusiasm. "Yeah, I tried to. It lasted maybe a second before he was pushing me away in horror."

"Oh Evie," Carlee murmurs, shifting closer to me. "It wasn't that bad, was it?"

It really was. I've never been so embarrassed in my life. Never felt so rejected. It's why I've avoided Rhett as much as possible over the last four years. Not an easy task when his best friend and teammate is my older brother.

"It was, actually. He said... He said, 'C'mon, Evie. You don't wanna do this.'" I do a rough approximation of Rhett's deep voice, biting it off in a harsh laugh. "Exactly what every girl who's just kissed her crush wants to hear."

Carlee winces as Lina leans back against the couch.

"Damn, girl. I'm sorry."

Picking up my glass again, I take a long drink. It's not often I wish I drank alcohol. Pretty much never, in fact. But right now, I wouldn't be all that opposed to this being more than a mocktail. Maybe the gross, out of control feeling of being drunk would ease the embarrassment that always comes when I relive that moment in my parents' hallway four years ago when I cornered Rhett while he was visiting with Kai. Oh, how wrong I was.

That's when I realized romantic ideas like that are for books and movies, not real life. Honestly, Rhett being out here was the only hesitation I had over moving to British Columbia for my master's degree. But being near the subject of my crush, and humiliation, was a risk I was willing to take for the chance to move away from my well-meaning family and have my own life.

And I have to admit, it hasn't been so bad. He's never brought up that time I embarrassed myself, and things are good between us now. Confusing at times, especially when I find myself wondering — no, hoping — that just maybe he's starting to see me as more than Kai's little sister, but things are overall good.

"Anyway. Let's change the subject, please?" I ask, looking between my two friends. They take pity on me, thank God.

"Yeah, I want to know what happened with the cute teacher at Selena's school." Carlee raises her eyebrows at Lina. "Did Ricky say anything at the last parent-teacher night?"

Lina drains her glass, then smacks her lips. "Ladies, let me tell you, that husband of mine had no idea what was coming. Mr. Myers walks in, and you should've seen all the moms swoon. It was kind of pathetic, honestly."

"As if you weren't seconds away from swooning yourself?" I tease, having heard many stories about the insanely handsome teacher at the elementary school Lina's kids go to. "Be honest. If Ricky wasn't there, you'd have swooned."

Lina considers my words, then lifts her shoulders in a shrug. "Fine, yeah, I would've swooned. Instead, I got to watch my husband get all possessive when Hottie McTeacher walked around handing out the kids' year-end folders. All the man did was smile and say Selena was a great student, and Ricky acted like he'd put the moves on me. His chest got all puffy and he wrapped his arm over my shoulders and glared at the poor man. Glared." Lina rolls her eyes, then falls back against the couch clutching her chest. "It was so damn sexy we couldn't even wait to get home. He made out with me in the car in the school parking lot."

"You didn't!" I gasp. "At the school? What if someone walked by? Another parent?"

"Or Hottie McTeacher!"

"I mean, maybe Ricky would've been open to a threesome?"

Lina smirks, and we all burst out laughing at the idea of her very masculine Mexican husband having a threesome with a much younger, preppy teacher.

We're still giggling when the front door opens and Rhett walks in.

He comes to an immediate stop, his face breaking into his trademark charming grin.

"Well, hello ladies, looks like you're havin' a good time," he drawls with a smirk and a wink.

Just as I expect them to, Lina and Carlee both respond with ridiculously girlish giggles. I can only hope they're not thinking about the cursed kiss story.

I give Rhett a small wave in greeting, but Ruthie is far more enthusiastic, bounding over to her favorite baseball player. Fine, maybe he's my favorite baseball player, too, but nobody needs to know that right now. Especially not my brother.

"Oh yeah, it's been a great night," Carlee says, emphasizing the word *great*. "You know, swapping secrets, talking about boys, typical girls night stuff."

"Sounds fun."

Swear to God, if Carlee says a single word about that dang kiss I told them about, she's dead to me. Normally, I wouldn't doubt my trust in my best friends, but right now, a few cocktails in, Carlee's usual filter is gone. And I feel sick thinking about her bringing up that story in front of Rhett.

Thankfully, she doesn't. And after another minute or two of small talk with my friends, Rhett turns to me.

"Alright, I think I'll make myself scarce and let you ladies enjoy your night. See you in the mornin', Evie." His smile at me seems different, softer than the one he gives my friends. Then he's gone, walking down the hallway with a confident swagger.

We're all silent until we hear his door snick shut, then the girls are on me, just as I expected they would be.

"Holy fuck, Evie. How could you not let us know he's even hotter in person?" Lina hisses, fanning herself.

"I don't know, he's just Rhett. I try not to think of him that way," I say, but my excuse is lost in Carlee's snort of laughter.

"Yeah, no. She didn't tell us because she wants to keep him all to herself. That's what's going on here, you still want to get with that hunk of a baseball player, don't you." Carlee nudges me, and I look at her, horrified.

"Oh my God, shut up! What if he hears you?" I hiss.

Carlee gives an unrepentant shrug as Lina waves her hand at me in dismissal. "Oh relax, he's not gonna hear us." At least she keeps her voice down. But then she gets a mischievous look on her face as she turns to Carlee, then back to me. "But our dear friend does have a point about you hitting that. I mean, it wouldn't be the worst thing in the world, now, would it? Pretty convenient, too, a summer of no-strings-attached sex sounds amazing to me."

I look at her, kind of confused for just a minute before understanding dawns on me. I feel hot and flustered, and I don't even have alcohol to blame. "Absolutely not," I whisper harshly, then repeat myself even firmer, "Absolutely. Not. There's no way anything is ever going to happen between Rhett and me. He's Kai's best friend, and he's helping me out by letting me stay here. The last thing I want is to make that awkward by opening the door for rejection again."

But Lina doesn't seem to be listening. She leans in, gesturing for Carlee and me to do the same. She drops her voice even lower, and that's the only reason I don't strangle her right then and there because of what she says next.

"I bet Rhett could take care of your little problem with having the big O."

I stare at my friend, wondering if she can sense the daggers I'm throwing at her in my mind. Carlee's hand smacks my thigh, breaking my mental attack on Lina.

"Oh my God, yes! Your whole never-had-an or-gasm-with-a-guy problem." She nods sagely, as if she didn't just spill my dirty little secret in a voice that's definitely louder than a whisper. "Yup, he's definitely the kind of guy who could help you with that. You know what they say about hot jocks, right? They've got two heads and only know how to use one of them, but dang, do they ever use that one well." She shimmies her shoulders as if she didn't just insult the intelligence of my brother, Rhett, and every other professional athlete out there.

"You two need to shut up right now. First of all, that's rude, Carlee. Rhett's a really smart guy, with a good head" — she starts to snicker and I glare at her — "*on his shoulders.* I'm not going to let you insult his intelligence or my brother's or any other athlete," I growl.

Carlee's face falls as she reaches over and takes my hand. "I'm sorry. You're right, that was super bitchy of me to say. I didn't mean it."

I give her a stiff nod to show I accept her apology, then stand and pick up their empty cocktail glasses before walking swiftly into the kitchen. When I return to the living room with two glasses of water instead, I set them down a little harder than I probably should. "Drink this. You're cut off from alcohol. Because you're both crazy if you think Rhett is going to be the first man to give me an orgasm. There's just no way."

Unfortunately, my friends might be tipsy, but they're not drunk. They both smile at me like the cat that got the cream.

"I give it a week," Lina says.

"I give it maybe a month," Carlee adds. "Definitely before she moves out."

I look between my two supposed best friends, my hands on my hips. "Are you seriously betting on whether or not Rhett and I are going to have sex?"

Both of my friends nod their heads, looking far too smug.

"You bet your butt we are." Lina smirks.

I fold my arms across my chest, my eyes narrowing into a glare. "Well, you're both going to lose because there's no chance of Rhett Darlington ever wanting to get close enough to me to do anything, especially not *that*."

"We'll see."

Lina's cryptic reply frustrates me. She's wrong, they're both wrong. There's nothing going on between Rhett and me, and there never will be. No matter my younger self's crush-fueled dreams or my current self's fantasies.

Chapter Twelve

Rhett

I definitely was not meant to hear what I just heard. But I did, and I know I won't be able to stop thinking about it.

Evie's never had an orgasm other than by herself.

Part of me is in denial. There's no goddamn way that's true. Another — more dangerous — part of me is seriously turned on by the idea of being the one man to make her orgasm. The one man to show her what true pleasure a good lover can bring.

God-fucking-damn.

There'll be no sleep tonight. Not for me.

I'll have to act natural tomorrow, pretend I never opened my bedroom door, planning on quickly going to the kitchen to grab a snack. Thank fuck I stopped in the doorway as soon as I heard my name. My mama didn't raise a fool, and I know Evie would be horrified if she knew I overheard their conversation.

Not that it stopped me from listening very intently.

When they move on to talking about other things, I slowly shut my door and tiptoe over to the edge of my bed. I sit, then let my body fall back and cover my face with my arms, exhaling under my breath.

"Fuck."

I stay in my bedroom even after her friends leave. I can hear her putter around the apartment, cleaning up, I guess. Then she takes Ruthie out, and when they come back, I hear her door quietly close.

Silence falls over the apartment. So quiet, I feel as if I can hear my own heart beating. After a while, a soft noise starts up, but I can't quite figure out what it is. Until I hear something else over that strange hum. Something that sounds almost like a whimper. But it's not coming from the dog. I don't think...

It happens again. And this time, I can tell it's not a whimper, it's a *moan*. Then a quiet bark that must be Ruthie. The humming sound stops, and I can just barely hear Evie's voice hushing the dog. Then the hum starts up again, and feeling like a complete knucklehead, I finally realize what it is.

Evie's playing with herself.

My mind immediately pictures her lying in bed, her long black hair spread out underneath her. I bet her eyes are closed as she arches back under the touch of the toy. Does she have her hands on her pussy? Is she wet? I bet she fucking is. Christ, what I wouldn't do to feel it for myself. To see her for myself.

I don't know how the fuck I'm gonna survive this. How the hell I'll just lay here and listen to her do this right down the hall from me. I hear another muffled moan. I stay quiet, feeling a little bit guilty for listening but not enough to stop. A couple more minutes go by of muffled moans and buzzing from what I now can presume is a vibrator. And then, I hear the sweetest sound of all.

"Rhett."

The sound stops, and everything falls silent again.

Even so, I stay in my room, not wanting to move a muscle.

If I move, I don't know if I trust myself to not go and do something stupid, like burst into Evie's room and make her say my name again.

But eventually, I realize I can't stay here any longer without losing my fucking mind. I get up as silently as I can and go into my bathroom. There's nothing I can do about the sound of the shower, but I gotta do it. I need to cool the inferno burning inside of me.

I step into the freezing cold stream of water and fight back a curse. But even standing under the icy spray doesn't calm down my thundering heartbeat and pulsing cock.

There's no choice but to give in to temptation.

Wrapping my hand around my cock, I squeeze tightly. But nothing is going to stop this from happening. No amount of denial, or torture, or punishment can stop the orgasm that is hurtling through me.

My mind goes back to the mental image of Evie naked, spread out in bed, only this time, I'm there with her. She's underneath me, and I'm the one bringing her to climax, not a damn sex toy.

I know I'm walking a dangerous line. Hell, I have been for days, weeks, even. Every time I entertain the slightest thought of Evie, I get closer to stepping over that line.

I know I shouldn't think of her like this. But I also can't stop myself, at least not right now. In no time at all, I'm painting the walls of my shower with my cum.

I stand there for a few minutes, panting as my heart rate slows down. Then I step out and dry off. Pulling my shorts back on, I stagger into my bedroom and fall into bed.

As I lie there, staring at the ceiling, trying to convince my dick that's already trying to get hard again to stand down, I start to consider all of the what-ifs.

What if I did go to Evie and she did welcome me into her bed? What if we did step over that line?

I'm so caught up in these dangerous thoughts that I don't realize Evie's door has opened until I hear a quiet yip from Ruthie coming from the hallway.

"Shhh." I hear Evie say, and then the click of puppy nails on the floor tells me they're on the move. But they pause outside my door.

Did she hear me in the shower earlier? Is she about to make the decision for us and come into my room? But then her soft footfalls carry on and I hear the front door open and close.

Guess not.

Which means it's up to me to decide how I handle this to-morrow when we come face-to-face.

The problem is, my head is telling me one thing and my dick is telling me something else. And what should be a clear decision is muddier than my truck used to get off-roading in the backwoods of Tennessee.

I want Evie. And she apparently wants me.

By the morning, courtesy of less than two hours of sleep, my mind is made up. It might be stupid and risky as all hell. But Evie needs a man who can teach her how she should be treated in bed. Who can teach her exactly how to get what she wants, what she deserves, and who can bring her the pleasure any woman is entitled to.

And I'll be damned if that's gonna be some random asshole who might not appreciate how fucking lucky he is.

It's gonna be me.

I head out to the kitchen just as the front door opens and Evie and Ruthie come inside from a morning walk.

"Oh. You're up." Evie comes to an abrupt halt just inside the door, but the little lady at her feet starts pulling on the end of her leash and whining.

"Mornin'." I'm actually kinda proud at how calm and normal I manage to say that as I walk over, crouch down, and unclip Ruthie's leash. She immediately jumps up on my chest, her little claws scratching me even through my shirt.

"Easy there, little one, that hurts," I scold gently, standing up and going back to the kitchen.

Evie follows me and takes care of feeding the puppy while I pour our coffees. But instead of handing it to her in the kitchen, I take both mugs over to the couch and sit down right in the middle, setting them on the table in front of me. She's got no choice but to sit next to me.

When she walks over and sees the setup, Evie frowns slightly, but I manage to keep my smirk to myself. "You don't want your coffee?" I lean back against the couch, sipping my own brew.

After a few seconds, she picks up her cup and sits down, tucking her feet underneath her at the end of the couch. I stay quiet, and for a few minutes, neither one of us says anything. We just sip the delicious nectar of the gods and wake up.

But the anticipation filling me can't be held back forever.

"So, did y'all have a good time last night?"

I'm not prepared for her reaction. Evie visibly startles, her mug swaying in her hands, in danger of spilling hot liquid all over her. I swiftly lean over and take it from her, setting it back on the table.

When I move back to Evie, I realize two things at the same damn time.

One, my hand is somehow gripping her upper thigh. Like, her *upper* upper thigh.

And two, if I turn my head just a little bit more, I'll be close enough to kiss her.

Judging by the sharp intake of her breath, Evie realizes it, too.

"Rhett?" she whispers. And those big brown eyes look up at me with so many unspoken thoughts and feelings simmering in them.

I lift my other hand up slowly, her gaze darting down to it, then back up to meet mine. My callused hand meets her soft cheek, and my thumb strokes gently.

"I heard what you said to your friend about me." My throat constricts. This isn't exactly what I planned on saying, but I realize now it's what I need to say. Before anything else. "Well, about athletes. And I just wanted to say thank you." My heart starts to race. Do I tell her about my dyslexia? About why the statement she made means so damn much?

Before I can work up the nerve to do just that, Evie's throat moves up and down as she swallows.

And then...

Her lips are soft landing on mine, her kiss tentative. I stay perfectly still, even though I'm desperate to take it deeper. My mind flashes back to a time four years ago when she kissed me. Back then, I couldn't let anything happen. She was so young and living on the opposite end of the country.

But now, we're both adults and she's here. Right here.

Stealing a kiss.

It only lasts a second before she pulls back. "Sorry," she whispers, and that's all it takes for me to lean forward and crush my lips to hers.

"Don't you dare apologize," I rumble against her mouth. Her hand fists in my shirt and I start to recount baseball stats to try and temper my reaction to feeling her touch me like this.

Then I remember what I *really* wanted to talk to her about. It would seem she might be even more open to the idea than I initially thought.

I break our kiss and lean against the back of the couch, letting my fingers lightly caress the bare skin at the base of her neck. Her eyes are a little glazed, and I'd imagine mine are, too. That was one hell of a kiss.

"Is the other thing true? What your friend said about you and...you know."

Her brow furrows slightly, but only for a second before she gasps and leans back, letting go of my shirt.

"Hold on, how long were you listening to us?"

Shit. Guilt swarms me, but Evie looks curious, and maybe a little nervous, but not angry.

Taking a breath, I come clean. "Long enough to hear you say you've never had a man give you an orgasm."

Evie folds her arms over her chest, but I still detect the slightest of trembles. "You weren't meant to hear that. But don't worry, I don't expect you to do anything about it."

That's not the reaction I was hoping for. "Why not?"

Evie scoffs, but her hands drop to her lap. "I tried to kiss you once before, Rhett, or have you forgotten? You pushed me away. Why would anything be different now?"

I knew we'd have to talk this out eventually, but goddamn, it's hard to focus with her so close. Her delicate scent invades my senses, making me want to bury my nose in her hair as I bury my dick in her pussy. But she needs to know I'm not messing around. Leaning forward slightly, I wait until her gaze is on me, and I hope she can see and hear my sincerity.

"Evie, when I turned you down, it was because you were twenty, still living at home, and I was on the other side of the country playing ball with your brother. It had nothing to do with me not being attracted to you. Or not wanting you. If anything, that was the problem. I did want you. I still fucking do, or did that kiss just now tell you nothing?"

"You...want me." She blinks slowly, her cute little mouth forming an O.

"And you want me, too. Because I heard more than just your confession last night." My voice is gravely, deep, and I wonder if she can hear the lust eating me up from the inside out. "Later. I heard you say my name."

"Later..." she says, her tongue darting out to moisten her lips. "You mean after. When I —"

"When you pulled out a toy and imagined it was me makin' you come? Yeah. I heard you. And it got me so fuckin' hot, I went into my shower and painted the walls as I pictured you ridin' me."

Evie lets out a small whine, her eyes fluttering closed. I don't think she realizes she's doing it, but she leans back in toward me before her eyes fly back open and her hand lands on my chest.

"What are we doing? What...what is going on?"

I take the chance and raise my hand again to tuck some hair behind her ear. "Well, I'd say we're admitting we've both got some feelings that might be worth exploring. Some mutual desires, you might say." I grin and wink at her, trailing my hand down to take hold of hers, bringing it up to my mouth so I can press a kiss to her knuckles.

As I lower her hand, I lift my gaze to hers. A perfect pink blush colours her cheeks. I lean in, moving slowly. But my intention is clear.

I'm gonna kiss her again, and this time, we might not stop at kissing.

But just as our lips are about to meet, the distinct sound of a key in my front lock penetrates the room and we spring apart.

"Shit. It's your brother." I forgot Yami was coming over this morning so we could go over some game footage. He wanted my help analyzing our upcoming opponents.

"Oh my God." Evie stands up, running her hand through her hair before her gaze drops down to my crotch. "Rhett!" she hisses.

I look down and curse again before leaping up and hustling toward my bedroom, leaving Evie to answer the door.

Her brother walking in and seeing my dick tenting my pants would be a fuck-ton worse than me abandoning her to deal with him herself.

And for the second time in less than twelve hours, I find

myself standing under a freezing cold shower.

Chapter Thirteen

Evie

Even after Rhett and Kai leave, it takes almost an hour for my heart rate to slow down to normal. I'm absolutely stunned, my brain is completely spinning, and I feel so out of my depth I don't quite know what to do.

This is not a normal feeling for me, and I can't say I like it very much. I'm used to having a clear mind, knowing exactly what to do, and how to handle things. I had to be that way from a young age so I didn't fall behind from missing school due to my asthma. Being organized and in control helped me graduate at the top of my class.

But apparently, I put too much effort into proving myself academically and intellectually, and not enough socially. Because when it comes to men, I'm clueless on what to do.

Rhett managed to flip my entire world upside down in only a handful of minutes. And the fact that I actually felt his lips on mine and could have felt even more, yet didn't, thanks to my stupid brother interrupting, has me feeling even more spun around in circles.

I eventually manage to get up off the couch and take Ruthie out for another walk. She doesn't seem to mind or notice that I feel so off-kilter. But I'm a distracted mess, almost walking into people and trees as we wander down the streets of Vancouver.

When we eventually make our way back home, I go through the motions of making something to eat even though I am anything but hungry. But I still feel the need to try and distract myself because fixating on what happened earlier won't give me any answers to the questions swirling in my brain.

I'm dumping eggs onto a plate with some fruit and toast when my phone vibrates on the kitchen counter. Turning it over slowly, I take a deep breath to steady myself.

Is it him? Is he texting me to say he regrets what he did this morning and it was all a big misunderstanding? I'm not sure how I would survive if that's the case.

But no, thank God, it's not Rhett.

> **CARLEE: Hey girl. I wanted to say again how sorry I am about last night. I was out of line, for sure, with my comment about Rhett and with teasing you about hooking up with him.**

> **CARLEE: I hope you forgive me. Buuuut. I do think you should at least consider testing the waters, seeing if maybe he'd be interested in something. I caught him looking at you for just a second last night, and that look was pure fire.**

I pick up my phone and press the button to call her on a video chat. Her image fills the screen, and I can see the remorse written all over her face.

"Hey, you," she says. "Everything okay this morning?"

I nod. "Everything's fine. I know you didn't mean it last night; we should have remembered tequila gives you no filter from your brain to your mouth."

We both laugh, and Carlee exhales in relief. "Seriously, it's worse than truth serum. I felt so bad when I woke up this morning."

"You sure that has nothing to do with you being almost thirty?" I tease, and Carlee narrows her brows at me.

"You shush."

Her phone moves as she walks over to her couch and sits down. And a glint comes into her eyes. "I do find it interesting how quickly you jumped to his defense, however. Are you sure there's nothing else you want to tell me?"

I laugh nervously. "Like what? The fact that I have a crush on him isn't new."

"Mm-hmm," Carlee says, her head moving up and down slowly. "Except I thought it *was* a crush. Not *is* a crush. One implies you're over it, the other implies you're very much not. And the way you defended him last night? That is the action of a woman who is definitely not over her crush."

There's absolutely no chance of hiding my blush. And I know the second Carlee sees the colour darkening my cheeks, because she points a finger at the screen. "Ah-ha! I knew it! No truth serum needed."

"We kissed this morning," I blurt out in a rush, dropping my face into my hands.

"Wait, what?"

I quickly explain what happened earlier, right up to Kai

showing up and letting himself into Rhett's apartment.

"I've never been cockblocked by my brother, and I don't exactly want to experience it again," I end dramatically.

"I'm pretty sure cockblocking is for dudes."

"Then whatever the female equivalent is."

"Clam jammed."

I snort a giggle at that. "Seriously? That sounds ridiculous."

"The other options are worse. How about beaver impeder? Cliterference? Taco blocko?"

I stare at the phone screen, horrified, and yet, also amused. "How come women get all the weird names like beaver and taco, and guys just get cock or dick?"

"Oh girl. You need to get out more," Carlee teases. "There's also pecker, joystick, tallywacker, soldier —"

"Stop! Oh my God, stop." We're both full-on laughing now. "Can you imagine being in bed with a guy and calling it a tallywacker?"

"Here, baby, let's put my tallywacker into your taco," Carlee says in a deep, ridiculous voice.

When our laughter eventually dies down, I slump back against the couch, my gaze going to the ceiling. "Thanks Carlee, I needed this."

My friend is silent for a beat before she answers. "You know I love you, and respect you and how smart you are. You think things through and don't make rash decisions. But sometimes, trusting your gut instead of your brain is the better choice. What's your gut telling you to do?"

It takes me even longer to think over my response. "Honestly? I don't even know. As enticing as it is to think about giving in to what I feel for Rhett, and what he might feel for me, I still worry about Kai. How he would feel if I hooked up with his best friend." I pause and think over what I've said. "But that's not even my biggest fear. What if I go to Rhett and he turns me down again? I still have to live with him, Carlee. I have nowhere else to go. And if he rejects me, there's no way I could stay here."

"First of all, based on what you said happened earlier, he's not going to reject you. And second, you might disagree, but I don't think your brother should have an influence in this decision at all. It's your life, and what you choose to do and who you choose to do it with is nobody's business but your own." She holds up a hand as if she can tell I'm about to protest. "I know it's messy with them being best friends and teammates. But do you really think Kai would be that upset?"

My head moves up and down emphatically. "He can be so overprotective of me sometimes. There's no way he would be okay with me dating any of his teammates. Besides, I'm pretty sure Kai thinks Rhett is just another older brother for me."

"I think it's pretty obvious Rhett doesn't feel that way," Carlee says candidly. "And aren't you the one who said he's a good guy? Any time he comes up in the media, it's always positive. Sure, he's been pictured with some women, but never anything serious, so maybe he'd be up for a no-strings-attached fling. Just some fun for the two of you this summer, and then that's it."

I consider what she's suggesting. The problem is, I don't know if I could do no strings attached. Not with Rhett. Not when I know he'll still be in my life afterward, even if only through my brother.

"All I'm saying is, I know you don't want a relationship right now, you want to focus on getting your life-after-university established and stuff. But I also know how self-conscious you are when it comes to guys and your lack of experience."

Carlee's voice is gentle and I know what she's saying is coming from a good place, but it still makes me uncomfortable and I shift in my seat.

"What if Rhett is the perfect man to help you get over that? Just consider it. That's all."

"I'll think about it," I reply quietly. And it's not a lie, if anything, I doubt I'll be able to think about anything else.

Chapter Fourteen

I've been playing ball since I was four years old.

I've had dyslexia my entire fucking life.

Yet I can count on two hands the number of times my fucked-up brain has impacted my game.

For the most part, I've been lucky with coaches who understand I might take longer to process certain things or that video analysis and visual aids help where written plans and play books are a disaster.

But every now and then, my disability likes to rear its ugly head and remind me I'm not that far off from the dumb jock Evie's friend suggested I am.

"Jesus fucking Christ, Darling, what's going on out there?" Coach slams his hand against his leg. "Didn't you see what Ramo was trying to tell you?"

I grunt in acknowledgment, my jaw clenched tight. Yeah, I saw the signals. But they were so fucking fast, I couldn't make sense of them quickly enough. Which fucked up my timing leaving second, and meant the Revs got an easy out on me at third.

Coach pulls his hat off, rubbing his bald head before slamming it back on. "Alright. Well. Get your eyes up next time." He walks back to the steps leading out of the dugout and leans against the railing.

There's not much I hate more than letting down my team. I rip off my sliding mitt and toss it to the ground before leaning forward and exhaling a curse.

The fucking truth is, I can't blame just my dyslexia for my performance on the field today.

Walking away from Evie this morning, with things so up in the air, felt wrong in all kinds of ways. And then having to sit in a car next to Yami and listen to him go on and on about some club he wants to hit up tonight since we have tomorrow morning off was like pouring salt in the wound.

My plans for tonight didn't involve Yami or any of the guys. And definitely not a club. No, my plans involved uninterrupted time with Evie, preferably including a bed, but I'd accept the couch as an alternative. Whichever she preferred.

Ladies choice and all.

And now the consequences of leaving things unfinished with Evie are hitting me where it hurts. Because I can't focus on anything but the conversation I want to get back to.

"What's going on with you, Darling?" Ronan Sinclair comes to sit beside me on the bench. I don't have to look at him to imagine the concerned expression I'm sure is on his face.

"Nothin', Sin. All good."

However, I guess my answer isn't enough for him.

"Not buying it. You're off your game. I won't push, but if there's anything I can do, let me know." He leans against the bench, folding his arms across his chest. "How's everything going with Evie? She still living with you?"

I abruptly stand, needing to get away from his stare that seems to see right through me. "Yeah. Everything's fine. Excuse me, I need some water." As I move away from Sin and his all-too-knowing questions, my stomach churns. The Tridents are a family. A protective family. We look after our own, and that includes partners, siblings, and kids. Which is why, if I get involved with Evie, even if it's a one-time thing, and anyone finds out...it's not just my best friend I'll have to worry about.

It's my entire team.

Somehow, I manage to pull my shit together for the rest of the game. We even eke out a narrow win, but I can't take any credit. At least I didn't fuck up again.

In the showers, all the guys are talking about their plans for tonight. Somehow, Yami's got everyone roped in, including the wives and girlfriends.

"C'mon, Mav, you and Sadie never come out," Yami says to our third baseman. To be fair, up until recently, Mav wasn't just antisocial. He kept himself apart from the rest of us and had a reputation in the league for causing trouble.

But he's different now.

Still not social, but he smiles once in a while.

"Fuck off, Yami. I'm spending tonight at home fucking my girlfriend. You enjoy your club full of sweaty strangers."

Yami just claps his hands together, walking over to me and draping his arm over my shoulder. "Fine, fine. I don't need your sexy bad boy energy ruining my chances anyway. Darling and I will quite happily find a sweaty stranger to have some fun with. Without you."

"Sounds kinky," Mav responds drily, and I shove Yami away.

"Seriously, man," I grumble. Even though every bone in my body is screaming at me to go home to Evie, my brain is back online and saying loud and clear that not going out with the guys would raise suspicion. And the last thing I need is any reason for Yami to suspect anything is going on.

I guess I'm going out tonight.

Thankfully, the club they want to hit is within walking distance of the stadium. The entire walk there, I'm palming my phone in my pocket, debating whether I should text Evie or not. Yami said he told her that we were going out, so technically, I don't have to. But I feel like shit for not touching base with her myself.

Except, what do I say?

I shouldn't have kissed you this morning, so I'm letting your brother take me to a club so I can try to forget about you.

Yeah, that'll go over really well. Besides, she kissed me first.

In the end, I don't send anything. Whatever I say to Evie, whatever we end up doing, it can't be figured out over a text message.

At the club, Yami leads us right past the line and inside where the music pulsates.

Normally, I can enjoy a night out with the best of them. There's a reason they call me Darling.

But tonight, I'm not feeling it.

Tonight, I'd rather be heading home than pressed into a

booth in the VIP area with a rookie on one side and some woman wearing a short silver dress on the other. She's turned to face me and is leaning forward in a way that makes it far too obvious she expects me to check her out.

Too bad for her, I don't have any interest. Instead, I look around the club. Anywhere but at her.

"So, like, you guys travel a lot. Do you get to go to cool places?" she asks, sipping what looks like a martini and leaving a lipstick stain on the glass.

"All we ever see are airports, hotels, and baseball stadiums. Not a lot of time for sightseeing."

I didn't think my answer was funny, but I guess I was wrong because she titters in laughter. Honestly, she reminds me of some of the girls back home that were too big for their britches. Acted like they were fancy debutantes when in reality their mama and daddy ran the feed store.

The act didn't work on me then, and it ain't working on me now.

"Excuse me, darlin', I need to find the little boys room." I gesture for her to let me out of the booth. She pouts but moves. Not enough for a clear path, of course. Oh no, I'm treated to a full-frontal brush against her body as I move past. I suppress a shudder and head for the restrooms.

Once inside, the noise level is slightly muted, and I lean against the black countertop, letting my head hang as I breathe deeply.

My peace is short-lived when the door opens, bringing in a burst of music and background noise before it closes again.

"Dude, what the fuck is going on?"

I look up at Yami. His feet are spread wide, one hand stuffed in a pocket, the other holding a drink.

Ah, shit.

"What do you mean?" I ask, my brain scrambling to come up with an explanation. The problem is, I don't know what the fuck he saw, or thinks he saw, or...shit. Stop. Focus, Rhett.

"I mean, where the hell is my best friend? My wingman? You've been off all fucking day, man. Hell, shit's felt weird ever since I got to your apartment this morning."

My throat feels like it's closing up as he tilts his head to the side.

"Did Evie's dog piss in your shoes or something?"

And just like that, he hands me the perfect excuse on a silver platter. Sorry, pup, you're getting thrown under the bus.

"Nah, man. Just not sleeping well, I guess. You know, the damn puppy's gettin' up at all hours." The lie slips off my tongue far too easily and I hate myself for it.

"Oh yeah, that would suck." He walks over and takes a piss before joining me back at the sinks and washes his hands. "I get it if you wanna head home. Honestly, your game sucked today, bro, you need to sleep."

I give him a tight smile. "Thanks, asshole."

Yami just laughs off the insult and heads to the door. "I'm heading back out there. You good?"

I nod. Once the door closes behind him, my head falls forward again. "Fuck." At least I can go home without Yami questioning me, but now I'm not so sure I want to face Evie.

I have no idea what to do about her.

That's not true. I know what I *want* to do, and I know what

I *should* do. And I'll be damned if I can figure out which is the better option.

I leave the club without saying goodbye to anyone. In my truck, driving home, the dark streets of Vancouver offer no answers to my dilemma.

In the parking garage of my building, I turn off the engine and sit there for a minute. I want Evie. But having her puts a lot at risk.

I've got to force the idea of being with her out of my head. She's a temporary roommate. A friend. My best friend's sister.

And she can't be anything more.

The door to my apartment opens silently, thank God. The lights are off except for the dim one in my kitchen that Evie leaves on when she knows I'm coming home late. My gaze lands on the two coffee mugs sitting beside the coffee maker.

A silent reminder that tomorrow morning I'll have to face her.

After stripping down to my underwear, I fall into bed and stare at my ceiling. No matter how hard I try to convince myself that I'm making the right decision by re-establishing a boundary with Evie before we fully cross it, I can't get my mind to settle enough to let me sleep.

Which is why I drag my sorry ass out of bed at six, pull on a pair of sweats and an old T-shirt, and stumble into the kitchen, needing coffee injected straight into my veins, preferably.

I'm halfway through my first cup when I hear a door open, and Ruthie comes scampering toward me. I bend down to give her some love, petting her head and scratching her floppy ears until I hear the sound of softer footfalls coming down the hall.

I straighten and slowly lift my gaze to her. She's standing at the edge of the hallway with one foot crossed on top of the other, looking adorably sleep mussed. Her long black hair cascades in messy waves over her shoulder, and she's wearing an oversized T-shirt that's so big, I can't tell if she's got anything on underneath.

And all of the logic I wrestled my way into believing last night, the decision that makes sense and protects both Evie and myself, flies out of my head as the blood rushes downward.

Maybe she's not meant to be mine forever, but for right now? She is.

It's only a few long strides to close the distance between us. One hand lands on her hip as I push her back against the wall. Her mouth falls open as she looks up at me with wide eyes.

"I really wanna kiss you right now, Evangeline."

This close, I can feel her chest rising and falling rapidly. But she doesn't answer. I'm about to step away, not willing to do something she doesn't want just as badly as I do, when three words are whispered into the tense silence between us.

"Then you should."

CHAPTER FIFTEEN

Evie

This kiss is so much more than yesterday's.

So. Much. More.

My senses explode.

At least that's what it feels like. I'm consumed by Rhett and the fire inside of me. His hand is gripping my hip tightly, the other is tangled in my hair. The press of his hips has my body back against the wall and it's a fight not to grind against him.

I may lack experience with men, but I'm far from innocent. I'd like to think I'm in touch with my own sensual side, and right now, every fibre of my being is vibrating with desire. I'm not nervous, not at all. Everything with him feels natural, perfect, like we were always meant to be doing this.

I clutch at his shoulders as his lips explore mine, our tongues tangling together. A small whimper escapes me when his teeth graze my lower lip and he goes to pull back, but I don't let him.

Pulling him closer, I press in deeper. His large hand moves from my hip and around to my ass, the heat from his touch leaving a trail of sensation. When his fingers dig into my flesh, he freezes, and I know what he's just discovered.

He wrenches his lips away from mine and our eyes meet. His

deep brown ones meet my own.

"Are you naked underneath, honey?"

His gravelly voice has me panting underneath him as I nod. But where I expect him to turn feral, Rhett turns sweet.

His forehead meets mine, as he moves the hand that's tangled in my hair around to cup my cheek. "Goddamn, you're perfect," he says on an exhale. Then he lifts his head, and any trace of sweetness has been replaced by something else, something far more enticing. "If you don't want this, then say something now, Evangeline. Otherwise, I'm gonna pin you to my bed and give you what you deserve from a man. You'll be screamin' my name, and it won't be a toy getting you there, it'll be me."

My mouth goes dry.

Lifting up on my tiptoes, I press my lips to the pulse point I can see throbbing in his neck. "I want that. All of that. I want you to be the first man to give me an orgasm. You're the only one I trust to take care of me."

A half groan, half growl is the only response I get to my babbling before strong hands are lifting me up, and I can feel his hips — no, his cock — pressing into my core through the thin fabric of his sweatpants as I'm pinned to the wall, just as promised.

It would be so easy to let go. And I'm right on the cusp of doing so when one horrifying thought hits me.

"Wait!" I mumble against his lips, pushing at his chest as best I can. Rhett freezes immediately and backs away, still holding me in place.

"What?"

"Is Kai going to show up again?"

Rhett drops his head to my shoulder with a throaty chuckle. "Not if he values his life."

"Okay, but he has a key," I say, wiggling to be let down.

"And he was out late last night. Plus, we have the day off, so knowing your brother, he won't wake before noon." Rhett glances down at his wrist, then back up at me with a smirk. "Which gives us just over four hours before we have to worry about him."

I give him a coy look. "Yeah? And what do you think we should do with those four hours?"

I'm back up in the air, my legs wrapped around Rhett's body as he walks down the hall. "I've got a few ideas, don't you worry."

We enter Rhett's room, and he closes the door behind us with one foot before carrying me over to the bed. That's where I discover a perk to being with an athlete as he showcases his incredible strength, lowering me to the bed and bringing himself over me, all without losing his grip on my hips.

"Fuck, Evie. You've been driving me wild for so long. I can't quite believe this is happening."

There's that sweetness again, and it makes me melt into a puddle of need. But I want more than just sweet words and sexy kisses.

I need him.

"Rhett, I don't need you to be the smooth-talking, charming southern gentleman right now."

He cocks an eyebrow at me. "Excuse me, what?"

"I need you to be the man who said he'd pin me to his bed and make me scream his name."

His face relaxes into a knowing smirk. "Oh yeah? What exactly do you want that man to do?"

"He promised to show me what I deserve, so I would imagine that involves several things."

Rhett's lips land on my neck in a slow, open kiss. "Such as?" His hand moves to the hem of my shirt, then underneath.

I fight not to wriggle, to try and move his hand to where I want it. "I think he'd be smart enough to figure it out," I say, barely above a whisper.

Rhett moves his hand slowly up to my bare hip. "Ah, and since you don't want the southern gentleman, is it safe to assume you would want this man to take control?"

"Oh yes," I breathe as he slowly, lightly drags his fingers across my hip bone from one side to the other. "I think that's an excellent idea."

"Hmm," he rumbles as he drags his hand higher, taking my shirt with it. I'm bare from the waist down, and I can now feel the rough fabric of his clothes rasping against my skin. But when I move my hands down to his pants, he stills.

"I think you need to keep those hands out of trouble, honey." Rearing back to sit on his heels, Rhett still doesn't take the opportunity to look down at my naked body. Instead, his gaze is trained on my face as he lifts my hands up above my head. Holding them there with one hand, he leans down and kisses me softly.

"Can you keep 'em there?"

I nod rapidly.

"Good girl."

I grip the pillow as he finally slides his body down mine at the same time as he tugs my shirt up farther, just above my breasts.

"Look at you. Fucking gorgeous." It seems as if he's murmuring to himself, so I don't answer. He glances back up at my face, bringing his hands to cover my breasts, thumb and forefinger pinching my nipples. My back arches as I gasp out his name.

"Rhett!"

He steals my breath with his next kiss, his fingers still playing with my nipples in ways I never imagined would feel so good. So satisfying while also making me desperate for more.

His lips trail down my neck again, over my bunched-up shirt, and onto my bare skin. As soon as his mouth closes over my breast, my hands come flying down to grip his hair, a moan escaping me at the feel of that wet heat.

Then it's gone.

"What did I tell you about keeping those hands out of trouble?" he growls, one hand pinning both of mine back up above my head. His expression is wild, his eyes burning as he stares at me. I can't help but whimper.

"Sorry."

His lips quirk up in a small grin, and there's that sweet side of him again. "Don't get me wrong. I like knowing you can't keep your hands off me. Feeling's mutual. But your first lesson starts now. You need to learn how important it is to trust your partner to know what you need. Okay?"

I nod again. "Okay."

His free hand strokes my cheek. "Good."

This time when his tongue laves my nipple, I manage to keep my hands where they are. Even as he swirls around, stiffening it into a hard peak, I just close my eyes, grip the pillow, and give in to his touch.

I've never done this — fully surrendered to letting someone else care for me. Even the few times I've gone to a spa, I have never been able to relax and just enjoy it. Always needing to be aware, involved, and in control. A therapist would probably tell me it's from being sick as a child, poked and prodded by doctors, my decisions made for me by my parents and care providers. Whatever the reason, in this moment, it doesn't matter.

With Rhett, that need for control is let go. I trust him. I trust him to take care of me.

He shifts, moving farther down my body, his lips covering every inch of me in kisses. But something's wrong.

"You're wearing too many clothes," I manage to say without it sounding too much like a needy whine. "I need to feel your skin on mine."

Rhett pauses, his lips hovering just below my ribs. "There's no rush. We've got plenty of time. But right now, these clothes are the only things stopping me from speeding things up way faster than I want to. Which is lesson number two. Sometimes, fast and dirty is good. Sometimes, you gotta slow down and feel everything."

He kisses my belly button and I clench the pillow even tighter. "Okay, but maybe a little bit faster wouldn't be a bad thing?"

His chuckle vibrates against my skin. "You feelin' needy?" His fingers drag lightly over my skin, circling just above my pubic bone.

"Rhett, *please.*"

He laughs again. "Not gonna lie, I like hearing you beg. But since this is all about you right now, I won't keep you waiting."

His nose moves down, dragging through the neatly trimmed hairs covering my pussy. "Damn, Evie," he groans, his hands coming back to grip my hips before sliding down and pressing my thighs open. "You smell so sweet. You're gonna wreck me, aren't you."

His southern drawl is so much stronger now. I love it, his dirty talk sliding over me like warm honey. Then a different kind of warmth hits me when he opens his mouth and laps up my slit with his tongue.

"Oh God, yes," I moan, my hands releasing the pillow. I don't get to hold onto his shoulders the way I want before he somehow senses what I'm doing and snakes one long arm up to pin my wrists down.

I'm trapped under his touch, with no choice but to let him drive me higher and higher. His lips, his tongue, his teeth, all of them working together, making me feel things no sex toy — and no man — ever has. And yet...

"I need more," I manage to gasp, not even fully knowing what that *more* could possibly be. But once again, Rhett proves that he knows.

"I've got you, honey." He lifts his head and lets go of my hands but gives me a wink. "Keep 'em there. My hands are needed elsewhere."

Raising that hand to his mouth, he pops two fingers in and sucks, pulling them out to show they're glistening wet. Bending back down, he sucks my clit into his mouth, his tongue circling around it a few times before doing another slow lap up and down my slit. Then, his eyes trained on mine, he slowly plunges his fingers inside of me.

My hips lift off the bed, seeking more, even as I feel like I couldn't possibly take it. A large, hot hand presses down on my pubic bone, holding me in place as Rhett destroys my pussy with his mouth and his fingers.

The one other time I've had a man go down on me, it was over in a few minutes, and he was thrusting his small dick into me before I even had a chance to feel anything.

This is not like that time.

Rhett plays me like a maestro with a violin. No, like a professional baseball player in game seven of the world series. He plays my body like it's the last thing he'll ever do. Like giving me pleasure gives him life.

Like making me orgasm is the *only* thing that matters.

"That's it, Evie. God, you taste so good. Flood me, baby. Cover me with it. Give it all to me."

His steady stream of dirty talk catapults me over the edge into an orgasm unlike anything I've ever given myself.

I'm just barely aware of the fact that I'm making some keening sound, my hands are gripping his hair so tightly I wouldn't be surprised if I came away with a few strands, and my body is bowed over his head as he gently licks and strokes me through my climax.

When my body finally relaxes back against the bed and I force my fingers to unclench from his hair, he lifts up on one hand and brings those fingers that were just inside of me to his mouth, sucking them once again.

"I was right. So sweet. And so fuckin' perfect when you let go." He moves up my body, pressing kisses along the way until he reaches my shirt that has fallen down a bit with all my move-ment. He lifts it over my head and tosses it behind me before pinning me in with one hand on either side of my head and a wicked smirk on his handsome face.

"But what are we gonna do about the fact that you didn't keep your hands outta trouble?"

Chapter Sixteen

Evie

Maybe having my mouth gape open and closed like a fish isn't the most attractive response to Rhett's statement, but it's such a perfectly delicious and dirty promise, with the tiny hint of a threat, that I honestly can't help it.

"You like that idea?" He chuckles again. "Of me punishing you for misbehaving?"

I try to swallow but my mouth is dry.

He bends down and kisses the hollow where my neck meets my chest. "Here's the thing, honey. You might have said you didn't want a smooth, charming gentleman. Except you can take the man out of the south, but you can't take the south out of the man. I'll always be a gentleman, just with a few rough edges sometimes." His stubble rasps against my sensitive skin, emphasizing that point.

I have to wiggle a bit, but I manage to get my hands between us and grip his head, bringing it back up to mine.

"Rough, charming, I don't care. I just want *you*."

"Good answer."

His lips are on mine again, and I lose myself in the kiss. My naked body is writhing underneath his very much still-clothed one.

"You're *still* wearing too many clothes," I pant, fumbling with the hem of his shirt. He ignores me, continuing to press kisses all over my upper body as his hips grind into my core. "Rhett. Ohhhh God," I moan when he presses right where I need him most.

He finally lifts his arms up, somehow managing to hold himself in place with my breast under his lips, and I tug his shirt over his head. His hair is a wild mess, but at last that bare chest I've drooled over for the last couple of weeks is mine to touch. And taste.

I push on his pecs, and he rolls us over so that I'm astride him. And it's abundantly clear that under the thin layer of fabric, his cock is long, thick, and very hard.

"Goddamn, this is a nice view," he drawls, his hands running up and down my thighs. "You'd look so fucking sexy riding a horse."

My brows lift as I bite back a smirk. "Really? You're picturing me riding a horse?" I grind my hips in a slow circle over his length. "I had something else in mind."

"Oh really?"

I nod slowly, raking my fingers down his chest. "It's my turn, Rhett. Should I tell you to keep your hands to yourself?" I ask pertly.

He laughs, low and rumbly, as he gathers my messy hair up in one hand. "You can try, but I'm no better at listening than you were."

In one smooth move, he lifts up to sitting, kisses me hard, then uses my hair to tug my head back, exposing my neck. He runs his nose up and down as he wraps his free hand around my waist, pulling me in close. The ridge of his cock fits perfectly between my legs, and I swear I can feel it throb beneath his sweatpants. Our chests are pressed together, and the tickle of the soft hair lightly covering his torso feels exquisite on my sensitive skin.

Rhett reaches a spot just below my collarbone and kisses it before lifting his head to look at me. "You mind if I mark you here?"

"Mark me?"

"I want you to remember this moment for a long time. Remember the way I made you feel."

His lips press to the spot again as I let out a breathy moan. "Trust me, I'm in no danger of forgetting."

I feel him start to suck, his teeth grazing the skin. He doesn't linger, but when he releases me, sure enough, there's a faint mark marring my skin.

"Makes you look good, baby," he rumbles. "Like you're mine." He kisses the spot again and again and again.

Oh God, that's everything I want, and nothing I can have. I don't say anything, because the hazy expression on his face makes me wonder if he's even fully aware of what he just said.

I want to be his. I want it so badly.

But if I can't have him for any more than just this once, I'm damn well going to enjoy every second of it. Which is why I push him away, smirking when he falls back on the bed. I shimmy my hips downward and tug those sweats down his legs until his cock is free.

Yep, just as I suspected. Thick, long, and definitely hard. My tongue darts out, moistening my lips.

"You keep staring at me like that and I'm gonna get a complex," Rhett says, his tone coloured with amusement.

Ignoring him, I gingerly run my finger down the rigid length of his cock, and it bounces under my touch, making me snatch my hand away.

Rhett laughs at me. "You've seen one before, haven't you?"

I lick my lips again, wrap my hand around his base, and look up at him with one eyebrow raised. "I have. But I've never had a chance to...explore." I give him an experimental stroke, and his fist clenches the sheet. "And never one so...impressive."

That's really the only word for it. I have no concept of what's average for men, but Rhett seems ideal to me. A nice length, not so long it'll impale me but long enough to hit where I want it. Thick, and with a long vein running up the underside that I suddenly want to run my tongue along.

So I do.

Dipping my head down quickly, I lick along his cock, taking in the slightly salty, slightly musky taste. Not too bad. And Rhett's moan makes me eager to do more. I swirl a circle on the tip, glancing up to see his jaw clenched, eyes closed, and face upturned. I smile to myself, and slide my lips over the head, taking some of him into my mouth.

"Fucking Christ," he bites out, rearing up, grabbing my hair, and pulling me off him. "No lesson needed here, honey, you're an expert. But if you keep doing that, this'll be over long before it should be."

I let him tug me up his body to meet him for a kiss, and when he lightly smacks his hand on my ass, I lay down on top of him.

My legs are still on either side, but when I try to shift so I'm resting more on the side of him, he holds me firmly in place. "Don't be thinking I'm lettin' you go anywhere," he says, gently kneading the globes of my ass. "You've got a lot more to learn."

"I assumed that was the case," I reply pertly. "I just didn't want to crush you."

Rhett throws back his head and roars with laughter before pulling me even more on top of him. "Honey, you couldn't crush me if you tried. Although, having your sweet little body on top of mine feels like heaven, so maybe you did and I've already died." He smirks, his eyes still alight with laughter. "Then again, if this was heaven, I'd already be inside of you."

My eyes roll as I hold back a snort. "That's cheesy, even for you, charming."

Wrapping his arms around me, Rhett rolls us over swiftly. And now I'm the one in danger of being crushed. Or I would be if he wasn't holding himself over me.

"Thought you didn't want charming?"

"Maybe I don't mind it so much." I run my hands up and down his back, feeling the muscles bunch and ripple under my touch. "Especially with a few rough edges."

Rhett moves his hips in a way that runs one of those edges along my pussy, making me ache to be filled.

"I've got condoms in the bathroom," he says, leaning down to kiss my neck. "But the team tests us at the start of each season. I was clear, and I haven't been with anyone since."

He thrusts his hips again, the friction of his cock sliding against me, making me dig my nails into his back.

"I've got an IUD, and —" I pause on a gasp as he moves

once more. "And I'm clear. Oh my God, Rhett, fuck me already. Please."

I've never begged a man for anything before. But after finally experiencing my first orgasm with a man and not a toy, I'm desperate for another. And I can now confirm my friends were right.

Rhett is the perfect man to make this happen.

"Do you realize what it does to me, hearing you beg like that?" he growls in my ear before capturing my earlobe between his teeth. "Fuck. I can feel how wet you are for me. You're gonna take me so good, aren't you."

"Yes, God! I'm so ready. Please." I try to reach my hand down between us but he beats me to it, lifting his hips, grabbing his cock, and notching it to my entrance.

"Evie," he says. Just my name. That's all. And then he's sliding inside, filling me, easing the ache that's been building for what feels like forever.

With just a few thrusts, Rhett settles over me, our hips pressed together as tightly as possible. He looks down at me with what almost looks like reverence in his gaze. His hips lift slightly, pumping in and out in slow, small movements that make me shiver as we stare at each other.

This changes everything.

We both know that.

And in this moment, that change feels like the best thing to ever happen to me.

His kiss is sweet, soft at first, but growing deeper and more insistent as he starts to move faster.

I moan into his mouth when he changes the angle, just

enough to stroke inside of me in almost the perfect spot. Almost — but not quite.

"I need... Rhett..." I don't know how to say what I need. I don't even know what it is. But something is building inside of me that feels like it will obliterate me. And I'm reaching for it, fumbling, unable to find it.

Until Rhett rears back, lifting my legs up onto his shoulders, damn near bending me in half. He kisses the inside of my calf and pulls out almost entirely before plunging back in.

"Yes!" I scream, and he does it again.

"Yes, yes, yes." I'm babbling incoherently as whatever he does ignites the coil that leads straight to my core. Minutes, or maybe even seconds later, I can't catch my breath until everything in me lets go all at once.

I feel Rhett pulse inside of me and hear him grunt out my name. "Fuck, Evie."

His hot, slightly-sticky-with-sweat body lands on mine, his head coming to the space between my head and my shoulder, his lips pressed to my neck. We stay like that for a few seconds, and I can feel his heart racing just as fast as mine.

"That...that was incredible," I manage to say as Rhett rolls off me and to the side. He laces his fingers with mine, drawing my hand up to kiss my knuckles.

"You are incredible," he murmurs against my skin, continuing to kiss the back of my hand.

I shift onto my side, and he brings our joined hands onto his chest, turning his head to look at me.

"So what happens now?" I ask quietly, not sure why I'm questioning him at this exact moment. Surely, the conversation could wait a little longer. At least until I've gotten up to use the bathroom and clean up.

Rhett seems to be considering my question, his eyes searching my face. "Well, in an ideal world, we'd do that all over again. Cover any material we missed the first time."

My lips quirk up in a smile. I can't deny I'm relieved he also doesn't want to burst the bubble we've created for ourselves quite yet.

"You sure you're up for that? I mean, you are *quite* a few years older than me," I tease. "I'd understand if your stamina wasn't quite up for it."

Rhett pulls me over him with a growl, smacking my ass. "My stamina is just fine."

He lifts my hips, and I grab his already-hard-again cock and line it up with my entrance.

"Oh yeah?" I smirk. "Prove it."

"Trust me. I will."

CHAPTER SEVENTEEN

Rhett

That was perfect. So goddamn perfect. We should be getting up; it's almost noon. But even two orgasms — three for Evie — later, I don't feel anywhere near done with her.

If we could, I'd stay here all goddamn day, fucking Evie, cuddling Evie, laughing with Evie.

We're both on our sides, our legs tangled together. My hand is lightly running up and down the slope of her hip. She's got her hands tucked under the pillow, her lips look well-kissed, and her eyes are soft and sleepy.

She's the most beautiful woman I've ever laid eyes on.

But we can't stay here forever. Hell, we probably shouldn't be here at all. I've committed the cardinal sin by sleeping with my best friend's little sister.

Except right now, I can't bring myself to give two shits about that.

"Rhett." Evie's tongue darts out and runs along her lips. "What are we going to do now?" It's an echo of her earlier question. But I can't avoid it by plying her with more sex any longer, no matter how enjoyable that would be for both of us.

"Well, first, I was thinkin' we'd take a shower," I start, but my smile doesn't become full-blown. I know that's not what she's asking, and it's not fair for me to deflect. "Then I suppose we need to decide what happens next between us."

I see her throat bob as she swallows. "Any thoughts on that?"

I reach out and run my fingers along a piece of midnight black hair. "Plenty. Not sure any of them make sense yet. You?"

"Same."

A beat of silence passes. And in that beat, a thousand thoughts fly through my head. Confusing, unfamiliar thoughts of a future with Evie.

A future I know I won't have.

This can't be more than just some casual fun.

She trails a finger over my chest. "I do know that I don't want this to be the only time I get to be with you."

"Me neither."

Relief flashes across her face, and her lips turn up in a quick smile. Then she's tugging her lip between her teeth, as if she's worried about what this all means.

She's not the only one. Because continuing to fool around with Evie is risky as all hell. For both of us. She's the kind of woman whose heart is so big, I know it'll be hard for her to avoid feelings becoming involved if we keep doing this. More than that, she's the kind of woman it would be easy for any man to develop feelings for.

Including me.

But that puts my friendship with her brother, hell, maybe even the dynamic on the team, in danger of falling apart when those feelings don't lead to anything more.

Yami is my best friend, my teammate, the closest thing to a

brother I have. We love each other like family. He trusted me with his baby sister when he didn't trust anyone else. And I worry he'll see this as the biggest betrayal of that trust.

As much as I don't want to, I ready myself to tell her that maybe we actually shouldn't do this again.

And then she says, "It won't ever be more than just sex, though. It can't be."

Just sex. With her.

I shouldn't agree. But I'll be fucked if I can say no.

"Yeah. Just sex."

I feel like the biggest piece of horse shit for more than one reason, even though I know it's the way it has to be unless I'm prepared to give her up. And after what just happened, I honestly don't know if I can do that.

She nods slowly, her face showing nothing about what she's feeling. "And it has to be secret. No one can know."

I take a full breath in and out before answering, part of me relieved at the thought I'll get to have her again, the other part spiraling over the shitstorm we're potentially opening ourselves up to. "I agree. Your brother..."

Evie rolls her eyes. "Kai should mind his own business. But he won't. I know that. And I don't want to get between the two of you or make things difficult for the team."

My chest feels tight. She's saying all the right things. Yet how can something feel so good but be so wrong all at the same time?

"You're a good man, Rhett."

I blink at Evie's words. I'm not sure what prompted her to say that, whether she could read my mind, or just sense the guilt I'm trying to ignore. But I lean in and kiss her.

"I try to be. You make me want to be bad, though, honey." Maybe it's not fair to turn her sweet comment into a joke, but I have to. I don't know how else to process everything I'm feeling.

"Rhett." She stops me with a hand on my chest just as I was about to roll her onto her back and go for round three. "I'm serious. You're a good guy. You're smart, and kind, and talented, and funny, and handsome. You're worth more than just some fun for a while." She looks down for a second as something crosses her face. "Even if that's all this is. I'm just saying, you deserve more. And someday I hope you let yourself have it with someone."

I want what she's describing. I really do. And as she's talking, my mind starts to picture a future with someone in it. Someone who looks a hell of a lot like Evie.

Which is stupid, and crazy, and not something I should be thinking about. We're just two adults attracted to each other who gave in to the inevitable and ended up in bed together.

That doesn't mean it's going to ever develop into something more.

That it *could* develop into something more.

I push those thoughts away and turn my focus back on the woman in my arms. The woman who just agreed to no-strings-attached sex with me.

My smile comes easily as I push my fingers through her hair. "Well, now, fun is what we're gonna have. So how about we —"

A small bark interrupts me, and Evie's eyes widen as she pushes at my chest, panic covering her face. "Oh my God, Ruthie!" she cries, throwing back the covers and jumping out of bed.

Shit. The dog.

She flings open the door, still completely naked, and I'm right behind her as we rush out into the living room to see what destruction might await us, having forgotten about the rambunctious pup living with us.

"I can't believe I forgot about her," Evie says, but then she comes up short in the living room. "Oh no."

The smell is unmistakable.

"Ah, shit."

Evie snorts, and after a second, I realize what I said and I start to laugh as well. Pretty soon we're just two naked fools laughing as we take in a sleeping puppy and a pile of dog shit on the floor.

"I'm sorry about this," Evie says when we finally calm down. She's already moving into the kitchen to get the cleaning supplies. "I'll take care of the mess if you want to shower." When she bends over, that beautiful ass is on display, and like a moth to a flame, I move over behind her and wrap my arm around her waist.

"I'd rather we clean up the mess together, then clean each other up together." I press a kiss to her spine as she straightens. The minx wiggles her ass back into my crotch, and my semi starts to stiffen even further.

"Seriously?" she says over her shoulder with a saucy grin. "Again?"

"Any time, honey." I wink, then move away, grabbing the paper towels and following her to the mess. We clean it up quickly, Ruthie still passed out on the couch, blissfully unaware of the fully nude humans cleaning up her shit.

When we're done, and the windows are open to air out the

foul stench, I take Evie's hand and lead her back down the hallway. If she finds it weird that we just did all of that with no clothes on, she doesn't say so, and I find it incredibly sexy that she's so comfortable in her own skin around me.

She tries to pull me to a stop outside the spare bathroom, but I keep going. "We're usin' my shower." Inside my room, I spin her into my arms and continue walking, guiding her since she's going backward into my bathroom. She's smiling, her arms around my neck as we go.

"And why's that?"

"First of all, it's bigger. And in case you hadn't noticed, I'm not a small guy."

She giggles, and I continue. "And second of all, I want you smelling like me when we're done. To remind you of what I can make you do."

Her breath catches on a moan as I bend down and cover her nipple with my mouth, tugging on it gently.

"As if I could forget," she manages to say, threading her fingers in my hair, and pulling my head back up so she can kiss me.

Never forget.

I don't know where that thought comes from, or the one that follows. I never want her to forget how I make her feel. Hell, I never want her to have an opportunity to forget. I want her in my bed, night after night, moaning my name. I want to be the only man to ever make her come.

I push those impossible ideas away, into a back corner of my mind.

The day will come when our fun ends and Evie will go off and find some lucky bastard who will get to be the one to give her a happy ending. In the bedroom and in life.

Right now, however, that bastard is me. And as we step under the warm spray of the shower, I vow to myself to bring her as much pleasure as I possibly can for as long as I have her.

Chapter Eighteen

Evie

I can't stop stealing glances at Rhett as we walk down the paved path that goes around the perimeter of Stanley Park, Ruthie zigzagging in front of us, sniffing at absolutely everything.

When we eventually got out of bed, and there was no word from Kai, Rhett asked about going for a walk. I said yes without thinking about how it might feel to do something so normal after he flipped my world upside down over the course of a couple of hours this morning.

There's a lingering ache between my legs. A pleasant one, but the beard burn on the inside of my thighs isn't loving the feel of my Lycra shorts as much. Small price to pay, I suppose.

My hand bumps Rhett's for the third time. "Sorry," I say quietly, shifting slightly over to the other side.

When he abruptly stops, it catches me by surprise. I turn, eyebrows raised. "Everything okay?"

"That depends. Are you gonna apologize every time you touch me? Seems a bit much, seein' as I saw you naked not that long ago."

I quickly close the distance between us, my gaze darting

around to make sure no one is in hearing range. "Rhett! You can't talk like that. What if someone hears you?"

"Why would that matter?"

I stare at him. He's a smart guy, surely he's not this obtuse. "All it takes is one person posting on their social media about seeing Rhett Darlington with a woman and talking about seeing her naked, and then..." I trail off. The rest doesn't need to be said.

Remorse flashes over his face. "Sorry, honey. I didn't think it through. I just wanted you to know, if you want to hold my hand, I won't complain."

Oh my heart.

No! Stop it, heart. We can't do that.

"We can't," I say gently. "Remember the whole secret thing?"

He grimaces but nods. "Yeah. I do. C'mon, let's keep going."

We continue walking with a touch more space between us now. I've never hated a couple of inches so much.

"You and your brother have both mentioned your asthma a time or two," he starts, looking over at me. "Is there anything I should know? Exercise restrictions?" He smirks, and even though I'm the one who just said we need to be careful, I nudge him with my shoulder.

"No, it's not that kind of asthma. Exercise is fine."

"Good. So, no worries about rapid heart rate or heavy breathing."

"Oh my God, stop." I laugh. But I'm grateful for the ease of the weird tension I'd managed to put between us. "It's when I get sick. My lungs can't handle viruses well, so those tend to result in a flare-up. Not always, but sometimes. I've got it under control now, though."

He nods in understanding. "Must've been scary when you were a kid."

"You have no idea. I still feel so much guilt for the stress my family went through trying to keep me healthy and out of the hospital. I know that's why Kai can be so protective, heck, my entire family sometimes treats me with kid gloves. They can't seem to trust that I'm capable of taking care of my own health now."

"They love you, there's no need to feel guilty for that." His hand brushes mine this time, his pinky hooking around mine for just the briefest of seconds.

I think back to all of Kai's baseball games that one of my parents had to miss because of me, or Josephine's piano recitals. All of the days my parents had to stay home from work because I couldn't go to school. It was a lot. I know it was. That's the only reason I don't get more upset with them when they hover, even now.

"I remember one time I was visiting, it might have been the second or third time Yami brought me home. You had been sick, but he didn't tell me how bad it was. We walked in the door, and he beelined over to the couch in the living room and hugged you for so long. All I could think was how lucky you were to have siblings who loved you like that."

Even though he says the words in an even, warm tone, I can detect a thread of longing. "You were an only child, right?"

Rhett nods. "Yeah, my mom struggled to get pregnant with me, so they decided to stop trying after that." A sad smile crests his lips. "Sometimes I'd wish for siblings, but looking back, I know my relationship with my mom wouldn't be as special as it is, if it hadn't been just me and her."

"How old were you when your dad died?"

"Fourteen. Old enough to know and miss him, young enough not to realize how precious my time with him was. Especially after he got his diagnosis." He lets out a pained laugh, and impulsively, I grab his hand, squeezing it tightly with my own. "There were so many times I chose to go to the field and mess around with my friends instead of staying home with him. I'd give anything to get those moments back."

We walk hand in hand for a couple of minutes before two joggers round the corner in front of us. Rhett drops my hand and takes a small step to the side, nodding at them as they pass us. We come upon a large tree that backs onto an empty field, and out of nowhere, he takes hold of my forearm and tugs me around it.

The next thing I know, my back is pressed into the knobbly bark of the tree, and his warm lips are pressing into mine. The kiss is over all too quickly, and then he's backing away. But those eyes. Those deep brown liquid pools are staring into mine so intently.

I wait for him to say something. To explain why he just did that. Then again, does it need an explanation? Apparently not, as Rhett simply tilts his head in the direction of the path, and we continue walking.

Only now, when our fingers brush together, we don't pull back right away. And those tiny touches are like little sparks. Not strong enough to catch into a flame, but enough to give me a tiny jolt every time.

By the time we make it back to Rhett's truck, it's late afternoon and the park is busy, full of tourists and locals all out exploring. It's a bit of a miracle we weren't stopped by anyone recognizing Rhett, to be honest.

"Should we teach this little lady how to play fetch?" Rhett asks, gesturing to the field near where we parked, only a couple of people sitting on a picnic blanket at one end.

"I didn't bring a ball," I say with a frown. "Otherwise, I'd say yes."

"Honey. I'm a baseball player. You think I go anywhere without a couple of balls?" Rhett winks, and then reaches into the back seat of his truck and pulls out a tennis ball.

I give him a delighted smile as Ruthie barks and lifts up on her hind legs to try and sniff the new toy. "Perfect."

Taking out the extra long leash I bought for training her recall, I switch her regular one out, and we move onto the grass. Rhett tosses it close to her the first few times, crouching down to cajole her back to him when she picks it up.

"She's a quick learner," I comment after she bounds back to him for the third time.

"She certainly is, let's try a longer throw." Rhett lobs the ball a little bit farther, and off she goes. "I knew she'd be a ball player." He winks at me, and Ruthie comes running back.

"Let me try." I move to his side, handing him the leash as I take the slobbery ball. "Ew, girl, this is gross."

Rhett chuckles. "We should get one of those long-handled throwing things for your princess hands."

"I do not have princess hands, I just don't love slimy wet balls," I say, pretending to be affronted.

He arches his brow at me, and after a second, I realize what I said. We both burst out laughing as Ruthie dances around our feet, barking for the ball to be thrown again.

"Okay, okay, patience, pup," I admonish after finally getting myself under control. I lean back and throw the ball, only to have it hit the ground way off to the side and roll to a stop in front of a runner.

A familiar runner.

"I see your aim still hasn't improved, Gigi," my brother calls out as he jogs over to us. "It's offensive to my pitcher soul that you still can't throw in a straight line."

Rhett, the traitor, laughs at my brother's not-so-funny statement. "Maybe I was trying to throw it over there to challenge her."

"Were you, though?" Kai teases. He tosses the ball effortlessly, and Ruthie runs after it. "This is mighty domestic looking, even for you, Darling."

Rhett makes a choking sound as I duck down to get the ball from my dog, trying to fight back a blush.

"I'm surprised you left your apartment. What time did you get home last night?"

"Listen. Not all of us are old men who need to go to bed before midnight," Kai fires back.

"Anyway, we should get going," I interrupt their banter, taking Ruthie's leash from Rhett and tugging her toward the truck. "Don't you have to pack, Rhett?" I give him a look that I hope he can interpret.

"Right, yes. I should do that," he says before reaching out and pulling Kai in for a man-hug. "See you tomorrow, Yami."

After I load Ruthie in the truck, I go and give my brother a quick hug of my own. "Good luck, Kai."

"See ya, Gigi. But seriously, we need to work on your arm." He rubs his knuckles over the top of my head like the obnoxious older brother he can be sometimes, and I scowl at him.

"You're annoying."

"And you love me." He smiles triumphantly.

I roll my eyes as he backs away. "Only sometimes."

When I get in the truck, Rhett's already buckled up but twisted around to face the back as he scratches Ruthie's head, murmuring to her under his breath.

"That was close." I sigh as I slump against my seat. "What are the chances we see him here?"

"Honestly? Pretty good. A lot of the guys run in this park."

I turn and stare at him in horror. "Then why the heck did we come for a walk here? Oh my God, you kissed me. What if one of your teammates saw us?"

In lieu of an answer, Rhett leans over and kisses me again.

"You're cute when you panic, honey. I made sure no one was around."

He turns forward again and pulls out of the parking lot, one hand on the steering wheel, the other resting on the center console between us.

"Somethin' on your mind?" he asks after a moment, and I realize he's caught me staring.

"You call most women darling."

His brows gather together briefly before he nods. "Guess it's a southern thing."

My lips hike up. "But you call me honey."

His hand moves to the top of my thigh, his fingers lightly stroking the bare skin below my shorts.

"Because you're not most women."

CHAPTER NINETEEN

RHETT: How my good girl doing

My jaw drops at Rhett's text. And not only because of the typo in the first word.

He left yesterday for another series of away games, and *this* is the first message he sends? Memories of him calling me a good girl in the bedroom flood me, making me feel hot all over.

RHETT: Just thought about how that sounds sorry to say I mean roofie

RHETT: Ruthie the dog

RHETT: But hope your doing good too

I frown at my phone for several minutes, trying to decipher his messages. Not that I can't tell what he's saying, but was he in a rush while typing? There's no punctuation, and the misspelling of Ruthie's name is kind of funny.

EVIE: Both girls are doing fine. I

> **watched the game last night, that hit in the third inning was amazing.**

His response takes a long time to come through, even though I see the three dots that tell me he's replying.

> **RHETT: I like knowing you are watching the game. Got to go now**

I set my phone back down, still a little confused by his messages.

Turning back to my computer, I sigh in frustration at the screen. Not that it's the computer's fault that I'm struggling with my job search, but still.

On a slightly hysterical whim, I open a new window and look up the website of the school board for the district where my family still lives. I click onto the open postings page, and just my luck, two great opportunities jump out at me almost immediately, and I slam the screen of my laptop down.

I slump back on the couch, jostling Ruthie who is sprawled out next to me. I can't help but smile as I stroke her fur. In just a few weeks, she's already grown so much. The vet I took her to gave her a clean bill of health, updated vaccinations, and agreed with my guess that there's some Great Dane in her somewhere, along with who knows what else.

She's a sweetheart, and so smart. I can't imagine not having her, even though it hasn't been all that long.

My phone alerts me to someone at the front door waiting to be let in. Assuming it's Lina, who's here to hang out before we go to the dojo for Aikido, I buzz her in and stand up to open the apartment door.

A few minutes later, we're in the kitchen as I fill a water bottle, and I'm spilling my guts to her about everything that has happened with Rhett.

After she finishes celebrating winning the bet with Carlee, she sobers, hopefully recognizing the turmoil I'm experiencing.

"You had great sex and you're bummed that you get to have great sex again."

Okay, maybe she doesn't fully understand the turmoil.

"I'm bummed because it's only ever going to be great sex. Nothing more."

"I thought you didn't want a relationship?"

I frown. "Sometimes it sucks having friends who know you so well."

"C'mon Evie, I'm just pointing out what you've been saying for the last few years. You don't want to think about dating, or finding someone, until you're settled into your career. Are you seriously going to give that up for a pretty dick?"

"You talk to your kids with that mouth?"

"Don't change the subject, young lady."

I give her a sad smile. "Fine. Sorry. And no, I'm not giving up on my goals, of course not. But it's not just a pretty dick. It's Rhett."

"Yeah, and isn't he still best friends with your brother? That was the other barrier, if I remember correctly."

I bite back my retort of thanking her for pointing out the obvious. "Maybe he wouldn't be that mad? I mean, this is Rhett we're talking about. His best friend. Kai knows he's a good guy, wouldn't he want that for me?"

"Are you really willing to test that theory on a guy who's only in it for casual sex?"

"No, I guess not." I mumble miserably. "Why are men so freaking annoying?" I huff out an exasperated breath. Ruthie doesn't answer, except to heave out her own sigh, rolling onto her back and presenting her belly to be rubbed.

I indulge her, of course. Only a heartless heathen would ignore a puppy wanting their belly rubbed.

"You made your bed when you got *into* Rhett's bed," Lina not so helpfully points out. "And you're the one who set the parameters by saying it couldn't be anything more than casual. You can't call him annoying for agreeing with you that this should just be a sexuationship."

An undignified snort escapes me at her description, but then again, it's not wrong. And she's right about another thing, too.

I was the one to blurt out that it could never be anything more than casual sex. I was the one who acted like I was cool with that and with keeping it a secret. In the moment, it seemed like the right thing to say. I could tell Rhett was conflicted, and the last thing I wanted was to give him any reason to regret what we'd done.

That would've hurt worse than if he'd rejected me in the first place.

But despite what I said that morning, it wasn't the complete truth, not by a long shot. I know Rhett thinks we can only be something casual, and maybe he's right. The risk of destroying his friendship with my brother and upsetting things with the Tridents—I understand how that risk might be too great.

That doesn't stop me from wishing it wasn't.

"I need to stop thinking about Rhett and my brother. Let's

go to the dojo. You better be ready to wear the pads, I need to hit stuff."

Lina wraps her hands around my shoulders, giving me a squeeze. "You're on. Sparring practice it is."

I wake up the next morning to another text message. One that sends my roller coaster emotions soaring high again.

RHETT: Morning hope pup didn't keep up last night

I bury my face in my pillow and squeal, startling Ruthie, who barks as she pounces on my hand. "No! Off, Ruthie." I scramble up, and she lowers her head into a play position, her tail wagging.

"We're not playing. Not right now." I snatch up my phone again and reread his message. It's not flirty, not at all. And there's those weird mistakes again. But still, he texted me first thing when he woke up if I'm calculating the time difference correctly.

The timing of his trip sucks. Not only because I've finally discovered just how good orgasms can really be, but to have the giver of said orgasms taken away from me so quickly is a mega bummer. I like being around him. We have fun together. And now that there's a new physical layer to the fun we can have?

Well, I'm wishing baseball players didn't have to travel quite so much right now. Or that I at least had something to occupy my time while he's gone.

Like a job or something. But that's a whole other source of frustration.

> **EVIE: She only woke up once! New record. Good luck today.**

> **RHETT: Need to talk to you after the game I'll call you**

My breath catches. Why does he need to talk to me? My pulse quickens as a thousand reasons fly through my mind. Which I know is an entirely foolish overreaction.

The thing is, we've never spoken on the phone. There's never been a reason to. I'm sure it's nothing, maybe he needs me to add milk to the grocery list or something, but what if it's more than that?

"What if he's hurt? He said his knee was bothering him the other day," I say aloud, my thoughts racing to all the worst-case scenarios. "Or Kai got hurt. Or Kai found out about us! Oh my God, after he saw us at the park, what if he figured out we had sex?"

Ruthie pounces on my hand again, this time her razor-sharp teeth graze the skin, making me wince. "Fine, I get it, I'm being crazy."

She barks, as if in agreement, and it forces a small laugh out of me, breaking the spiral a little bit. The logical side of my brain recognizes it's stupid to be overthinking this so much, but I guess I'm so tied up in knots between the stress of job hunting and the uncertainty of whatever Rhett and I are doing.

I throw off the covers and get out of bed.

"C'mon, girl, we're going for a walk. They say exercise gives you good endorphins. Maybe that'll help." I pull on the first clothes I find, which happen to be some bike shorts and a big T-shirt. Throwing my hair up in a ponytail, I call for Ruthie as I walk out into the main living area. I hear her following me and head straight for the front door, grabbing her leash and my keys.

Half an hour later, Ruthie is panting and I'm dripping with sweat as I unlock the front door and we enter the blissfully cool apartment.

Vancouver is headed into an unseasonably early heat wave, and no matter how much I wanted to keep walking in hopes of draining my nervous energy, I knew it wasn't fair to Ruthie to be out in the heat.

The problem is, I'm still antsy, and I've got hours to go until Rhett's game is done, when I can find out why he wants to call.

Ruthie finishes slurping down her water and comes over to look at me, her tail wagging.

"Don't look at me like that. I'm allowed to be impatient."

She cocks her head to the side, her expression clearly saying *Stop talking and feed me.*

I sigh and move over to her food bowl. "Yeah, yeah, I get it. You don't care about my craziness, you just want your breakfast. Dogs are so lucky, not having to worry about pesky things like relationships. Or sexuationships."

CHAPTER TWENTY

Rhett

"Fucking hell, where did the Stars find that pitcher? Swear to God, I saw smoke come off that ball." Monty sinks down on the bench next to me after getting struck out by our opponent's pitcher.

"Heard he's from their farm team in Minnesota," I comment, keeping my eyes trained on the pitcher's mound. Monty's right, this guy is fast. Real fucking fast. And I'm gonna be up against him next inning.

"Someone needs to tell Mike we should try and poach him next season."

"You cheating on me, Monty?" Yami chimes in, turning from where he's leaning against the railing. "Or just looking for a sidepiece."

Monty bats his eyes at Yami. "You know you're my number one guy."

"Glad you added that last word or I'd be worried Lark would have my balls."

"Sorry, bro, no one beats my Birdie for the top spot."

"Not even that new guy?"

"Not while he's playing against us."

"Oh, so if he was on our team, he might have a chance of topping Lark?"

"The only one topping Lark is me."

The guys in the dugout all jeer at Monty's comment just as the woman in question walks out of the tunnel leading from the locker room. The silence that falls is almost comical, especially since she's clueless, looking around at everyone avoiding her gaze. When her eyes land on me, I give her a smirk.

"Hey, Larky, Monty was just telling us all about your bedroom dynamics."

"I was not, Darling, shut the fuck up!" Monty closes the distance between him and Lark and wraps his arms around her from behind, his hands landing on her very pregnant belly. "Ignore them, Birdie. They're being shitheads."

"Tell me something I don't know," she replies, rolling her eyes. "I just came out to let you know I'm leaving early."

"Everything okay?" I ask as we all give her our full attention. Lark's special, not just to Monty, but to all of us. And she's carrying the next generation of Tridents in that belly.

"Yeah." She grimaces, rubbing her stomach. "Just swollen, sore, tired, cranky, and ready to no longer be pregnant."

"Do you have someone taking you back to the hotel?" Monty turns Lark to face him.

"No, but I'll be fine. And I'll see you after you win this game."

They kiss, then Lark leaves with a wave for all of us and Monty sits down on the bench with a ridiculous smile on his face. "I can't wait to be a dad."

I punch his shoulder lightly. "You'll be great, man."

"Thanks. I know."

"Keep that confidence for the field, Monty."

We win the game, but not by much. So when Yami and some of the other guys try to convince me to grab a beer with them at the hotel bar and I decline, no one gives a shit.

The truth is, I'm tired, but not that tired.

I want to call Evie.

She never answered my last couple of texts, but I'm guessing she's busy with the dog. I didn't think I'd miss her, but I do. Both of them. More than I did the last time I went away. Guess it's more the sex I'm missing, but whatever.

When I get back to my room, I open the door and curse. Moving to the thermostat, I see the AC never got turned on, leaving the room a disgustingly hot temperature for the Midwest in summer. I crank it on, then strip out of my clothes until I'm just in my boxers. Then, grabbing a bottle of water from the mini fridge, I settle on the bed and lean back against the headboard.

After draining half the bottle, I set it down and pick up my phone. I open my message thread with Evie, and since I'm sending a short one, I type it out.

RHETT: Good to talk?

Her answer comes through almost immediately.

EVIE: Sure.

I grin and immediately hit the video call button. Her face fills the screen in seconds, but my smile falls when I see her chewing on her lower lip.

"Hey honey, what's wrong?"

She lets go of her lip and her tongue swipes along it instead. "Oh, nothing. How was your game?"

I'm not buying it for a second. "Game was fine. We won. Now tell the truth, honey. Why do you look upset? Is Ruthie okay?"

She glances away, and my stomach churns. I'm just worried about her because we're friends. I care about her. That's all.

"Ruthie's fine. What did you want to talk about tonight?" Her gaze darts to me, then away again, and suddenly, I know what's wrong.

Obviously, I fucked up with what I sent in my text earlier, and she's been worried about this call for some reason. "Maybe I just wanted to hear your pretty voice and see my good girls," I say, trying to make my voice as sweet and charming as I can. It works enough to earn me a small smile, so I continue. "Sorry if my text was confusing."

My heart starts to speed up. Once again, I find myself wishing I was brave enough to just tell her the truth. But everything feels good between us right now and I don't want to mess that up. "I was busy and had to dictate it, and y'know, voice-to-text can fuck things up with punctuation and all that." I force out a laugh.

What I don't say is that I *know* my texts can easily be misunderstood sometimes. But I can never figure out what's wrong to fix them, so I just leave it. My friends and family that know about my dyslexia are used to it by now. They know not to try and read too much into my texts, but she doesn't know that.

Which makes it my damn fault if she was worried about this call.

I feel like a piece of shit.

But thankfully, she gives me a relieved smile. A bigger one this time.

"That makes sense. So it's nothing serious?"

"Nah, I just figured you'd be better company than the boys I spent all day with. Instead of going for a beer, I'd rather see you and Ruthie. Is that okay with you?" I give her a wink, and I know the second the tension fully leaves her because her shoulders drop.

"Yeah, that's okay with me."

I look in the background of the screen, trying to figure out where she is in the apartment. Her bedroom, I think.

"Where's my puppy?"

"Oh, so she's your puppy now?" Evie teases, and I love seeing the smile back on her face. "And here I thought I was the one who rescued her."

"Well, you know, I did rescue you both, in a way, giving you a place to stay and all that." I wink again and her smile grows as she giggles.

"Hold on, let me go and get her. She's asleep on the couch."

"No, don't bother her. If she's sleeping, let her sleep. It's like with a baby, you never wake 'em when they're sleeping." I pause, an idea coming to me. I pitch my voice low, making it clear what I'm implying. "Besides, this way I get you all to myself."

Evie's eyes widen and I see that tongue dart out again, only this time, she's not licking her lips because of nerves. "Yeah?

What are you going to do about it? You're so far away."

"Well," I say, drawing the word out as long as I can. "I know you can already orgasm with a toy, and now we know you can orgasm with me. I wonder if you can do it with me and the toy. Well, the toy will have to do the work, I suppose." I smirk.

"Are...are...are you suggesting phone sex?" Evie stammers and the innocence in her wide eyes, the incredulity of her question, almost makes me want to laugh. But I don't, because I don't want to embarrass her.

"Could be a fun *lesson*. If you're interested."

I wait to see how she'll respond. It takes a minute, and then she slowly nods her head.

"I've never done this before."

"That's okay, neither have I."

She snorts out a small laugh. "Are you serious? You've never had phone sex? I find that kind of hard to believe."

I shrug my shoulders, not letting her doubt bother me. "It's true. I'm not exactly a relationship guy, and phone sex isn't the kind of thing you do with just anyone."

She's silent for a second and I wonder if I've said something wrong. I'm about to apologize when she speaks again. "So how do we start?"

And just like that, my dick starts to get hard. Maybe I should have left my clothes on to slow things down a bit. Because this might all be over before it even starts. And I don't particularly want to explain that to Evie, when she has no idea how she affects me.

"Why don't you tell me what you're wearin', honey."

I see her eyes glance down and then back up to the screen.

"Just my pajamas, some shorts and a tank top."

There's nothing sexy about what she describes, but it *is* sexy simply because it's her. I adjust myself a little bit, trying to appear relaxed, even though my body feels tight with tension already. And we're not even naked.

"Let's start with you peeling off that tank top nice and slow." I see her hesitating, and for a brief second, I worry this is too much for her.

I'm about to ask what's wrong when she blurts out, "What do I do with the phone? I can't hold it and do, you know, everything."

This time, I can't hold back my chuckle. "That's okay, you can always prop it up on the table. Doesn't matter how much I can see, just knowing you're there and I'm making you feel good is enough for me."

That seems to put her at ease as I see her nod and then she shifts to set the phone down on the bedside table. She goes out of frame a little bit, but when she comes back, her shirt's off and I can see those perfect, plump little tits of hers as she lies back down. She moves onto her side and looks at me.

"Now what?"

I smile, loving how quickly and easily she seems to trust me to take the lead. "Well, honey, how about now you pull out some of those toys you like to use. Maybe the one you were using that night you called out my name." I close my eyes and let out a low groan. "You don't know how hard it was not to walk down the hall, go into your room, and take over for that damn thing. It's haunted me ever since. Let me see what my competition is."

She leans out of frame again, and I can hear the sound of

a drawer opening and things being moved around. When she comes back this time, she's holding a small black vibrator.

"That's it? That's the one that had you fightin' not to scream my name?"

She nods and bites her lip. "There's no competition, Rhett. You win every time."

I reach down and cup my junk, squeezing it to try and ease the ache I feel at her soft voice. Holy hell, she doesn't know the power she has over me.

"I think it's about time you turn that thing on and slide it over your pussy for me."

"I'm still wearing my shorts," she says, her voice already raspy with need.

"Good. Keep 'em on. Tease yourself over the fabric and tell me how it feels." I can hear the low vibration of the toy turning on and it takes me back to that night when I overheard her making herself come. Only this time is so much better because I can see her. I might not be in the room, but I get to be a part of her pleasure, no matter what.

"It's...God, Rhett. It's not enough, but it's a lot, you know?" she babbles, and I smirk.

"Yeah, I know. You're doin' so good, honey. Slide it back and forth. Tease yourself, soak those little shorts of yours, pretend it's me gettin' covered in you."

Her eyes flutter closed. I see her arm move and assume she's moving the toy over her pussy because a pretty flush starts to cover her cheeks. "That's it, Evie, what a good fucking girl you are, playing with yourself for me. Are your shorts wet?"

She nods, letting out a whimper of acknowledgment. "Good,

honey, so good. I want you drenched."

"What about you?" she manages to ask, her eyes blinking open. "What are you doing?"

I tilt the phone down so she can see my hand gripping my dick that's poking out of the top of my shorts. "I'm trying not to blow too early. Just looking at you, knowing what you're doing, it's enough to make me hard as a rock."

"Take it out. I want to see you."

Fucking hell, hearing her demand what she wants makes a fresh wave of precum leak from me. I shuck off my shorts as quickly as I can, then pan the phone back down so she can see my cock glistening. "That's all because of you, Evie."

She moans, and I tilt the phone back up. "Take off your shorts, honey. As gorgeous as your face is, I need to see that pussy. Tilt the phone so I can see you. One hand uses the toy, the other pretends to be my fingers. Fuck, I wish I was there to taste you."

Evie does what I say, tugging off her own shorts and angling the phone down. As soon as her pussy comes into view, shiny and plump, I groan. "Goddamn, Evie."

"Rhett," she says, half moan, half whine. "I wish you were here."

"Me too, honey. But we're gonna have some fun anyway. Okay?"

"Mm-hmm."

"Show me that toy on your pussy."

From this angle, I can see her hand move between her legs, the small black toy already turned on and buzzing. As soon as she touches it to her skin, her hips jump and then start to move in a rhythmic motion, chasing the pleasure that we're both after.

"Good girl, good girl," I croon, sliding my own hand up and down my cock. "Now take those fingers, lick them to get 'em wet, and then slide them inside. Start with one, then add another, baby."

Her other hand goes out of the frame, and when it comes back, I can see that it's wet. She slides it up and down her slit first, and I love that she's taking the time to tease herself. Sure, I want her to listen to me and follow my instructions, but seeing her do what she knows works, that's also fucking sexy as hell.

When she skips the first step and plunges two fingers straight into her pussy, I groan out her name. "Goddamn, Evie, that's so fucking hot to watch. Does it feel good?"

"You'd feel better," she pants, and I let out a harsh laugh.

"Fuckin' tease. Trust me, when I'm back, we're gonna do this all over again." She moans, her fingers speeding up. "You like that idea? Me sitting on a chair, watching you pleasure yourself?"

"I'd like it more if you were pleasing me, Rhett."

"Whatever you want, Evie. Whatever you want."

Seconds later, I can't fight back my orgasm any longer. "Ah shit, Evie, I'm coming, baby. I'm sorry, I can't wait. You with me?"

"God yes, Rhett, I'm with you." She moans low and slow as I grunt through my own climax, cum splattering all over my stomach.

A minute or two later, I hear a soft giggle. "Um, hey Rhett? I'm staring at the ceiling."

"Oh shit." I grab the phone that I hadn't even realized I

dropped and grin when I see her sleepy, satisfied face. "Sorry."

"Don't apologize. That was fun."

Fun.

"Yeah. It was. You feelin' better now about me wanting to call?" I tease, and she giggles again, nodding with her face buried in her pillow.

"Alright. So if I text you that I'd like to call again another night, you'd be okay with that?"

She lifts her head back up. "Is every call going to be like this one?"

"I mean, would that be so bad?"

Her laugh is full-on now, and I fucking love it.

"No, that wouldn't be so bad."

CHAPTER TWENTY-ONE

Evie

I didn't know what to expect when Rhett came home this time. Would we immediately jump back into bed? Or would we dance around each other like we had before everything changed?

I didn't have long to wonder, seeing as the day he came home, he burst through the door, scooped me up and threw me over his shoulder, and carried me into his bedroom where he kept me hostage for over two hours.

I was a very willing hostage, but still.

That was four days ago, and things are subtly shifting between us.

I've spent every night in his bed, after the first night when he moved my toothbrush into his en suite and told me his mattress was more comfortable than the one in the spare room.

If by mattress he means his chest, he's right.

But I can't shake the disappointment from knowing that this will never be more than just sex. Because my heart is most definitely getting involved, no matter how much I try to deny it.

"Hand me the coconut milk, will you?" Rhett asks, holding

his hand out over his shoulder. We're in the kitchen cooking dinner, Rhett having played an afternoon game earlier today.

And by we, I mean Rhett is cooking and directing me on tasks that I can do to help him. I hand him the open can of coconut milk and he dumps it into whatever he's stirring on the stove. It smells absolutely delicious. I lean back against the counter, watching him and fighting back a yawn. Exhaustion is riding me hard today, and it's not only from all the great sex I'm having.

My period is due any day now, and for me, that means wicked cramps will kick in soon. If I'm really lucky, I'll be fighting a migraine on the first day as well.

I can only hope my body cooperates and goes easy on me this month. I'm not sure how much experience Rhett has with being around a woman during her period, but it's not a fun time for anyone. And it's certainly not something I want my new sex buddy witnessing.

Too bad I won't have any control over it.

I push away the impending doom of my monthly cycle and hop up to sit on the counter. "Where did you learn to cook? I thought southern food was all deep-fried this and okra that."

Rhett chuckles as he turns to me, pretending to look insulted.

"Woman, I'm gonna assume you've just never had proper southern food if that's really what you think." He turns back to the stove. "I learned to cook from my mom and my nana when we lived on the ranch after my daddy died. Nana cooks southern comfort food better than anybody I know. Her mac and cheese comes straight from heaven, I swear. But Mama loves to try new things and was always finding recipes from all over the world for us to try. This curry, for example," — he nods to the pot on the stove — "is one of her favorites. She always said her dream was to visit Thailand and eat Massaman curry from a street vendor."

"Has she traveled there?" I ask. "I'd love to visit Thailand, heck, I'd love to go anywhere in Asia."

Rhett looks at me curiously as he replies, "She hasn't made it yet, but someday. Have you ever been back to Japan?"

I nod. "Once, when I was much younger, before my grandfather died and my grandmother moved in with us, Mom and Dad took us all over. But it was so expensive. Six plane tickets is a lot."

"You know, sometimes I forget there's four of you," Rhett says. "Yami mostly only talks about you, not your older sisters."

I sip my water before I answer. "Josephine and Vivienne are a few years older than Kai, and a lot of years older than me, so we were never that close. With them being twins, they always kept to themselves, so it was the two of them against the two of us. I guess maybe that's why Kai and I are so close."

"You mean the world to him," Rhett says softly. "You know that, right? He'd do anything for you."

"I know I'm lucky to have a brother like him."

We both fall silent after that, and I wonder if Rhett is thinking about how Kai would feel if he found out about us. I know I don't ever want my brother to come between me and whoever I end up with, but with Rhett, it's kind of unavoidable.

"Alright, dinner is served."

He turns around with two bowls of steaming food that smells absolutely phenomenal. My mouth starts to salivate as I take one and we go over to the couch. Rhett picks up the remote control and hands it to me.

"Your turn to pick the movie tonight."

I just shrug, blowing on a spoonful of curry. "I don't care, whatever you want is fine."

Rhett turns on some action movie and picks up his own dinner. The truth is, I don't pay attention to the movies we watch together. I'm too busy trying not to be distracted by him. He sits so close beside me, I can feel the heat coming off his body. I'm forever trying to hold back from climbing into his lap and kissing him.

My bowl is half empty and there's some sort of car chase happening on the screen when we hear a key turn in Rhett's front door. "Goddamn it, I really need to take that key back from your brother," he grumbles under his breath as he shifts away from me on the couch. Sure enough, Kai strides in as if he owns the place, stooping down to pet Ruthie, who's run over to greet him.

"What's up, my brother from another mother and my sister from a... Wait. Same mister."

I roll my eyes, grateful Kai can't see my face.

"Dude, dinner smells amazing, you didn't tell me you were making Massaman curry tonight. I would have been over earlier."

"Help yourself," Rhett says casually, and I wonder how he feels right now. Is it awkward for him, too? The three of us together with no one else around to act as a buffer? If it is, he's not letting it show.

Kai walks over with his food, but instead of going to the empty chair, he steps over my legs and forces his way in between the two of us. "Jesus, give a guy some room," he complains and I blink slowly.

"You're the one squishing us," I shoot back. "What's wrong with the chair?"

Rhett coughs, and I realize I shouldn't be making a fuss about sitting next to Rhett.

Thank God my brother is oblivious. "The couch is more comfortable. And I'm the best friend, I was here first. You go to the chair."

The little sister in me wants to fight back, but the rational adult in me realizes it's probably better to just move off the damn couch. After all, the last thing I need is my brother getting suspicious about why I want to be on the couch with Rhett. I move to the chair and sit back down.

"So what are we watching?" Kai asks, slurping down a spoonful of his food.

He and Rhett fall into an easy conversation about the movie, which both of them have already seen. I sit there quietly eating my dinner, trying not to resent the fact that my brother has taken over my evening with Rhett.

I finish eating first and seeing as I've got zero interest in watching a movie with the two of them commentating through the entire thing, I stand up.

"I'm going to take Ruthie for a walk."

"'Kay" is all I get from my brother, and nothing from Rhett.

Until I go to move between the couch and the chair, and a hand brushes against mine. I pause. His eyes are still trained forward on the movie as Kai rambles on about something, but Rhett's finger twists around mine in the smallest of caresses. He drops my hand, and I carry on into the kitchen.

But my annoyance at my brother is somehow lifted just from the touch of Rhett's hand.

By the time I get back from walking Ruthie, the movie is over and the guys are watching a baseball game.

Seeing me come in, Kai stretches and stands up. "Hey, baby sis. Was waiting for you to get back."

I unclip Ruthie, who goes straight to her water bowl and starts drinking noisily.

"What's up?" I ask, hanging up the leash. Rhett's now stood up as well but is moving toward the hallway, I guess to give Kai and me some privacy.

"Just wanted to see if you've talked to Mom lately. After you nagged me, I called her, and she said Oba-chan wasn't feeling so great. Have you heard anything?"

I try not to get too worried as I realize, no, I haven't. "We talked a while ago when I first moved in here, but nothing since. Shoot, I really should call her."

Kai swipes a hand through his black hair. "Damn, and you said I was the bad kid for not calling more often. What's up with that? You normally talk to Mom all the time."

"I've been busy," I reply, somewhat defensively. It's a lie. The truth is, I haven't wanted to take the risk that Mom would once again figure out I'm not at Kai's. Which, come to think of it, he should consider that, too. "By the way, I didn't tell her I was staying here and not at your place."

Kai just looks at me, confused. "Why not?"

"Because —" I start, not exactly sure how to explain it in a way he won't dismiss me as being silly.

"She loves Rhett. He's like another son. She'd be totally cool knowing he's looking out for you."

Great. Another reminder of how everyone in my family views Rhett. Everyone except me, I suppose.

"Yeah, you're probably right," I say lamely. "I'll tell her next time we talk."

"And let me know if she says anything about Oba-chan?" he asks hopefully, moving to the door to get his shoes.

"Or you could call her yourself." I fold my arms across my chest.

"Eh, she likes you better."

"You headin' out?" Rhett says, coming to join us. He stands apart from me, leaning against the counter.

"Yeah, man. See you tomorrow? Want to squeeze in some extra BP before warm-up?"

"You betcha."

They bump fists, Kai gives me a hug, and then he leaves.

I turn and slump against the closed door. "Well, that was fun."

Rhett moves and leans against the door next to me. "Wasn't so bad."

"I guess."

He leans over and kisses the side of my head. "C'mon, honey. Let's go to bed. I'm in the mood for some dessert."

"Dessert in bed? Won't that be messy?" I ask, completely clueless, until I see the wolfish grin on his face. "Oh. Oh!"

Rhett pulls me away from the door and straight into his arms. "Never change, Evangeline Yamaki. The absolute delight I get in watching your pretty, good girl face realize how much fun it can be to behave badly is like nothing else."

He starts to walk me backward toward his bedroom. Thank God he knows where he's going since he certainly isn't looking as he peppers kisses all over my skin.

When we reach his room, I'm airborne, tossed onto the bed as if I weigh nothing.

"Now, I need to eat quick and get some sleep. Long day tomorrow." Rhett flops onto his back and gestures to me. "So get up here and gimme that sweetness."

All thoughts of my brother disappear when he grabs my hips and lifts me on top of him.

Rhett stays true to what he says and gets me off quickly. And after we've cleaned up and get ready for bed, I don't think twice before climbing back under his covers and snuggling up against him, already feeling drowsy and relaxed from my orgasm.

Unfortunately, sometime in the early hours of the morning, my uterus decides to put a temporary pause on our sleepovers.

Chapter Twenty-Two

Rhett

Waking up to an empty bed was not how I expected to start the day. I frown as I lift my head and feel the cool pillow that should instead have a beautiful naked woman resting her head on it.

Ruthie has started sleeping in her crate all night without needing to go out, but maybe last night she needed to pee and I slept through it somehow? Still doesn't explain why Evie didn't come back to my bed.

I get up and go down the short hall to her room, only to find the door closed.

Weird, but I can respect if she needs some privacy. I move into the kitchen and get the coffee going.

But a short while later, there's still no sign of life from Evie's room, and I'm guessing the pup is gonna be getting desperate. I crack the door open, and sure enough, the room is still dark and there's a lump on the bed.

The dog crate is right beside the door, so it's easy to quietly open it and let the pup out. Ruthie darts between my legs, and I gently close the door, all with no sign of movement from the bed.

I take the puppy out and feed her breakfast, waiting for Evie to emerge. When she still doesn't, I start to get worried.

I shower, get dressed, and by the time I have to leave for the stadium, it's been over an hour with no sign of Evie.

Deciding I can't leave without at least making sure she's okay, I slowly open her door again. I pitch my voice low. "Evie? Honey, I'm sorry to wake you up, but I gotta leave for the stadium. You okay in there?"

There's a shift on the bed, and then a quiet reply. "Yeah, I'm fine, just tired. See you later?"

Her voice is muffled and sounds pained. I briefly debate going in there and getting a closer look at her, but I'm conflicted. Just because we're having great sex, does that give me the right to be nosy when she so clearly is dismissing me? I suppose it's none of my business if she's having a day in bed.

Even if I've never seen her act quite like this…

"Okay. I dealt with Ruthie already, but I'm gonna leave your door open so she can get in. Alright?"

"Mm-hmm. Thanks, Rhett."

"I'll see you later, honey."

I pull the door halfway shut, hesitating, still wondering if I'm making the right call leaving her like this.

But in the end, I gotta get to work, and she's not my girl. If she says she's okay, then I gotta believe her.

Still, when I get to the stadium, I go straight to Yami. "Hey man, your sister's normally up pretty early, right?"

He laughs. "Fuck, yeah, she doesn't know how to sleep in. I hated it as a kid because she was always so damn loud and I just wanted to not be up before eight during summer break, you know?"

"Okay, yeah. So is there ever a time she stays in bed?"

Yami gives me a funny look, and I realize how weird that question might sound, so I hurry to explain. "Today. She didn't get up to let Ruthie out, and by the time I was leaving to come here, she was still lying in the dark. She said she's fine, but" — I lift my cap off my head and put it back down — "I dunno."

"Ah, shit. I bet she's got her period."

My eyebrows shoot up. "What?"

"You obviously don't have sisters." He rolls his eyes, then his face sobers. "Evie gets wicked bad cramps and migraines sometimes. It's brutal on her. If she was still in the dark when you left this morning, I'm guessing that's it."

"Fuck. Does she need anything? Should she have someone with her right now?"

Again, Yami looks at me strangely. "Dude, she's been dealing with this for years. She's fine."

I don't say anything more. The last thing I need is Yami wondering why I care so much that his sister's suffering.

But I hate knowing that she's at home, alone, in pain.

I head out of the locker room and straight to the gym to do some warm-up on an exercise bike. It's the safest option right now with how distracted I am, thinking about Evie. Should I text her? Have some food delivered? Fuck. No. She's my room-mate and fuck buddy, not my girlfriend.

Except, somewhere along the line, she became more than a fuck buddy. I care about her. She's my friend, of course I do. Only, is this level of caring...more than what a friend would feel?

God-fucking-damn it.

"Rhett Darlington, just the man I need."

I keep my legs pedaling as I turn my head to see Willow strutting toward me. She's got her brown hair up in a slicked-back ponytail, and a take-no-shit energy that's clear as day.

"What kind of shit does a woman need if she's got real bad cramps and migraines?"

Willow's head actually moves back, that's how stunned she is by my question.

"Shit. I'm sorry. I didn't mean to dump that on you. Can we forget I said anything?" I ask, cursing myself out inside my head. Why the hell did I say that? Fuck.

"Ah, no, we absolutely cannot forget that. Why are you asking?" Willow says, folding her arms across her chest. "Wait. Kai's sister is living with you." Her face softens, and I know I'm fucked.

"Rhett, is something going on with you and Evie Yamaki?"

"Hush your mouth, will ya?" I hiss, glancing around. But the gym is, fortunately for me, empty right now.

"That's all the confirmation I need." She smirks. "But Rhett. Does Kai know?"

I think about how to respond. "No. And there's nothing to tell. Not really. We're just friends." The words feel like sawdust in my mouth.

"Mm-hmm, sure," she says, arching a brow at me.

"Listen, I know, it's complicated. But right now, I need your help."

Willow moves closer. "Fine, fine. We'll discuss your choices later."

Great, can't wait for that conversation…

"She's at home, still in bed with the lights off. She wouldn't tell me why, but then Yami said she gets real bad cramps and migraines. I hate that she's there alone. What kinda stuff might she need?"

"You're such a softie." Willow smiles as she pulls out her phone. "Okay, I'd assume she has the basics covered, but she could probably use some electrolytes, maybe a sweet treat of some kind, or a bath bomb to help her relax. Oh, an eye mask. You could get one that you can either cool or heat up so she can choose what she likes. Cozy sweaters and blankets. Hmm. I don't know what else, just comfort items."

Willow's typing away on her phone, and after a couple of minutes, she turns the screen to face me. Thankfully, it's got pictures, so I can see it's a cart for a local store that offers same-day delivery, and it's filled with all the stuff she just mentioned.

"That's perfect." I take the phone and type out my address and payment info without too much trouble, and hand it back. "Thanks, Wills."

She smiles, pocketing her phone. "You know, any woman would be lucky to have a guy like you. And I would think any woman's brother would be able to see that."

I run my hand over my head, not meeting her gaze. I don't want to think about whether or not she's right. That's too much right now.

"Okay, well. Movin' on. You came here for a reason, what can I do for ya?"

"Oh, right. You're up for schmooze duty after the game. We've got some VIPs coming from the children's hospital, and

Sadie wants you, Monty, Yami, and Wilson."

"Not Mav?" I smirk, and Willow scoffs.

"Yeah, no. As much as Sadie loves him, even she knows better than to make him be social after a game."

"You mean anytime."

"Good point." We both chuckle. My legs start to slow down.

"Thanks, Wills. I appreciate you doing this. And..." — I swallow — "and keeping things to yourself."

"I've got you, Rhett. Just take it from me, secrets don't last forever around here. And it's always better if you're in control of how they come out." She gives me a knowing look, and I nod in understanding.

Willow leaves, and I climb off the bike, toweling it down before going to get changed for pregame.

And my head is feeling a hell of a lot less fucked-up. I've got a game plan now. Even though I can't be with Evie until later, at least I feel like I can relax, believing she'll have whatever she needs.

Somehow, luck is on my side. We win the game and I manage to get away from the meet and greet before Yami.

The drive home feels annoyingly long, but eventually, I'm parking my truck in my spot and getting on the elevator. My keys rattle in my hand as I wait impatiently for it to reach my floor.

As soon as the doors open, I'm squeezing through and hurrying down the hall to my apartment. I unlock the door and open it to find the lights on but dimmed. Ruthie comes racing over, and I stoop to give her some love.

When I straighten, I realize there's someone on the couch.

"Um, hi."

It's Carlee, Evie's old roommate, and she's got her hands clasped in front of her.

"Hi. Carlee, right?" I say, keeping my voice low. "Is Evie okay?"

Her friend nods quickly. "Oh yeah, I was actually just about to go. She called me a while ago asking if I could drop off some soup. She, um —"

"Her brother filled me in," I add quickly, saving Carlee from having to decide whether or not to share Evie's current situation.

Carlee's face brightens. "Oh, she must have told Kai. That explains the delivery earlier. Hope it's okay I signed for it, he sent over a bunch of stuff." She points to the kitchen counter, where several of the items Willow and I ordered have been opened.

"Ah, no, he didn't, actually." I grasp the back of my neck.

"Then who..." Carlee trails off, biting her lip. It looks like she's trying hard not to smile. "Oh. I see."

I turn away so she can't see me blush. "Anyway. Thanks for being here for her."

"She's my best friend."

The sound of her gathering her things is in the background as I busy myself getting a drink of water. I turn back when I hear her slide her feet into shoes. "I just took Ruthie out, so she's good. And Evie will be fine soon, the migraines don't last long. And when it eases, I think she'll love that bath bomb. For now, just make sure she has something to drink, and keep the lights off as much as you can."

I nod. "Will do."

Carlee opens my front door and pauses. "And Rhett? Don't fuck this up, and don't play games. She won't know how to handle it."

She closes the door before I can object and try to defend myself, but her words stay with me anyway.

I move to lock the front door. Ruthie is contentedly playing with a toy, so I quietly walk over to Evie's bedroom and crack the door open.

It's still dark, and in case she's asleep, I speak softly. "Hey. Just wanted to let you know I'm home. You need anything?"

"Rhett?" comes her quiet reply.

I step into her room, pulling the door mostly closed behind me to keep out the light. Going around to the side of the bed she's on, I crouch down. The light is dim, but I can see enough to stroke back some long dark hair from her face.

"Hey there."

"Hi." She licks her lips. "Sorry about this."

I lean in and press the lightest of kisses to her forehead. "You've got nothing to apologize for. Your brother told me you get hit hard some months. Why didn't you tell me what was going on?"

"It didn't seem like the kind of thing to tell your hookup," she replies, her voice raspy. "But I'm feeling better. The headache is easing."

It shouldn't feel like an arrow to the chest hearing her call me a hookup, but damn, it does. Then again, I said it was nothing serious earlier, too, so maybe it's good we're on the same page.

I clear my throat before I reply. "Good. Next time, tell me. Okay? I can make sure you got what you need."

"Thanks, but I'm okay. I had stuff, and Kai sent some things over. Not sure how he knew."

"I sent that stuff, not Yami."

Silence follows my statement. Maybe I should have let her believe it was her brother, but for some reason, it mattered to me that she knew I was thinking about her.

"You want me to run you a bath?" I ask, picking up her hand and holding it in mine. "Or just let you rest."

"A bath would be great later. Could you..." — she pauses, and I hear her breathe in and out slowly — "could you just hold me for a while?"

Oh damn.

"You bet I can, honey." I stand up and whip off my shirt before pulling down my jeans. Then, carefully, I slide into bed behind her and gather her in my arms. She moves willingly, tucking her little body back against mine. My hand lands on her stomach, and she covers it with hers, letting out a sigh.

"Thank you, Rhett."

CHAPTER TWENTY-THREE

The week leading up to the All-Star break somehow feels like the longest and shortest week of the entire year.

We're only halfway through the season, and I'm fucking exhausted from playing close to eighty games. We all are. I'm glad I'm not on the All-Star team this year, partly because I want a break, but mostly because I'm hoping to spend more time with Evie.

Things between us are shifting, there's no question. I like her way more than I should, and I don't have the first clue what to do about it. I'm hoping that the break will give me — give us — a chance to maybe figure that shit out.

I grab my mail on the way upstairs after a grueling few hours at the stadium. We didn't have a game today, but Coach Stirling still kicked our asses in an intense practice.

Tomorrow we leave for a quick three-day road trip down to Oregon for a series against the Rose City Roasters, then it's back up here for another three-day series before the break.

Six games. I can do this.

I'm flipping through my mail when I get to a large envelope with the logo of the bank my mom has her mortgage with down in Tennessee. Which means it's the paperwork I've been waiting for.

Which also means it's paperwork I can't afford to not understand properly. My goal of paying off Mama's mortgage hinges on me getting through this damn paperwork.

When I open the door to the apartment, I can hear the shower running, so I quickly unlock my phone and call Kai.

"Dude, what did I tell you about phone calls. Just text me," he complains by way of greeting.

"I would, but I don't have time to fight the goddamn voice-to-text. I got that stuff from the lawyer. Can you come over tonight and gimme a hand readin' it? Evie's going out with some friends," I say quickly in a quiet voice, one ear on the shower to make sure it's still running.

"Oh. Yeah, sure, man. You got dinner covered?"

My eyes roll. Like the guy can't afford his own dinner. "I'll order food."

"Deal. See you in an hour."

I hang up and head to my bedroom where I leave the envelope on my dresser. I'm halfway through changing into some shorts when arms wrap around me from behind.

"Hey, when did you get home?" Evie's lips press a kiss to my spine.

I turn in her arms and lift her up into mine, carrying her over so I can sit on the bed. "Just a few minutes ago. You were in the shower." I thread my fingers through her hair and pull her in for a proper kiss. "Hi."

"Hi." She smiles against my lips.

We stay like that, kissing on my bed for several minutes. It would be so easy to lose myself in this.

In her.

Evie's the one to pull back first, standing up with a small sound of discontent. "You have to stop being so distracting, Rhett Darlington," she teases. "Or I'm going to be late for class."

I frown in confusion. "I thought you were going out with Carlee?"

She shakes her head. "No, my sensei called and needs my help with one of his classes tonight."

Shit. I was counting on her being out late with her friend so that Kai and I would have time to go through all of the paperwork. Her Aikido class is only an hour and a half, which doesn't leave much time at all.

"Oh, okay," I say distractedly, rubbing the back of my neck. "Well, you know, if you want to go out with Carlee after, I'll be here to look after Ruthie. Your brother's coming over to hang out."

Evie strokes my hair back from my forehead with a small smile. "I gotta say, it's kind of nice having you co-parenting my dog with me." She laughs lightly. "Although, I do feel like I'm getting off easy with the whole new puppy chaos."

"Oh yeah?" I tease right back. "Is that the only reason you're happy to be here? Because I help you with the dog? And here I thought I had other qualities that interested you."

She slides her arms around my neck and presses a soft kiss to my forehead. "Trust me, there are plenty of ways you keep me interested. But I really should go." She steps back and I follow her as she leaves my room, Ruthie trotting along beside me.

Like we're two lost little puppy dogs following our beloved owner.

In her room, the bag she takes to the dojo is open on her bed. I watch as she throws a few more things in it, then zips it shut and picks it up.

"I'll let you know what I end up doing," she says as she moves into the living room and slides her feet into a pair of shoes.

I nod, stuffing my hands in my pockets so I don't reach for her again. I really need to figure out what the fuck I'm feeling, because it's a hell of a lot more than just casual at this point. Lines are more than blurred; she's more than a roommate or a woman I'm only having sex with.

"Sure, sounds good. Have a fun night." I stay where I am, waiting to see if she reaches for me, or if I'm the only one having a hard time fighting my desire to constantly be near her.

But Evie just bends down to give Ruthie a pet and then gives me one more smile before she walks out the door.

And even though she'll be home in a few hours, I instantly regret not kissing her goodbye.

I'm so fucked.

Kai shows up an hour later, unlocking the door and letting himself in like always.

"Yo, dude, where's the food?" he says instead of a "hello" like a normal person.

"It'll be here any minute," I reply, opening the fridge and pulling out two bottles of the nonalcoholic beer I have on hand.

As if on cue, there's a knock at the door, and it's my doorman with the bag of Mexican I ordered. I thank him and close the door. Sometimes, the perks of living in a nice building are good.

Like not having to go downstairs and deal with delivery people gawking over the baseball player who just wants to eat a damn burrito.

I hand Yami his drink and then dish out our burritos. We head over to the living room and sit down on the couch.

"Fuck, this is good," Yami groans around a mouthful of beans and beef.

I turn on the sports highlights and we sink into the couch, filling our faces with food and watching the game that's being discussed on TV.

"Did you hear the Roasters are giving Pink the series off? We might actually have a chance to get on base." Yami's voice is a mixture of admiration and annoyance.

The Rose City Roasters, a newer team to the league, are who we play next, and their star pitcher has a killer arm.

"Thank fuck for that. We need those wins going into the break."

Yami grunts in acknowledgment and we go back to eating.

I finish first, Yami soon after. He pushes his plate back onto the table before leaning back on the couch with a groan. Ruthie immediately jumps up on the couch, putting her paws on his chest and attempting to lick his face, but he pushes her away.

"Not gonna lie, brother, I'm kind of glad you're stuck with this ball of fur. I don't think I'm a dog person." He pushes her away again and glares. "Stay away from my fucking face."

"C'mon, Yami, it's the most action you've had in a while," I tease with a grin, earning a punch to my shoulder.

"Shut it, Darling. When was the last time you got any?"

I am *not* answering that...

Instead, I stand up. "Want another beer?" Without waiting for him to respond, I grab both of our plates and toss them in the kitchen sink.

I return to the couch and deposit two more beers on the table. Ruthie is still relentlessly trying to get Kai to pay attention to her, and it seems he's finally given in when I see him heave a sigh, then start petting her back once she settles down on his lap.

"Even you can't resist that face, can you." I grin.

Yami rolls his eyes but doesn't stop petting the puppy. "Yeah, yeah. Go get those damn papers. Let's get this over with."

He's right. A glance at the clock tells me Evie's class will be over soon, so we don't have long. Even less if she doesn't go out after.

I go into my bedroom and grab the envelope off my dresser and take it back to the living room, dropping it in front of Yami.

"Thanks for doing this, man. I appreciate it," I say gruffly, sitting back down beside him.

"All good, you know it's no big deal," Yami says. "But why wouldn't you ask Evie to help? She's already here."

"Because she doesn't know about my dyslexia. And the last thing I need is anybody else knowin' that I can't fucking read." I try not to snap at him, but is he serious right now?

Apparently he is, and he isn't done.

"Yeah, but Evie's different. She wouldn't give a fuck. I mean, hell, look at what she's doing for work. Her job is literally going to be helping kids that struggle in school and can't read."

"Kids," I growl. "Not an almost-thirty-year-old grown-ass man. Just help me get through the papers."

He looks at me for a long few seconds, making me wonder

if I'm gonna have to deal with him pushing me to explain why I'm so adamant on Evie not knowing about my dyslexia, but thankfully, he doesn't.

He tears open the envelope and pulls out the stack of papers, and sure enough, the printed words are so small there's not a chance I would have been able to make sense of them.

"Why do they have to type this shit so small?" he complains.

I get a small amount of satisfaction knowing it's not just me.

"Hell if I know, what's it say?"

Yami takes a minute and scans the document. "Looks like it's pretty basic. They want to confirm your personal information and the fact that you've got your mom's power of attorney. Then there's the section asking you to confirm the amount you're giving."

His eyes bug out a bit when he scans the number. "Dude, you've been holding out on me. How the hell did you save up this much money?"

I just shrug. "I don't spend a lot on stupid shit, and my last signing bonus was good. Who better to spend it on than my mom? She deserves it."

Kai nods. He knows my mom and how amazing she is.

"That she does," he says. "The woman is a saint. Okay, well, everything looks good on this page, you just have to initial in a few places and sign the bottom to approve the transfer." He turns the page and starts reading the terms and conditions aloud.

I stand up and go to grab a pen from the kitchen drawer when all of a sudden there's the unmistakable sound of a key in the lock.

"Shit." Evie's back, a hell of a lot sooner than I anticipated. I race back to the couch to snatch the papers from Yami and hide them somehow.

"Dude, stop panicking. It's fine."

All I can do is glare at him because the door is opening and Evie's walking in just as I shove the papers under a throw pillow.

Hopefully, she didn't notice.

"Hey, Gigi," Yami says, and Evie frowns as she drops her bag and toes off her shoes.

"Are you ever going to stop calling me that?"

"Maybe when it stops bugging you so much."

I take advantage of their sibling bickering and try to slow my breathing down from panic level to normal. In the entryway, Evie bends over to pet Ruthie.

When I finally feel like I'm not ten seconds from losing it, I say, "I didn't think you'd be home so soon. What happened to going out with Carlee after your class?"

"It was a short class, and Carlee has a headache." Evie straightens and flashes me a soft smile. "But don't worry. I'll go into my room and leave you two alone."

I'm nodding in agreement when Yami stands up, giving me a meaningful look. "Nah, it's all good, sis. I'm gonna take off. That burrito I ate is moving through me quick." He rubs his stomach.

"Gross, Kai." Evie wrinkles her nose. He walks over and gives her a one-armed hug, despite her trying to push him away.

I stand, trying to be subtle about checking that the papers are out of sight, and follow him to the door.

The look I'm giving him sends a clear *where the fuck are you going* message, and the one he sends back is just as clear. *Talk to her.*

No thanks. I'd rather be covered in dog shit. No offense, Ruthie.

The door closes behind my supposed best friend, and I stand there for a second, wondering if maybe Evie didn't notice my crazy panic when she first walked in. If she doesn't ask about it, I don't have to tell her.

But if she does, well, Mama didn't raise me to be a liar.

I go to the kitchen and try to act busy putting dishes in the dishwasher and finish tidying up. But a minute or two later, I can sense her walking up behind me.

"So that was kind of weird when I walked in." She pauses and the burrito in my stomach turns to stone. "What's going on? I thought we were the ones keeping a secret from Kai, not the other way around."

Well, shit.

Chapter Twenty-Four

Evie

My heart is pounding. I hate confrontation. I don't want to be a pushover, or a doormat, but I also hate the feeling I get when I have to stand up to someone.

The thing is, I hate being lied to even more.

And Rhett might not be lying, but he is keeping something from me.

There's no denying that when I walked in tonight, both my brother and Rhett looked incredibly guilty.

I know I was early getting home, what with Carlee canceling our tentative plans. But that doesn't excuse the fact that they clearly had something to hide. Did Rhett think I didn't notice him fussing around with that stack of papers or see him shove them under a throw pillow?

He's still standing at the kitchen sink with a strange defensiveness to his posture. His jaw is clenched, his arms are folded across his chest, and he's looking everywhere but at me.

I've never seen him look like this, at least, not toward me. It's unsettling in a way because I don't know what I did wrong. Wait, no. I didn't do anything wrong. I'm not the one keeping secrets. He is.

I decide to just wait, hoping he'll answer me and tell me what is going on. But after several minutes of silence, he still doesn't say a word.

I nod. "Okay." I turn to walk away, planning to go to my bedroom and try to figure out what to do. I can't stand liars, which is ironic given the situation I'm currently in and the things I'm hiding from my brother. But Rhett hiding things from me feels even worse.

I only get two steps down the hallway when he finally says something.

"Wait. Fuck, Evie, this isn't easy."

I slowly turn around and face him. He's staring at the floor, his hand gripping the back of his neck. I wait until his gaze finally lifts to meet mine.

"I'm sure it isn't. But it's not easy for me, either, realizing that you're hiding something from me. I know what we have is nothing serious, that we're just friends hooking up and you don't owe me anything." I breathe in and out, long and slow, centering myself. "If you really don't want to tell me what's going on, I'm not going to force you. I've got no right to."

I'm about to turn and leave again when Rhett takes his turn to slowly exhale as his head falls forward, his chin hitting his chest.

"I can't read," he mumbles under his breath.

"What?" I say, trying to make sense of what I think I just heard.

He lifts his head, and embarrassment, anger, defeat, all of it is written across his handsome face, etching it with misery.

"I. Can't. Read." This time, there's no mistaking the anger

in his voice. "Okay? That's the big secret. Sin's five-year-old can probably read better than me. I have dyslexia. Real bad. Tennessee didn't have people like you to help kids like me, so I never learned how to fuckin' read."

"But you graduated from high school," I say like an idiot, still dumbfounded by what he's revealed. My mind is battling between jumping to solutions, ways I could help him, and absolute shock that after all this time of knowing Rhett, I never knew *this*.

Rhett's oblivious to my spinning thoughts and lets out a harsh laugh. "Sure, I did. You know those southern charms you like to tease me about? Turns out, they're helpful when it comes to convincing teachers to let me graduate."

"So tonight, what was Kai doing here?"

Rhett moves to the living room and sits down on the armchair. It's not lost on me that he doesn't sit on the couch where I could maybe sit next to him. He chooses to sit by himself in the chair.

So I choose to go over and lean against the arm of the couch facing him.

"Because Yami is the only guy on the team who knows how bad it is. The others know I have a learning disability, and that I don't do well with stuff that's written out, but only Yami, Coach Stirling, and my agent know exactly how fuckin' stupid I am. That I can't read worth shit."

"You're not stupid, Rhett." I reach a hand out but snatch it back at his scoff.

"Sure. Just not smart enough to learn to read."

"It's not about being smart enough, it's about being taught

the right way."

Rhett stands up and starts pacing. "I don't need you to fix me. I'm fine. I've managed this long."

I stand up, too, my hands out. "I'm sorry. I don't mean to imply that you need to be fixed. I'm just surprised, is all. I never suspected this. I mean, I've heard you and Kai talk about books. You and my dad used to talk about that old sci-fi series you both love. But there's no actual books here." I'm rambling, processing my thoughts out loud, I suppose. All it earns me is another harsh laugh.

"Yeah, I love science fiction. And autobiographies and history books. I just listen to them all on audio."

"That makes sense." I start to nod, but Rhett's already shaking his head.

"Sure, except it's not actually reading, now, is it? It's cheating. I listen to the words. I don't read them."

My mouth falls open in outrage. "Okay, *now* you're being stupid. Audiobooks are not cheating. They count. They're just as much a way of reading as e-books or paperbacks. You're consuming literature. It doesn't matter how you do it." I fold my arms across my chest, narrowing my gaze at Rhett in defense of not only him, but all the kids I want to help in the future. All the kids who I know struggle with the narrow-viewed teaching styles prevalent in many schools.

He drops back down into the chair, resting his elbows on his knees and letting his head hang low. Dejection is clear in his voice. "Tell that to all of my teachers. Tell that to a younger me who didn't have even audiobooks to help get through. I had to flirt, charm, and cheat my way through school. Evie, I barely graduated. Scraped by, passing only thanks to my high school baseball coach who begged the teachers to let me. He knew my future was on the field, not in a classroom. Thank fuck I had baseball. You know how rare it is to go straight from high school into the minors without playin' on a college team?" Rhett lifts his head, only to shake it slowly from side to side. "It doesn't happen. I was the youngest kid drafted into the minors. I was fucking terrified, I didn't feel ready at all, but I had to make it work. Because my only fallback was to work on my grandparents' farm. If it weren't for Coach back then, pushing for me to graduate somehow, I wouldn't be here. I'd be back in Tennessee, shoveling cow shit."

He falls silent, and I take a second to think over everything he's just shared. It's all starting to make sense, and a part of me is surprised I didn't see it sooner.

The lack of books in his apartment, the way his text messages don't always make sense.

When Rhett speaks again, he sounds tired, but the anger is gone from his tone. Resignation is in its place. "Tonight, your brother was here to help me go through some paperwork that arrived. Stuff for my mom. Stuff I have to deal with quickly. But stuff that I can't make sense of. There's not a chance in hell of me bein' able to read it and understand it."

"It's never too late to learn," I say cautiously. Rhett stands up abruptly with a snort and I instantly regret it.

"What did I say about tryin' to fix me. I've managed for almost thirty years by myself, and I'll keep managing."

I hold my hands up. "You've done incredibly well for yourself. I'm not trying to argue that. All I'm saying is that if you wanted,

I could maybe suggest some resources or tools to help." His glare softens, not all the way, but closer to the sweet man I know him to be. So I take a chance and continue. "For the record, I don't think dyslexia is necessarily a bad thing. Your brain is wired a little bit differently, and you need to learn things in a different style from most other people. But it's also what makes you creative and kind and caring and empathetic. It's what makes you, you."

He stares at me, almost in disbelief. Has he never had anyone tell him that? "Christ. Evie, you don't know what I would have done to have someone like you tell me that when I was growing up."

I take a chance that he won't push me away and move to kneel on the floor in front of him, my hands going to his knees. "You didn't have me then, but you have me now."

There's a moment of silence. And I wait to see if I've crossed a line that I shouldn't have ever crossed. If I've pushed him too far and he's going to push me away. But when he finally lifts his head and looks at me, all the tension bleeds from me.

That anger, that defeat that was written all over his face be-fore, it's all gone now. And something indescribable is shining back at me from his big brown eyes. Something that makes my heart skip a beat and my stomach fill with butterflies.

"I don't deserve you, Evangeline," he says in a low rumble.

I rise up, my hands moving to cup his face as I pull him in for a kiss. "Yes, you do," I whisper against his lips. "Yes, you do."

Chapter Twenty-Five

Rhett

"Evie," I whisper, gently stroking my hand down her face. "Wake up."

She lets out an adorable grumbly noise and rolls over, taking my hand with her and hugging it in between her breasts.

"It's too early," she mumbles.

I chuckle. "I know it's early, but trust me, this will be worth it. Come on, honey. I'll get your coffee. You just have to get up and get dressed. I'll even give you one of my hoodies to wear."

She slowly rolls back over, letting out an adorable yawn. "Where are we going?"

"You'll see. It's a surprise." I pull my hand free and stand up from beside the bed. "But you gotta get up and get going, honey."

She pushes herself to sitting, and man, she looks so fucking adorable all sleep mussed. It's tempting to give in and just push her right back down onto that bed and cuddle her for another hour or two. But when I got the idea for this morning, I couldn't shake it. And since the All-Star break is finally here, now's the perfect time to sacrifice some sleep.

I leave her to get dressed and head out into the living room to gather the few other things I want to take with us. I'm in the middle of pouring coffee into two travel cups when Evie finally emerges, stumbling out of her bedroom, rubbing her eyes.

She looks perfect wearing my oversized hoodie and a pair of joggers. I hand her a cup of coffee before moving around behind her, and then I begin raking my fingers through her hair to untangle the knots.

"What are you doing?" she asks sleepily.

"Just drink your coffee."

Slowly, I carefully split her hair into three sections and start to braid it together.

Evie turns her head slightly as I continue braiding. "You know how to braid hair?" She's sounding a little bit more awake and very surprised by my actions, which makes me smile in satisfaction.

"My mama taught me how to braid our horses' manes and tails. I figured this would be the same idea," I say conversationally as I apply a tie to the end of her hair. Then I lean in and kiss the top of her head. "Now, come on. We gotta go." I grab my Tridents hat, flip it around, and put it on my head before grabbing an extra and setting it down over her braid and lightly flicking the brim.

Then I pick up Ruthie's leash, clip it on her, and lead them both out the door. We're in my truck a few minutes later, headed for North Vancouver.

"Are you going to tell me where we're going?" Evie asks, taking another sip of coffee.

"Nope." I shake my head, earning a huff of half-hearted annoyance.

"Well, did we have to go wherever it is so early?" she sasses, and I smirk.

"Yep."

We drive in silence for the next few minutes. The streets are empty, with most of the city still fast asleep.

A little while later, we're almost to the spot on top of Mount Seymour where I wanted to take her. It's the perfect spot to watch the sunrise. I pull into the empty parking lot and hop out of the truck, jogging around to open Evie's door before she can.

I help her down and drop a kiss to her forehead. Then I go to the back and get Ruthie after changing out her regular leash for the extra long one so she can roam a bit while we watch the sunrise.

"C'mon, it's almost time." I nod my head toward the short trail that leads to a bench at the lookout. The light is dim, dawn just starting to break, but there's enough to see our way to the lookout.

"Wait, what about your coffee?" Evie asks, looking back as I close the truck door.

"Leave it. If I'm holding that, I can't do this." I drape my arm over her shoulders, tucking her into my side. "You'll just have to share yours if I need a sip."

She giggles and snuggles in under my arm.

The lookout is empty. Of course it is, not many people are brave enough to get up so early for a sunrise. We sit down on the bench that overlooks all of downtown Vancouver, and Ruthie wanders around a bit, sniffing at the grass.

On the bench, Evie turns sideways, lifting her feet up and leaning against my side. I wrap my arms around her, taking off her hat so I can rest my cheek on her head.

I know we need to talk about what we're doing. There's no avoiding the truth, things have shifted between us. And I can't find it in myself at this moment to be worried about that. Sure, there's shit we gotta figure out. Like telling Yami the truth. But right now, nothing else matters except how right it feels having Evie in my arms.

"You woke me up before dawn and brought me all the way out here to watch the sunrise."

I tilt her face up to meet mine before dropping my lips to hers for a kiss. "Sure did. It's one of my favorite things to do when I have a day off. There's nothin' more beautiful than watching the world wake up. Those first rays of sunshine somehow feel the warmest and most pure. It gives me hope that the rest of the day will be just as beautiful."

Evie looks at me for a minute with a soft smile on her gorgeous face. "I always thought you were charming, but now I know you're actually a romantic, aren't you?"

I laugh, ducking my head down onto her shoulder. "Guess so. You can thank my mama for that. I grew up listening to her and my nana talk about all the romance novels they read. I guess some of it rubbed off on me."

That makes Evie giggle again, and she snuggles even deeper into my side just as the first rays of sun start peeking over the city. We stay like that for quite some time, watching the sky grow brighter. I lose track of how long we're there, content to just be in the moment with her.

"When did you first start loving the sunrise?"

I smile, even though she can't see it. "When we lived on my

grandparents' ranch. Farm animals don't wait for no one, not even the sun when they're hungry. Gramps and I would get up to do chores before school, and he made sure that no matter what, we always took a moment to watch the sun come up."

"I love that. You must miss your family."

"I do, but I get back to see them each year, and Mama comes up to watch games a few times a season."

She tilts her head to look up at me, chewing on her lower lip. I reach a thumb out to free it before giving her a soft kiss.

"Do you ever think about transferring to a team closer to home?"

"Now, that's a tough question. I did, before I ended up with the Tridents. But now Vancouver feels like home, and I can't imagine playin' anywhere else."

She turns her head back to face the sunrise with a quiet sigh. And a few seconds later, her hand squeezes my leg. "I'm glad you're here."

"Me too, honey."

Soon, the sun has fully risen, and when Ruthie comes over with a whine, lifting her paws up onto our knees, I reluctantly accept that it's time to go.

"I think she's hungry," I comment, kissing the top of Evie's head again.

"She's not the only one," Evie replies, placing her hands over her stomach. "My body can't figure out why we've been awake for so long and haven't eaten."

As if on cue, my own stomach lets out a rumble, making us both laugh. "That settles it. Breakfast for my girls."

My girls. I'm not sure what made me say that.

Evie stands first, and when she turns to me, I'm glad I'm still seated. The depth of the connection between us when she looks at me is so intense, I reach a hand up to rub my chest.

"Do you mean that?"

I stand up, stuffing my hands in my pockets. "That depends," I say, knowing I'm taking the coward's way out but not quite ready to put it all out there.

"On what?"

"On whether you want me to mean it."

Evie turns slightly, wrapping her arms around her waist as she looks out over the city. I instantly miss her gaze being on me. Which should be enough of a sign that I'm in deep. But there's a tiny kernel of doubt buried within. Small enough that it's easy to ignore right now.

"I've wanted that for a long time."

Her whisper is almost stolen by the wind. But I feel it as much as I hear it. And I close the small distance between us, turning her to face me, taking her hands in mine and lifting them both up to my lips for a kiss.

"Can I tell you something?"

She nods.

I exhale a shaky laugh. "This scares me more than facing down a fastball in the bottom of the ninth." She squeezes my hands, and I swallow down my nerves and uncertainty. "I do mean it. You and Ruthie. You feel like you're mine. And I've never felt that before. But I swear, if you want this, then I do, too. I want nothing more than to see if this can be somethin' real. Because it sure as shit feels real to me."

"Same." This time, Evie is the one lifting our hands and

catching me by surprise when she kisses *my* knuckles. "To the scared part, and to the something real part."

There's no point holding back my smile any longer. "That's damn good to hear, honey." I pull my hands free, only to cup her face, and draw her in for a long, slow, lingering kiss. One that solidifies everything.

My damn stomach chooses that moment to interrupt the romance with another loud grumble.

Evie pulls back with a laugh. "Have you got a granola bar in your truck before your stomach starts to eat itself?"

I nod and drape my arm over her shoulders as we turn toward the truck. "I'm a professional athlete, I don't go anywhere without snacks."

Her laughter rings out in the early morning air, and it's the most beautiful sound.

We decide to make breakfast together at home instead of going out to eat. Which suits me just fine since the sooner we get home, the sooner I can get Evie naked.

Maybe we'll just eat breakfast naked.

I bet I can convince her...

The drive home is quiet, but not a sleepy quiet like the drive up the mountain earlier. No, this time, there's a charged energy crackling between us. My hand is high up on Evie's thigh, my thumb stroking back and forth slowly. I can feel her twitch and shift in her seat, and I try not to let her see me smirk. It's good to know my goal of mildly edging her the entire drive is successful.

When I finally pull into my parking spot, I turn off the engine and slowly lift my hand from her leg, leaning against my door.

"Whatcha thinking for breakfast? I make a mean pancake."

Evie turns to me, her cheeks pink and her eyes full of fire. "Really. Pancakes? That's what you're thinking about right now?"

I rub my stomach, biting my cheek to stop smiling. "Yeah, I'm hungry, remember? That granola bar wasn't nearly enough to satisfy me." I wink when I say the word *satisfy* so that she knows exactly what *will* satisfy me.

But instead of lunging for me like I half expected her to, Evie blinks slowly, then turns and gets out of the truck without a word. I scramble to get out myself, but she's already opened the back and has Ruthie in hand and is halfway to the elevator before I can grab our coffee cups and catch up.

I slide into the elevator just as it starts to close, scooping Ruthie up before she has a chance to start whining. "So that's a no to pancakes?" I ask, leaning against the wall of the elevator. It's getting harder to act unaffected.

Ruthie starts chewing on her leash. Normally, I'd correct her behaviour, but there's no chance of my gaze dropping from Evie's.

The door opens on my floor, and Evie brushes past me, still silent. She waits for me at my door, allowing me to unlock and hold it open for her. Her silence is more than a little unnerving, but at the same time, I'm so fucking turned on, waiting to see what she does next. Waiting to see when she'll explode. Because it's coming. The buildup is like a fuse, growing shorter with every passing second.

I have the good sense to lock the door behind me, still staring at her back as she sashays toward the bedroom. She pauses at the entrance to the hall and looks over her shoulder at me.

"It's a no to pancakes."

Her shirt lands on the floor a second later, her pants following immediately after.

That's my girl.

CHAPTER TWENTY-SIX

Rhett

I poke my head into the bedroom that now only serves as a place for Evie to keep her clothes, finding her wearing blue panties and a bra, her head in the closet.

"Evie, you better hurry your sexy self up. Your brother's gonna be here any minute, and I don't know if he wants to see my reaction to you walking around half naked," I say.

"I'm almost ready," she calls back and I stifle the urge to go over there and squeeze that pert ass.

Instead, I head into the living room and tidy up a couple things left out from our earlier lunch. Then I get Ruthie's dinner ready and carry it back into the guest bedroom. The plan is to leave her in her crate tonight since we'll be gone for a few hours. It's the longest she's ever been left alone during the day, and I'm not lying when I say we're both a little nervous.

But tonight's important. Each year, Monty's Little Brother Grayson's baseball league does one major fundraising event. This year happens to be a bowling night, and since it falls during the All-Star break, a lot of the guys from the team are going.

It'll be good to hang out with everyone and support a good cause, and I've been looking forward to tonight for a while. But the change in my and Evie's relationship means I'll have to work extra hard to resist touching her the way I want to and not let anyone in on the fact that we're more than just temporary roommates.

"See? I'm ready, and Kai's not even here yet," Evie says triumphantly as she walks into the room.

I let out a low wolf whistle as I take her in. "Damn, I was just thinking about how hard it would be to keep my hands off you tonight. And you just had to go and look that good. Woman, you're torturing me."

I walk over and run my hands down her sides to land on her hips. I turn her around, taking in the way her dark jeans cup her perfect, pert little ass. And how her long black hair falls in soft curls halfway down her back.

"I've never seen you with curls." I lightly run my fingers down one section, feeling the silky strands slide through. "I like it."

Evie blushes. "It won't stay. Asian hair is rarely good with curls unless we get a perm or something."

She's babbling. I love that I can affect her like this. I lean in and kiss the tip of her nose. "Your hair shines like the brightest night sky. Straight or curly, it doesn't matter. It's gorgeous. *You* are gorgeous."

And she really fucking is. She's wearing a Tridents T-shirt, but it's got her brother's last name on the back. Okay, fine, it's her last name as well. Doesn't matter that it makes sense for her to wear it, some possessive part of me doesn't like seeing another guy's name on her.

I guess the grumbling sound that escapes me makes that evident, because Evie's eyebrows raise. "What was that for?"

"No reason. Just something in my throat, I guess." There's no way I'm drawing attention to the fact that a part of me wishes it was my name she was wearing.

The front door opens and Yami lets himself in. I just barely manage to step away from his sister in time.

I really need to find a way to take back his key.

"Hey, hey, let's get going. Party doesn't start until we get there. Well, until I get there." He walks over to his sister and ruffles her hair.

"Kai, stop it. I just finished getting ready," she complains, ducking out from under his hand.

I can understand her annoyance on a deeper level now that I know Evie as well as I do. Yami obviously loves her and respects her, but sometimes he really does treat her like a kid sister, and not the fully capable woman she is.

I remember when we first met, he would joke about chasing away anyone who tried to get close to Evie. I thought nothing of it, she was a teenager, and he was her older brother. It was his job to be protective like that.

But now, I wonder how he'd react to the idea of *me* being the one getting close to her. Would he be mad that we kept it from him? Or would he somehow be okay with it?

These questions have crossed my mind more than once over the last several days, and the God's honest truth is, I have no idea what the answer would be.

All I know is that if I want any kind of future with her, we're going to have to find out.

Yami drives to the bowling alley in his stupid low-slung sports car that's a pain in the ass to fold myself into.

"I don't know why the hell you drive this thing," I complain, once again trying to shift into a comfortable position in the back seat.

"Because it looks cool, dumbass. And normally I don't have big-as-fuck baseball players in the back seat," he fires back.

"If you would have let me sit back there, you could have been up front where there's more leg room." Evie shakes her head.

"You're the lady, you get the front. It's just good manners," I retort.

She turns in her seat to face me. "Thanks, Rhett. I appreciate it, but I'm sorry you're so uncomfortable. You have to promise that you'll sit in the front seat on the way home."

I give her a soft smile after confirming that Yami's not looking at us in the rearview mirror. "Fine, honey. I will. Thank you."

Her eyes widen a fraction, and I realize my mistake. I've never called her honey in front of anyone before. Thankfully, her brother seems to have missed my slipup, or maybe he assumes it's no different from when I call everybody darlin', because he doesn't say a word.

But it is different. Very different. Because what I feel about Evie *is different*.

When we arrive at the bowling alley, half the team's already there. Evie and I go separate ways, with her heading off to say hi to Willow and Lark and me following Yami over to where our teammates are standing around a table with a couple pitchers of beer and some pizza.

Even with a lot of the parents and siblings from the youth baseball players here, no one's acting crazy about our presence, which is nice.

"Gentlemen," Yami says, holding his arms out wide. "Who's ready to have their ass handed to them by a bowling ball?" He lifts his right arm up to kiss his bicep, earning a groan from several of us. "Don't hate, don't hate. This arm isn't only the best pitching arm in the western division, you know." He might sound like he's talking smack, but the truth is, I've been bowling with him before and he's not lying. The guy is good. Annoyingly good.

"I don't know about that Yami. If it's anything like your cornhole skills, I'm feeling good about my chances." Sin takes a sip of his beer, smirking at Yami. Laughter rings out from all of us who were at that team barbecue in the fall at Sin and Willow's house.

"Listen. It was the end of the season, my arm was tired, and I'd had three beers. Don't judge me on that performance."

"Sit down, Yami, your cocky side is showing," calls out Wilson, another younger player.

Yami looks down at his crotch, then back up at the group with a grin. "My cocky side is my best side. Just ask your mom."

I groan and slap Yami's back. "Don't go getting started with the yo mama jokes, Yami. They're not funny. Never have been."

The other guys all chime in with their agreement, and with an eye roll, Yami allows the subject to change to the players on the All-Star teams and who we think will win.

Eventually, Monty and Grayson join us, along with a couple other kids from the league. We spend the next half hour signing autographs and taking pictures with the kids. Not Grayson, however. He's known most of us for years, from all the times we would join Monty in helping out at training camps or supporting Grayson's team. He's a cool kid.

"Time to start bowling." The announcement comes from the overhead speakers. "Teams have been chosen at random, please look to the screens overhead to see who you're playing with."

I stroll down the walkway behind the lanes until I find my name. And right below mine is Evie Yamaki. Along with Willow, a couple of youth league kids, and their parents.

Even though Yami is several lanes away, I'm hyperaware of how close I stand to Evie and whether our body language is giving anything away.

Subtlety is the name of the game. Willow is the only one with even the slightest hint that maybe there's more than meets the eye between us. Every now and then, I feel her staring like she's trying to figure us out.

I'm determined not to give her anything.

But when Evie takes her turn, walking up to the lane, bending over to pick up a ball, I'm treated to the perfect view of her ass in those jeans. And my own jeans become a little bit tighter each time she does it.

I think I'm doing a good job of exercising restraint until her final turn, when she throws her first strike of the game. She skips back to the rest of us with her arms in the air as we all cheer. It's impossible not to be excited for her, and I jump up to give her a hug, spinning her around. I set her back down just before I completely fuck up and kiss her. She stares up at me for a second before whirling around to high five the rest of our group.

"For someone who's just friends with his teammate's little sister, that sure did look like one hell of a hug. It almost makes me wonder if somebody's in a secret relationship or something."

Willow slides across the plastic bench closer to me, leaning in so she can — thank fuck — keep her voice low. "I should know. I'm practically an expert on them."

My body stiffens, and I keep my head facing forward, not even looking at her. "I don't know what you're talking about, darlin'. There's nothing to see."

"Uh-huh. You're still playing it that way, are you?"

I turn my head to her, fixing her with a serious stare. "I'm not playin' at a single damn thing, Willow." The lie feels wrong coming off my tongue.

Willow goes quiet for a moment before giving me a small nod. "Okay, if you say so. I'll leave it for now. But trust me when I say you're not being as subtle as you might think. It's clear to anyone looking hard enough that there's more than friendship between the two of you. And my only advice is to be careful. Think about how long you want to keep this ruse going, because sooner or later, the truth will come out and you want to be in control of it when it does." Regret laces her tone, and I notice her gaze search the bowling alley. The second she sees Ronan, her lips turn up in a smile. "Trust me, I've got some experience with this. It can get messy if you don't have a plan for telling everyone the truth."

Someone calls her name at that moment and Willow stands up to leave, but not without one last parting comment, an echo of what she said to me that day she helped get supplies for Evie's migraine. "You're a good man, Rhett Darlington. Remember that."

Willow walks away, and my gaze scans the bowling alley, finding Yami laughing with some of our other teammates. Then I turn back to look at Evie, who's moved over a couple of lanes and is talking to Lark and Sadie. Her eyes land on mine, and a smile breaks across her face, and I know there's an answering one on mine.

Willow is right. We're doing a terrible job of hiding how we feel. And I don't want to hide it any longer.

But how and when do we tell her brother?

Chapter Twenty-Seven

Evie

"Last night was fun," I say, my fingers drawing lazy circles on Rhett's bare chest. I'm on my stomach beside him, my head and one arm propped up on his torso as his hand runs up and down my back.

We're in bed, both of us barely clothed — Rhett in boxer briefs, me in one of his T-shirts and a pair of panties, but the subtle desperation I used to feel when we'd be in bed together is gone. There's no longer a ticking clock over my head, reminding me that my time with him is limited, and I had best soak up every second of intimacy I can.

Now we're free to relax and enjoy these moments of closeness.

Well, as free as we can be, given that we're still a secret.

Rhett makes a rumbling noise of agreement, his hand moving up to rake through my hair. "It was. And seein' you get a higher score than your brother was the highlight of my night."

I giggle, dropping my face down to his chest, feeling his answering chuckle vibrate under me. "He really was not happy about that."

"We men need to be put in our place by beautiful woman on

a regular basis."

I lift my head again, shifting upward to press a soft kiss to his lips. "Spoken like a *true* man."

"Nah, spoken like a mama's boy, raised by a strong woman and a father who taught me the most important thing in life is to respect everyone, no matter what."

I breathe in slowly and hold it for a second before exhaling as I drop my head back down, laying my cheek on his warm chest. "We should talk about my brother. Telling him, I mean."

Rhett's hand stills for a moment before resuming the slow, methodical stroke of my hair. "Yes. I suppose we should. It doesn't feel so good, keeping it from him. Especially now."

I nod. "Yeah. Especially now."

He shifts under me, and his other hand moves to tilt my chin up. "It's not that I thought what we were doing before, when it was just sex, was anything to be ashamed of. I hope you know that, Evie."

"I know." I nod against his touch. "It was my decision not to tell him. I didn't want to come between the two of you or make things weird with the team, not when it wasn't anything serious."

I see his Adam's apple bob up and down as he swallows, his hands coming to cup both sides of my face.

"Even when we were pretending it was just sex, I didn't think it ever really was. Not for me, if I'm being totally honest."

"Oh." His words feel like a warm blanket over my heart, everything settling into place.

His thumbs move back and forth once, twice, as his deep brown eyes sear into my own.

"I've been fightin' my attraction to you for a lot longer than the last few weeks. It felt wrong to want you like that, like I was betraying Yami somehow. But I've realized how stupid that was. He'll always be my best friend. That doesn't give him any goddamn right to say who I get to care for."

I want to cry. I want to jump up on the bed and scream with happiness. And I want to kiss Rhett, over and over again.

I've waited so long, dreaming of the day Rhett Darlington might return my feelings for him. And now that day has come, and he's admitted he cares for me.

And fast on the heels of wanting to cry and smile and all the things comes the crushing fear that this beautiful man could still break my heart into pieces.

Because while he might finally be in a place to acknowledge there's *something* between us, I'm already in the place where I think I'm falling in love with him. And his words that first time we ever slept together have never left me.

He said he wasn't the guy I should be in a relationship with. That I deserved more.

I don't want more. I just want him.

I muster a smile, covering his hands with mine. "And he'll always be my brother, but he has no right to say who I get to be with, either."

Rhett lifts his head, meeting me halfway for a long kiss, cementing those words.

"So we tell him. Soon," I say when our lips break apart. Rhett nods.

"Soon."

All of a sudden, I'm flipped onto my back, and now Rhett is

hovering over my torso.

"But not right now." Hands lift my shirt up and over my head, and then he's kissing his way down my neck, all the way over to one breast. "Right now, I think there's an inch or two of your gorgeous body I haven't paid attention to in a day or so."

I giggle as he wraps his lips around my nipple, that giggle turning into a gasp when his teeth graze it as he releases it with a pop.

"Well, we can't have that," I say, my voice coming out breathy and high.

Rhett gives me a devilish look, his eyes gleaming with desire. "We most definitely cannot."

"Good thing you've got time to rectify the situation."

"We've got all the time in the world, honey."

Several hours and orgasms later, I'm in the kitchen wearing one of Rhett's shirts when strong arms band around my waist, soft lips landing on my neck. "This is why I love All-Star break."

"Grilled cheese sandwiches?" I giggle as he tickles my side.

"No, uninterrupted access to you. We've got four days left and I want to spend as much of that time naked as we possibly can." Rhett swats my ass, and I yelp and dance away.

"Rhett, I'm cooking!"

"Mm-hmm, and I'm hungry for more than just a sandwich, honey." He hops up on the counter and leans back on his hands. All that muscled, tanned skin on display, ripples of abs, and a very prominent outline underneath his shorts.

I drag my gaze away as he chuckles, fully catching me gawking.

"Food first. You just" — I wave the spatula around in the air, blushing — "ate...not that long ago."

"Let's get somethin' straight. I will never *not* be hungry for you, honey."

"That's...you're..."

Rhett slides off the counter and smacks a kiss to my lips along with a grope of my ass. "Addicted to you? Guilty."

A couple of minutes later, we're eating our sandwiches on the couch. Well, I'm still eating. Rhett polished his off in a few bites. He leans forward and picks up the book I'm currently reading. I fight not to blush. It's a very steamy paranormal romance about bear shifters.

"This looks...interesting," he says. "Tell me. Do they fuck as bears or as men?"

I almost choke on my bite of grilled cheese.

"Men, Rhett. Oh my God." I go to snatch the book away from him, but he holds it out of reach.

"Now, now, I want to know what my competition is when it comes to turning you on. What's your favourite part?"

It just so happens I've read this book a few times already. "Chapter sixteen. Take a look."

His cheeks darken and he goes to set the book down, but I reach over and stop him. "Read to me?"

"Evie," he cautions, but I push. Just a little.

"I'm willing to bet you know more than you think you do. Your brain has created coping skills and strategies to handle situations when you have to read. Don't sell yourself short. And if you mess up, oh well, it's just me here and I won't judge. Trust me?"

He inhales deeply, then blows it out just as slowly. "You know I do, honey. Okay, sixteen, you said?"

I hide my exhilaration as he flips the pages. But before he's read even a single word, we're interrupted by my cell ringing on the table in front of us.

"Saved by the bell," he says, stretching to pick up my phone. "It's your mom."

I pout but quickly follow it with a peck to his cheek. "This isn't over, Rhett Darlington. I want to hear you read some shifter romance. Got it?"

All I get in response is a wan smile as I answer the phone. "Hey, Mom."

"Evie? Hi honey, is Kai with you?"

Dread settles into me, both at her somber tone, and at her question. "No, he's not here right now." *Not a lie...*

"Okay. I'll have to try him again later. Sweetie, I've got some bad news." Mom pauses, and my hand comes up to twist the hem of Rhett's shirt. My mind starts racing with all the things that it could possibly be. My sisters? Dad? Grandma?

"Oba-chan is in the hospital. They think it's pneumonia."

"Oh my God," I whisper. I hadn't even noticed Ruthie in front of me until I hear her whine and feel her press her cold nose into my knee. My hand drifts down to pet her head. "Is she going to be okay?"

"I don't know." Mom sounds broken. A far cry from the strong, positive woman she normally is. "Your dad thinks you and Kai should come home, though. Your sisters are heading to the hospital to see her today. Dad has been there since he took her in last night."

A warm hand lands on my thigh. I turn to Rhett, my eyes filling with tears. He squeezes my leg softly, his face wreathed in concern.

"Okay, I'll look for a flight."

Rhett's eyebrows raise at my whisper.

"I'm so sorry, Evie. I hope we're being overly cautious, but the doctors warned us that with people her age, it can go downhill quickly." Her voice catches on the last word, and a tear escapes my eye, trailing down my cheek. Rhett's thumb lifts and he strokes it away. I let myself lean into his side, seeking comfort.

"I understand," I whisper. "I'll find Kai and tell him."

"Would you? I came home to get a few things for Oba-chan and to call you two, but I really want to get back to the hospital."

I hear sounds of her moving around in the background and nod before realizing she can't see me. "Yeah, Mom. I'm sure he'll be home soon. I can tell him."

"Thank you, sweetie. If he has any questions, tell him to call me, not your dad. And let me know your flight info when you get it booked. We can help pay for it if needed. The important thing is that you get here."

"I know. I love you, Mom. Can you tell Dad and Oba-chan that for me?" I'm openly crying now, my stomach in knots with worry for my grandmother.

"Of course. I love you, too."

The call ends, and my phone falls from my hands. Rhett catches it, those baseball reflexes coming out. I'm numb, staring forward, trying to breathe.

"Evie, please honey, tell me what's wrong," Rhett says, drawing me into his embrace.

My tears fall onto his chest as my mind begins playing a reel of memories, moments with my grandmother over my entire life.

"My grandmother is in the hospital. Pneumonia. Mom said it's not looking good, and Kai and I should go home."

"Oh shit, honey." Rhett holds me tighter. "I'm sorry. We'll get you on a plane as soon as possible."

I nod, and then the words start pouring out of me. "She's the most amazing woman." I hiccup, drawing in a ragged breath. "When my grandfather died, she moved out to Canada to be with my parents. Turns out, she'd always wanted to travel the world, but my grandfather was more traditional and didn't see the point. He hated that my dad moved to Canada to be with my mom, but she always supported them." My eyes close, a small smile crossing my face as I remember sitting with her in the living room of my parents' house, doing my homework as she practiced her English. "She's the reason I learned Japanese. So I could talk to her. But she wanted to learn English as well, so we taught each other."

"I remember when I first met her, I tried to greet her in Japanese and she scolded me." Rhett chuckles, his hand rubbing my back in comforting circles. "Then she said, 'In Canada, we speak English, Rhett.'"

I giggle, even as I sniff back another tear. "Sounds like something she'd say."

"Okay. So. We need to get you and Kai on a plane to Ontario, today."

I swipe away the remaining tears, and move to sit up, but Rhett doesn't let me, holding me against him tightly. It takes only a second for me to give in to the comfort he's offering.

"Just let me hold you, honey."

I nod against his chest, snaking my arms around him so I can hold him right back.

But I have to talk to my brother, and book a flight, and pack. So a few minutes later, I pull away again. This time, he lets me.

"Okay. How can I help?" he asks, his hand returning to rub my back. I take a slow, deep breath.

"Could you try to get a hold of Kai? I'm going to search for flights."

"You got it."

He turns to his phone, and I pick mine back up. A few minutes later, he hands his to me. "It's your brother."

I take it, and he moves to stand up but I grab his arm to stop him. "Stay?" I whisper, and with a soft kiss to the top my head, he sinks back down beside me. I give him a grateful smile before turning to the phone.

"Kai? I have to tell you something."

Chapter Twenty-Eight

Evie

In no time at all, I'm at the front door of Rhett's apartment, waiting for my brother to arrive. Kai's on his way over to pick me up, and we're heading straight to the airport, to see if we can get on an earlier flight than the one we booked that doesn't take off for several hours.

After holding me for several minutes, helping me get my emotions slightly more under control, Rhett helped me pack. I've got one of his hoodies and a T-shirt to sleep in. Although, how I'll keep that from my brother, I'm not sure. It feels comforting to have something of his with me, though.

"Make sure you let me know how your grandmother is." He kisses my forehead again, then my lips. "Ruthie and I will be waiting to hear from you when you land."

I look up into his face. This man, who is so calm, so steady, so present for me, as I feel like I'm falling apart. "I wish you were coming with us," I say impulsively, burrowing back into his strong embrace as my heart races to catch up to what I just said.

I never wanted to feel dependent on someone who could so easily break my heart, but in this moment, I need Rhett. I need his strength and his warmth; I need *him*.

My phone dings with an incoming text before he can respond, and Rhett pulls it out of my back pocket, handing it to me.

KAI: I'm parked out front.

"He's here." I pocket my phone and look up at Rhett.

He gives me a slow nod and an easy smile. "I'll see you in a few days. Your grandma's gonna be fine."

"I hope so," I whisper, letting him guide me in for a soft kiss. "Bye."

"Bye." Another kiss, then another. Then he opens the door, passing me the handle for my suitcase.

I move to the hallway, pausing at the elevator to look back at him. He's leaning in the doorway, one hand on Ruthie's collar as she whines, wanting to follow me. I give him a small smile, then step into the elevator.

Kai hugs me when I reach his car, helping me load my suitcase in the trunk. "Here's hoping for an earlier flight."

I nod in agreement, sliding into the passenger seat. The drive is silent, both of us lost in our own thoughts, I suppose.

I can't stop thinking about Rhett. About how he made me feel so comforted, even in the midst of receiving such terrible news. How he took care of me automatically, comforting me and helping me pack. And how it didn't feel wrong letting him do that. It felt good, not being alone, being supported and cared for.

I've spent so long trying to prove my independence that I never stopped to think about how good it can feel to have a partner in the hard times.

At the airport, Kai lifts my suitcase out of the trunk, and I take both his and mine to the sidewalk as he pays the valet to deal with his car.

"C'mon, let's see about that earlier flight"

I nod and follow my brother inside. Unfortunately the flight before ours is full, so we go through security, and find one of the bars to settle in for a long wait. Kai orders some food, but I opt for only a drink.

"I have to say, traveling with you is convenient," I say lightly, trying to brighten the mood.

Kai snorts. "Yeah? Shorter security lines are a perk, I guess."

We smile at each other, but the smiles fade quickly. Kai tugs his baseball hat down lower. "Fuck, Gigi. What if Oba-chan isn't okay."

I swallow, my drink suddenly turning to dust in my mouth. "She has to be."

He leans forward, covering my hand with his. "She will be."

A long moment passes, and I wonder if he's trying to picture life without our grandmother in it the same way I am.

His phone rings, and my gaze flies to it as he snatches it up.

"Mom? Hey. Yeah, we're both here, we're at the airport. Our flight doesn't leave for a few hours."

I bite my lips as I watch his face, hoping to see some indication of what Mom's saying. When his eyes widen and he exhales, I fight to not get my hopes up.

"Really? That's fucking awesome." He winces. "Sorry. Yeah, I'll tell her." He gives me a thumbs-up that has me filling with relief, but then his face falls again. "I get it. Yeah. We'll see you soon. Love you, Mom."

He hangs up and I gesture wildly at him. "Well? What's going on?"

"The doctors think Oba-chan will be okay, but it's still early. Mom said she's improving with the antibiotics, but she's not out of the woods."

I sag back into my seat, feeling like I'm on a ride that I really want to get off. "So it's good news? Or not good."

"A bit of both, I guess."

"Okay."

We fall silent again. Until Kai straightens in his seat, staring at something behind me. "What the fuck?"

I turn, and my hand flies up to cover the gasp that escapes me.

"Rhett?" On trembling legs, I push up to stand.

"Dude, what the hell are you doing here?" Kai grins, arms open wide. *Shoot.* He thinks Rhett is here for him?

Rhett sidesteps him, ignoring my brother, staring only at me.

"Did you mean it? That you wished I was comin' with you?"

My mouth falls open, even as I nod. "I mean, yes. But —" My gaze darts over to Kai, who's now frowning, arms folded across his chest as his gaze bounces between the two of us.

Rhett takes a step forward, taking my hands in his. That's when I register the suitcase at his side. "If you want me, if you need me, then I'm here, honey."

"Honey?" Kai growls, but both of us ignore him.

It's my turn to take a step forward, and then I'm back in Rhett's arms. He's holding me tightly, kissing the top of my head. And the knot in my stomach loosens.

"Okay, seriously. What the actual fuck is going on?"

Kai's hand is on my shoulder, forcing me to let Rhett go and turn to face my brother. But Rhett doesn't let me go far, shifting so that his arms hold me from behind.

"Evie and I are together, Yami. I care about her a hell of a lot. And *not* like a sister."

Kai's jaw clenches so hard I can see the muscles bunch under his skin. "How long."

"Kai," I start, but he holds up his hand, and that's when I realize he's glaring at Rhett.

"How long, Darling? How long have you wanted my baby sister?"

"I've thought she was beautiful for years. I'm not gonna lie to you about that. But I swear on my mama's heart, nothin' happened between us until recently."

He doesn't mention my attempt at kissing him all those years ago, and I'm grateful. Because when I see Kai's face relax, I realize where his anger was coming from.

This time, when I go to speak, neither one of them stops me.

"Kai. I'm an adult. And I get that you think I'm your baby sister, and that you have to protect me from everything, but you don't. And you certainly don't have to protect me from Rhett." I lean back into his chest, tilting my head up to smile at him. "You of all people should know the kind of man he is."

Rhett's answering smile is soft and full of emotion. But it's Kai who draws my attention. When I look back at him, his shoulders have dropped, and he's scrubbing his hands up and down his face.

"Jesus, you guys, because I didn't have enough going on with Oba-chan being sick, now I gotta deal with you two being all…"

He waves his hands at us, grimacing slightly. "Whatever this is."

Rhett's chuckle vibrates through my body. "We're together. Deal with it, Yami."

"Fuck," Kai groans, but he sinks back into his seat. "Fine. Sit. I'm starving."

Rhett pulls out my chair before sitting down beside me, his arm coming around my back. The waitress arrives at that moment with our orders. Her eyes widen as she takes in Rhett, but I have to give her credit, she just sets down our dishes before looking back at him.

"Can I get you anything?"

"Just some water, thank you darlin'." Rhett gives her a smile and she walks away.

"What the fuck was that smile for? You can't call her darlin', my sister's right there." Kai's defense of me is sweet, but not necessary. I want to laugh, only then I look at Rhett, and realize he looks completely freaked out.

"Evie, I wasn't flirting, I swear."

I pat his arm reassuringly before glaring at my brother. "I know you weren't. You call everyone darlin'. You were just being yourself." I lean in and kiss his cheek. "Southern charmer and all."

Relief covers his face as he leans in as well, cupping my chin. "Exactly. But only *you* are my honey."

"Gross. No, stop. Right the fuck now, stop."

We pull apart and look at Kai, who's grimacing again, his hand lifting to cover his eyes.

He peeks between his fingers, and I giggle. "You're gonna have to get used to it, Kai. I happen to quite enjoy kissing him."

Kai pretends to retch, and I turn to Rhett, shaking my head. "Can you believe they worry about *my* maturity when he acts like this?"

Rhett's fighting back a smile as he strokes his fingers across my shoulder. "No surprise to me." He leans in and kisses me, keeping it soft and short for my poor brother, who I have to admit is actually taking this better than I expected.

When we face him again, Kai's beer is empty and the frown is gone from his face. "Fine. This is happening. I can deal." He turns to Rhett and leans forward. "But my sister is never to be discussed in the fucking locker room. Am I clear?"

Rhett gives him a firm nod. "Crystal."

Kai leans back. "And if you hurt her, I will end you. Sisters before misters and all that shit."

"I'm not entirely sure this is the right use of that phrase," I interject, but Kai holds up his hand in a stop sign at me.

"Doesn't matter. I mean it. He fucks up, he's dead to me."

"Kai," I start to try and reason with him, but Rhett's hand on my arm stops me.

"No, Evie, he's right. You come first. I'd expect nothin' less." He reaches a hand across to Kai, who slowly takes it in a firm handshake. "She's safe with me, Yami."

They stare at each other for a tense moment before my brother finally smiles. "I know she is, Darling. If it had to be any guy from the team, I'm glad it's you. But *you* might not be so safe when my mom hears about this."

Rhett scoffs. "Your mom loves me."

Kai's smile turns positively wicked. "Exactly. Get ready to state your intentions for my little sister, dude. Because she's the baby of the family. The Yamakis are gonna be ruthless."

Chapter Twenty-Nine

I've known the Yamaki family for years. They're great. They love me.

So why the hell does my stomach start to twist up in knots tighter than the fly fishing lures my grandpa taught me to tie as soon as our plane touches down in Toronto?

It's probably because of the way my best friend keeps looking at me and laughing under his breath.

"Kai. Stop it," Evie chides when he does it again as we're walking to the baggage carousel. "You're acting like Rhett's about to walk the plank."

Yami just shrugs and gives an unrepentant smirk. "Mom and Dad like him well enough as my best friend. But as your boyfriend? That's different, Gigi, and you know it. You've never brought a guy home. I'm just looking forward to the show." He mimes eating popcorn as Evie shoves him.

I try not to clench my jaw too tightly as I walk on ahead. This is gonna be fine. All I have to do is be my usual polite, charming, respectful self with their parents, and there won't be a problem.

And try not to be too obvious about how much I want to fuck their daughter every waking second of my goddamn life.

Outside the airport, Evie and Yami's dad Kenji is waiting for us.

"Dad!" Evie cries, abandoning her suitcase and running into her father's arms. "I didn't expect you to be here. How's Oba-chan? Can we see her today?"

"Slow down, Evangeline. She's doing better." Kenji hugs his daughter tight, giving Yami and me a smile over her shoulder. He looks tired but happy to see his kids. "Your grandmother is the one who kicked me out and told me to come and get you." He releases Evie and pulls Yami in for a shorter hug before turning to me with an outstretched hand. "I didn't realize I was picking up three of you. Hello, Rhett. It's good to see you."

"You as well, Ken. I'm sorry to hear about your mother."

He gives me a firm shake. "Thank you. It was kind of you to accompany Kai."

There it is. I expected Evie's family to assume I was there for Yami. But somehow I never thought through how to answer this kind of question. My gaze darts over to Evie, but she's just staring wide-eyed back at me.

Shit.

How did we not figure this out on the plane ride over?

"Nah, Dad, get this: Rhett and Evie started dating this summer." Yami slings his arm over my shoulder. "It's cool, I'm keeping an eye on them. But yeah, he's here for her." He juts his chin at his sister before dropping his arm.

Evie's father looks at me, and thankfully, there's no judgment on his face, only curiosity. "I see. This is quite the development."

"Dad," Evie finally says, moving to stand beside me and slipping her hand in mine. "Don't be weird about this, okay?"

His face softens into a loving smile for his daughter and I feel my chest relax. "Sorry, Evangeline. You just took me by surprise." He turns to me and nods. "Rhett. You're a good man. Thank you for being here."

That's all he says before turning and leading us to the car. I shoot a glare at Yami, who mouths, *you're welcome* with a smirk.

I stay quiet for the drive back to the Yamaki house, letting Evie and her brother chat with their dad. Evie's hand is on my leg, but after I catch her father looking at us in the rearview mirror, I refrain from putting mine on hers.

I'm relieved she seems okay with being affectionate in front of her family, but I'll be damned if I mess things up in any way. She's gonna have to take the lead, and I'll follow when it comes to how we interact.

I'd rather die than lose the respect of her family, or worse, have them disapprove of our being together.

When we reach the house, I get out of the car after Evie. "I'll grab the bags, you go see your family," I say, giving her hand a squeeze. She smiles and goes with her brother and dad to the house. Truthfully, I'm happy to have a couple of minutes to myself.

My decision to come to Ontario was impulsive, and incredibly last minute. I had to scramble to get Monty and Lark to look after Ruthie, struggle through trying to book a ticket online, pack a bag, and hustle my ass to the airport.

I don't regret my decision. Not for one goddamn second. But I am wishing I'd had a chance to think it through. To maybe talk to Evie about how to handle this. Because I'm realizing now that I threw her a massive curveball when it comes to telling her entire family about us. And we had no chance to talk about it on the plane with Yami sitting right beside us.

By the time I get inside, Evie is standing in the living room with her two older sisters, Josephine and Vivienne. Seeing the three of them together, despite their similarly old-fashioned names, courtesy of their mother's love for historical fiction, they couldn't appear more different.

Where Evie smiles easily, and has a wide-open heart, I've always found the older Yamaki girls to be a lot more reserved.

They turn to me, and judging by Evie's hesitant smile, she told them about our relationship. Josephine approaches and gives me a perfunctory hug. "Hi, Rhett. Good to see you."

"Thanks," I say. "I'm sorry it's not under better circumstances."

She gives me a nod and steps aside to follow her father into the kitchen. I look at Vivienne, who's still standing next to Evie with her arms folded across her chest and a slight frown on her face.

"Vivienne," I say with a nod of my head, unsure how to proceed. We've never had an issue with each other, but I also can't say I know her very well.

"Rhett," she says. And that's it. She turns and follows her sister to the kitchen. Evie watches her go, her brows furrowed, as I make my way to her side.

"That was weird," she says, leaning into my side. "I guess we took them by surprise."

"About that," I say, running my hands up and down her arms. "I'm sorry for springing this on you so last minute. I wasn't planning on coming, but when you left and you said you wanted me..." I trail off, my hands stilling. "Well, I guess I didn't really think it through. I just wanted to be here for you."

Evie turns in my arms and flings her arms around my neck. "I'm so happy you're here. Honestly."

Relief courses through me. *Thank fuck.*

"Evangeline, we're going to head to the hospital now. Your grandmother is waiting to see you."

I drop my arms and step back quickly at the sound of Kenji's voice, but he doesn't seem angry to walk in and see us embracing.

"Okay, Dad." She looks up at me. "Will you be okay here?"

I nod. "Of course. I'll head out for a run or hit the gym down the street. Go, take your time with your grandmother."

She flashes me a quick smile, and I start to lean down to kiss her lips before pausing, fully aware her father and now her sisters are all in the room with us. I change trajectories and press a very short kiss to her cheek instead.

Kenji nods at me. "There's a spare key in the kitchen, lock up when you leave."

"Will do," I say, grateful for the offer and the trust that comes so easily from this family.

After the Yamakis all leave, I exhale in the quiet. Everything is feeling a hell of a lot more real now that our relationship is out in the open. And with that comes the pressure I can feel building in my chest. In some ways, it felt like there was less at stake when it was just sex. Now, there's feelings involved. And not just mine and Evie's, but the team and her family.

I make my feet move to carry me down the hall toward the stairs that lead to the second floor. I've walked up these stairs countless times during offseason trips with Yami to visit his family. I follow the usual path to his bedroom that was converted into a guest room with two twin beds. I know without even looking that the girls' rooms were converted into a sewing room and another guest room with a queen bed.

Family photos line the hall, and even though I've seen them before, I catch myself looking at them differently now. I'm seeing Evie not only as the little sister held by her brother or dad, but as the girl who grew up into an incredible woman.

I peer into the first bedroom and see Evie's suitcase sitting beside the bed, but not mine. Not that it surprises me to find mine down the hall on one of the beds in Yami's old room. I held no expectation of being able to be with Evie under her parents' roof.

But spending the next three days not being able to touch her the way I'm used to means I'm gonna need that workout.

Chapter Thirty

Evie

I'm not a fan of hospitals. Never have been. I spent way too much time in them as a child.

Apparently, I like them even less when it's someone I love inside.

Dad leads us to the medical floor and into Oba-chan's private room. She's sitting up in bed with oxygen cannulas in her nose and my mother by her side.

"Kai, Evie." Mom stands up and walks over to us, pulling me in first for a long hug. I inhale the comforting, earthy scent I always associate with my mom, letting it fill me with peace.

"Hey, Mom." We break apart and she cups my face, looking into my eyes with a smile before releasing us and moving to Kai. I make my way to the bed where my grandmother waits.

She looks so old, so frail. It takes me aback for a second, but I don't think I let it show. I sit down and pick up one of her hands, covered in fine wrinkles. I lift it to my cheek and close my eyes. "Hi, Oba-chan."

"Hello, Evie." Her voice is strong, and clear, and sends a wave of relief through me.

"How are you feeling?" I take her in more closely now and see the usual warmth and intelligence in her eyes.

"I am improving with the antibiotics they are giving me. The doctors have said I will be home soon. You did not have to come visit."

Her formal speech patterns are so familiar and take me back to long days spent learning Japanese at her side as she learned English at mine.

I give her a smile, but it's Kai who answers first.

"Sure we did, Oba-chan. You're kinda important, you know, so quit it with this whole getting sick business."

She laughs, but it turns into a coughing fit that has Kai frowning and all of us crowding around her bed. She waves us off after Dad gives her a cup of water with a straw.

"Jokes are not welcome right now."

"Sorry, Oba-chan," Kai says, taking her other hand.

"You are forgiven. Now. Tell me, Evangeline. Have you found a job yet?"

All eyes turn to me. I've never felt pressure from my family quite like I am in this particular moment. And I know, deep down, that it's not so much pressure from them as it is pressure from myself. I hate the fact that I still haven't secured a job. But if I'm being completely honest, I haven't been searching quite as actively as I could be. I may like living with Rhett a little too much, and knowing when I find work, that situation will end, which makes me feel less motivated than I should.

"Not yet," I say, clearing my throat and forcing a smile. "There haven't been many postings near Vancouver this year, but I'm still looking."

"You could always look in a different province," Vivienne

says, her tone mild but with something critical underlying.

"We'd love it if you moved back here, honey." My mom places her hand on my shoulder. "You've always got a room at home, for as long as you need it. And we could help —"

I put up my hand to cover hers and interrupt. "Thank you, but no. I love it in British Columbia. I want to stay there."

"And that decision has nothing to do with a certain baseball player," Viv says, and everyone turns their attention to her.

"Evie?" my mom asks, and I realize she doesn't know. "What does your sister mean?"

"Um, well, Rhett and I..." I pause, glancing at Kai to see if he'll help me out, but he's carefully *not* looking at me. "Rhett and I are dating now."

"Oh honey, that's wonderful, he's a good man."

"He flew out with her and Kai," Viv interjects, her arms folded across her chest. "He's back at the house right now."

"Really? Well, isn't that lovely."

Viv makes a snorting sound.

At least my mother seems happy with my news. And Dad seems to have accepted it, along with one of my sisters. But my focus narrows in on Vivienne. Why is she so upset by this? I can't help but wonder what the heck is wrong with her.

"Anyway. Oba-chan, can I get you anything?" I squeeze my grandmother's hand, desperate to move the focus away from me.

Somehow, the elderly woman always sees exactly what I need. Giving me a knowing smile, she inclines her head. "Some fresh water would be lovely, thank you."

I stand and snatch up the plastic water jug. "Great. Be right back."

In the hall outside her room, I take a quick breath in and blow it all out. I know I've never been close to my older sisters, but the frustration emanating off Viv is unsettling. Especially since it's so clearly directed at me.

I take a bit longer than I should filling the water jug, but I can't avoid my family for long. I don't want to. I came here to be with my grandmother, and I'll be damned if Viv's judgmental attitude is going to keep me from her. She's always had a haughty, better-than-everyone attitude, but for the life of me I can't figure out why she seems so angry at me.

But as I pivot on my feet to head back to the room, my sister walks up to me, her hands clutching her purse that's strapped across her chest.

"Viv, whatever has you mad at me, can it wait? Oba-chan needs her water," I say, attempting to move past her.

"No, Evie, it can't." Her hand comes to my arm, bringing me to a stop. "What the heck is going on right now? You don't have a job, you're mooching off our brother and now you're dating his best friend? Come on. It's time to grow up."

I take a minute to breathe in and out slowly. I will not rise to her bait. "Grow up? Last time I checked, I'm twenty-four with two degrees. Pretty sure that's considered grown up."

Viv scoffs. "Yeah, and instead of focusing on finding a job with those two degrees, you're messing around with a guy. What about your future?" The absurdity of her statement has me dropping my mouth open in shock.

But fast on the heels of that surprise is a sinking feeling in my stomach.

"It's not like I'm not looking," I argue. "I don't want to settle for a job that isn't right for me."

Still, my gut churns at her accusation.

"You know that if you had come back here when you graduated, you probably would have a job already. And you'd be with your family. You would have been here when Oba-chan first got sick."

"That's a low blow, Viv," I say, somehow remaining calm despite the sharp pain her words cause me.

My older sister doesn't break my stare. "I'm not the one setting aside my goals, my priorities, my *family*, because of a guy."

"Viv. Stop."

We both turn at the sound of Kai's angry voice. He's striding toward us, fists clenched. He comes to a stop, shooting daggers at our sister from his hard eyes.

"You're out of line."

"Am I?" Vivienne goes toe-to-toe with Kai. "Did you know she was dating Rhett? You're meant to be looking after her out there, ensuring she doesn't make foolish decisions. What happened, Kai?"

"What happened is that I decided to treat Evie like an adult, not a fucking child, Viv."

"Mom and Dad told us —"

"Mom and Dad would tell you that you're being insane right now," he interrupts Vivienne. I'm frozen between them, unable to move or say anything as one sibling attacks me and the other defends. "C'mon. They wanted us to watch out for her when she was a kid and sick all the time. It was the right thing for us to do. But not anymore." He looks over at me, his face softening. "Given recent… events, I've had a come-to-Jesus moment. She's a grown-ass adult, no matter how weird it is to think of her dating my best friend. But Evie doesn't need us to be so overprotective anymore. So back off and leave her alone."

If Vivienne is listening to him, it doesn't show. Instead, she turns to me, putting her back to Kai.

"You're putting a guy who's gone half the year for his job above your own career."

"She's not," Kai says, stepping around Viv and taking my hand in his. I appreciate his solidarity, but Vivienne's words are hitting their mark.

"She is, Kai. Or don't you remember last Christmas when she so boldly proclaimed her only focus would be finding a job. That's why she's staying with you, so she can put all her energy and time into that. Except now, she's distracted by Rhett."

It's impossible to hide the guilt I feel when she mistakenly assumes I'm staying with Kai. And of course, Viv picks up on it.

"Wait. What's that all about?" She waves her hand at my face. "Hold on." Her hand comes up to cover her mouth. "You're not staying with Kai, are you? Oh my God, Evie. Because dating him wasn't enough, you had to move in with him?"

"It's not like that!" I finally find my voice. "I couldn't stay with Kai, and Rhett was able to help out. We didn't expect to fall for each other."

"Why couldn't you stay with Kai?"

I look at my brother, beseeching him to help me find a way out of this inquisition. But he's just as lost as I am as to how to handle our out-of-control sister.

"Why, Evie? What possible reason could there be for you not staying with our brother where he can look out for you?"

I'm guessing that telling her I rescued a puppy from the side of the road and Kai's building doesn't allow dogs isn't the answer she wants to hear. Instead, I focus on the long-standing wound she's pouring salt into.

"I don't need looking out for!" I cry, finally losing my cool. My ability to stay calm and be the mature one has reached it's limit. "For God's sake, Vivienne, I'm an adult. You do realize that, right? I'm not a little kid, I'm a freaking adult. Fully capable of making my own decisions, whether you agree with them or not."

Viv's mouth narrows into a thin line. "If you're so grown up, then start acting like one. You need a job, Evie, not a boyfriend."

She turns on her heel and walks away, not toward Oba-chan's room, but toward the elevators.

"Fucking hell," Kai mutters, turning me to face him with his hands on my shoulders. "Are you okay?"

I reach up and dash away the tears building in my eyes. "Not really."

"She's wrong, Gigi and totally out of line. That was not cool for her to blow up like that. You're not being a fool. Rhett's a good guy."

I nod and let him pull me in for a hug.

"But," he starts with a more cautious tone. "What *are* you going to do about a job?"

"I can't make one appear out of nowhere," I mumble into his shirt, then I pull back. "I swear I'm looking for one. I'm just not ready to give up on staying in BC."

"Then don't. Mom and Dad always encouraged us to follow our hearts. And if you want to stay out west, not for a guy but for yourself, then do it. I'll be there to help every step of the way."

His words help, but not enough to fully erase the damage done by my sister's accusations.

Or fill the pit that has opened up in my stomach.

CHAPTER THIRTY-ONE

"Come, Evie, drive home with me." Mom's invitation is more of a gentle demand than a request.

"Okay." I lean down and give Oba-chan one more hug. "I'll come by again before we leave, okay?"

She nods and pats my hand. "I'd like that."

We walk as a group out of the hospital. Vivienne thankfully left earlier, saving me from having to interact with her any longer. At least for today. Apparently, Mom has a family dinner planned for tomorrow before Kai, Rhett, and I return home the next day.

In the parking lot, we split up, Dad and Kai going in one car back to the house, Josephine headed home on her own. Leaving Mom and I to drive back together.

My mother has always known when I need time to process, and when I need to be drawn out of myself and pushed to talk things through.

A talent she clearly still possesses, as the first ten minutes of our drive are silent. I stare out the window, watching the city I grew up in pass by outside. I don't miss it. I do miss the mountains of Vancouver.

After a while, I realize Mom has veered off from the route that would take us directly home. I turn to ask her where we're going, but she answers me before I can say a word.

"I thought we might go and get some tea." Her gaze is forward, but a knowing warmth is in her smile.

A moment later, we're pulling up in front of a bakery. Inside, we place our orders. I insist on paying, and Mom eventually acquiesces. We take our cups of steaming tea and find two comfortable-looking chairs tucked into the corner.

Even though I know Mom didn't bring me here just for tea, I wait. I'm not even sure what to say.

"I heard your sister talking to you."

Startled, I lower my cup without taking a sip and stare wide-eyed at her. "You did?" I had no idea she was anywhere near us when Viv was berating me.

"Yes." She nods, sipping calmly from her tea. "She loves you, Evie. You know that's where she's coming from. Love."

"She's got a funny way of showing it," I mumble, half under my breath.

"Evangeline," Mom chides gently, and I lift my gaze again to hers.

"Love shouldn't make me feel like crap about myself, Mom."

She shakes her head. "No, it shouldn't. And I'll be speaking to your sister later about how she handled things. But love does mean being honest, even when it might hurt. Vivienne is so proud of you, we all are. She's also worried about you, and some of that is my fault. When you were little, you were so sick all the time. You know your father and I asked your siblings to look out for you, but I didn't realize they were still taking that to heart."

She takes another sip, her gaze direct but full of affection. "But her concern does come from a good place. You're such a bright star, Evie, and your sister doesn't want you to deny yourself how high you could climb."

"I'm not," I protest. "I'm looking for jobs. Being with Rhett hasn't changed that."

"Of course. You're not going to abandon everything you've worked hard for, not for anyone, I know that, and so does your sister." Mom reaches a hand over and covers mine with hers. "But I want you to be honest with yourself. Is there a chance you are perhaps limiting your searches because of him? Your relationship is new, and I assume, wonderful and exciting. That can make it very tempting to shift your priorities to include him."

"Is that a bad thing?" I fiddle with the tag from my tea bag.

"Not at all." Mom shakes her head, squeezing my hand again. "If you and Rhett are happy, and if things are serious between the two of you, then following your heart is all I could ever want for you." Her smile takes on a hint of nostalgia. "After all, your father followed his heart all the way across the world to be with me."

I force a smile back at her. It helps, knowing Mom doesn't feel the same way as Viv. But telling me to follow my heart only works if Rhett's heart is in the same place as mine. And the harsh reality I've been avoiding is that I don't know if that's the case.

"I won't lie, when you told us you wanted to move out west, I was heartbroken. You're my baby girl. I will always want you close by. But I also want you to live your own life and find your own happiness. If that's with Rhett, that's wonderful. If it's not, then you'll find it somewhere else." She pauses, her head tilting to the side, those all-knowing eyes reaching down straight to my soul. "Just make sure the happiness you seek isn't dependent on someone else."

I nod but don't say a word.

Mom pushes back from the table, standing and picking up her cup. "Come, we had better get home and start making dinner before your dad decides to take matters in his own hands."

Her laugh is rich and full of love for my father, terrible cooking skills and all.

That's what I want. That deep, unending love and respect they share. The kind of love that made my father leave his home in Japan, defying his father's wishes, to move all the way to Canada for the girl he met when she studied abroad for a year.

He sacrificed everything for her. He showed her there was nothing they couldn't overcome, because they both knew they were meant to be together.

That knowing, that belief in fate or destiny, that's what I've dreamed of having some day. While I might feel strongly for Rhett, possibly even love him, everything is still so new, and so undefined. Does he believe we could have a future? That some force has been bringing us together all this time?

Do I believe that?

Or am I subconsciously sacrificing my career goals for the fantasy of a future with him?

If things were different, would he even consider doing the same for me?

Mom's well-intentioned intervention has only left me with more questions instead of answers.

All of which have me trying to swallow around a lump in my throat because I don't know *how* to answer them, or if I even want to.

I just know I have to.

Rhett is waiting for me when we get home, as everyone else is already home. The concerned look on his face when he pulls me in for a hug, his gaze searching my expression for answers of what might be wrong, is almost my undoing. He kisses the top of my head and quietly whispers, "Everything okay, honey?"

I want to melt into his arms and tell him everything that is so jumbled up inside of me, in hopes that he can untangle it.

But I don't. I find the strength — or maybe cowardice — to pull back and paste a smile on my face as I lie to him. "Yep, everything's fine. Mom and I just wanted to catch up quickly and hear more about Ruthie."

I step farther away from him, forcing myself not to acknowledge how his brows furrow.

"Okay. Well, I'm glad your grandmother is doin' better."

I give another short nod. "Me too." I gesture to the kitchen. "I'm gonna help Mom with dinner."

Making my escape, I can feel his gaze on my back, and my face flushes with all the conflicting emotions. How can I be falling in love with him, and want forever with him, but be so scared of saying anything to him?

Where are we going as a couple if I am so clueless as to how he feels that I can't trust he won't break my heart if I reveal it to him?

Unanswered questions rattle around in my brain like a pile of bingo balls being mixed around in the spinning cage.

"Evie, I think that's good." Mom gently takes the spoon from me, and I blink back to awareness, realizing I had been stirring the pasta sauce for a lot longer than she asked me to.

I take a step back and brush my hands on my pants. "Sorry."

"You need to take a breath, my girl. That beautiful brain of yours is overthinking and overanalyzing everything, and all that will do is drive you crazy."

I smile guiltily. "I know. It's hard not to, though."

Mom just rubs my arm. "It is, especially when something," — she leans in closer — "or someone, is so important. You need to talk to him, Evie. Even if you're scared."

I nod because it's what she expects. "Right. I know."

But as we sit around the dinner table later, and I watch Rhett with my family, seeing how easily he fits in, like he always has, the lump in my throat doesn't ease. If anything, it grows bigger.

The realization of how much is at stake, how big the impact would be if things went further between Rhett and me, starts hitting me in waves, one after another.

It's not just Kai and Rhett's friendship.

It's his connection to our family.

It's his career and the team.

It's my career and finding a job I love.

There's so much on the line. What started as pure fantasy fulfillment, a chance to be with the man I'd crushed on for so many years, has become a ticking time bomb.

A bomb that only Rhett can disarm, and only if he does see

a future with me.

Not only that, but only if we can somehow find a way to make our two lives, our two careers and goals, somehow align.

All of which terrifies me. Because I have no idea if he wants any of that.

And asking him outright feels like setting myself up for rejection. I did that once, and I can't do it again. Or I really will be the foolish, naive little girl my sister thinks I am.

Chapter Thirty-Two

Rhett

Something is very wrong.

It's hard fucking work to put on a smile and act as if everything's fine and after twenty-four hours of doing it, I'm drained. And tonight, our last dinner with the Yamakis before we fly home tomorrow, is proving to be the hardest. I want to grab Evie, drive away from this house to find somewhere private, and beg her to tell me what's hurting her so I can fix it.

"Next time we see you, we'll be celebrating your new job." Evie's mom Helen raises her glass toward Evie with a fond smile. "I know it's waiting somewhere for you."

"Maybe it's waiting here in Ontario?" Kenji jokes, but it's anything but funny to me.

Would she really consider moving back here? Judging by the grimace she barely manages to hide, I don't think so. Then again, she needs a job. I can't ask her to stay in BC just because I'm not ready to give her up.

I don't want to give her up.

But I want what's best for her. And that means I'll support whatever decision she makes. She means too much to me for me to ever try to hold her back from her future.

Evie deflects her father's question, her gaze downward. No one else seems to notice she's not herself, but I do. At one point, when I see her mother looking at her, I realize so does Helen.

Obviously, that catching up they did was about more than just Ruthie.

Later, after dinner is cleaned up and everyone is relaxing for the evening, I knock softly on the open door to Evie's room.

"Need any help packing up?" I lean against the frame, hoping my smile doesn't show how mixed up I am inside.

Evie looks up from the shirt she's folding. "No, thanks. I'm almost done."

Swallowing down my nerves, I step inside and move to stand behind her, running my hands down her arms a couple of times before wrapping them around her. I feel her freeze and almost step back.

No. Damn it, no. I'm not letting her get away, not now.

"Evie. Honey. What's goin' on?" I ask, daring to rest my forehead on her soft hair. My eyes close as I fight not to hold her tighter, as if that would keep her with me.

"Nothing."

When she pushes against my arms, they drop away. No matter how I feel, I won't ever force her.

"That's a lie, and we both know it." My voice is deceptively calm and quiet, given how I'm feeling. "Something's got you spooked like a wild horse. All I'm askin' is you tell me what it is. Let me in."

She sits down on the edge of her bed and twists her hands together. I move in front of her and sink down to my knees, taking her hands in mine and lifting them to my lips.

"Please. Talk to me."

She draws in a shaky breath before finally lifting those beautiful dark eyes to mine. "At the hospital yesterday, my sister said some things that were hard to hear. But..." she trails off, dropping her gaze for a second. "But I needed to hear them." She looks back up and straightens her spine. "I have to focus on finding a job. Not that I haven't been looking," she's quick to add, "but I don't think I've been as serious about it as I should have been. Maybe Ruthie distracted me, maybe we..." Again, her words drop off, and my stomach clenches. "Maybe I got caught up in whatever we've been doing. But what Viv said, about my goals, I have to stay focused on that. My work is important to me, helping kids who need it, that's what I've always wanted to do. There's a job out there for me, and I have to go and find it."

I nod slowly, taking in what she's said and trying to make sense of it. Her job search? That's what has her acting distant?

"Okay, well, when we get back, we'll buckle down and search." I smile, squeezing her hands. "Any school would be damn lucky to have you."

Evie gives me a small smile. "Yeah. And." She exhales. "That job, that school, it could be anywhere." Her eyes seem to search my face, gauging my reaction, I guess, so I give her an encouraging smile.

"Sure could. Wherever it is, you're gonna be exactly what they're looking for." I drop her hands and move up to sit beside her on the bed. Draping one arm over her shoulders, I tug her into my side. "I wish I had been lucky enough to have someone like you when I was a kid. You're gonna change some lives, honey."

She lets herself lean into me, but I can tell she's still holding back. And when she speaks, her voice is small and quiet. "There's a lot of jobs here in Ontario. I did a quick look when Mom and I were driving home yesterday."

I force my grip on her shoulders to stay loose, but my other hand clenches into a tight fist.

"Really," I say in what I hope is a casual voice. "Well, I'm sure your family would love to have you close by again."

"Mm-hmm."

Oh God. Is that a *she's considering it* mm-hmm? Fuck. What am I meant to say?

"Well. You'll make the decision that's right. I know you will." I press a kiss to the top of her head, hoping that's what she wants to hear.

"Thanks."

I need to see her face. I force my fist to unclench and reach up to cup her chin, turning her to me. It's impossible to figure out what she's feeling, but her cheeks are red, and something dangerously close to tears are shining in her eyes. I lean in and kiss her lightly at first. "Hey. It's gonna be okay, honey. You'll find a job."

"I know I will," she whispers back.

I kiss her again, and again, keeping it light until I feel her start to relax underneath me. Until, that is, she speaks again.

"I just wish I knew..." She stops suddenly, pulling back.

I keep hold of her chin and look at her. "Knew what?"

A small, obviously forced smile flashes across her face. "Nothing. Sorry. I was going to say I wish I knew when I'd find a job." A fake laugh, very unlike her, escapes. "But that would require a magic crystal ball or something. Anyway, I'm good. Thanks for the talk."

When she pulls back again, my hands drop. She stands and moves around to the other side of her bed. "I better finish packing. We leave pretty early tomorrow."

I'm staring at her, trying to figure out what the hell just happened, when she looks up at me. "You should pack too."

"Right. Yeah. I'll do that."

Slowly, I stand up and make my way to the doorway, where I pause and look back. Evie's refolding the same shirt she was folding when I first walked in.

"You sure you're okay?" It's a stupid question. Because she's obviously not. But I don't have a goddamn clue what else to say.

She looks up at me, that forced smile back on her face. "Yup. Just lots to think about."

No kidding.

After leaving Evie's room, I go to the one I'm sharing with Kai and toss my things into a bag, all while listening to him ramble on about some shit.

And later, while lying in bed, staring up at the ceiling, I run over the conversation with Evie again and again, trying to make sense of it.

She's stressed about finding a job. Okay, that makes sense. But what doesn't make sense is why that has her pulling away from me. Unless there's more going on. Unless whatever her sister said to her has her believing I could be standing in the way of her future.

Which is the last thing I'd ever want to do. I thought that was clear, that I want her to reach all her dreams, but maybe not?

That crystal ball she was joking about would be pretty useful right about now. For the first time, I've got something other than baseball and my family that I deeply care about.

And I don't have a goddamn clue how to tell her.

Chapter Thirty-Three

Rhett

The first day back after the All-Star break should be fun. It normally is. Everyone's relaxed after a week off, the guys that played are amped up, and we're all ready to get back to business and win some goddamn games.

At least, that's how it's been for me every year until now.

Today, parking my truck in the lot behind the stadium doesn't fill me with excitement.

Leaving Evie at home after our quiet flight home and even quieter night together was the last thing I wanted to do.

Sure, she sat next to me and cuddled into my arms while we watched a movie. But we didn't talk. Not about her job search, not about what her sister said or what we're doing, none of it.

As I'm getting out of my truck, I hear a voice call my name. Turning, I see Sin jogging toward me, a wide smile on his face.

"Hey, how was your break?" he asks as we pull each other in for a quick back-slapping hug.

"Good, good," I reply. "Went back to Ontario with Yami and his sister for a couple days."

Sin's face sobers. "Yeah, I heard his grandmother was sick. That was nice of you to go with them. You're close to the family?"

I nod. "You could say that."

A confused frown draws his brows together. "Okay."

I don't elaborate. "What did you get up to?"

Sin fills the time on the rest of our walk inside telling me all about how he and Willow took their kids down to California to hit up Disneyland.

And by the time we get to the doors of the locker room, we're both laughing.

"I'm not even joking, man, Peyton had Willow wearing princess headbands the entire time. I had to buy them each a new one for every day we were there."

"Be honest," I joke, "How many did *you* wear?"

"None, dude, none. That's not a photo I need in the tabloids."

I scoff. "You're with the head of PR. You think she'd let that happen?"

"True." Sin laughs as we head into the locker room.

"There he is," Yami calls out as soon as he sees us. Before I can say or do anything, he strides over to my side and drops his arm over my shoulders. "Listen up, fuckers. Darling has decided to take his life into his own hands and date my baby sister. Don't worry, I'm cool with it." He points to the other guys in turn. "But you're all responsible for reporting back to me if he does anything stupid that I need to kick his ass."

I stare at him, open mouthed. "What the fuck, Yami," I growl, shrugging off his arm. He just laughs, slapping my back as I stomp over to my locker.

"Dude, that's a bold move, making a play on a teammate's

sister."

I glare at Cortana, one of the second basemen who's been around almost as long as I have.

"Fuck off, Cort. It's none of your damn business."

"Sounds like Yami just made it all of our business," he fires back, a smirk on his face as he stands in front of me.

"Yami's an idiot. It wasn't his news to share."

"Actually, my brother from another mother, it kinda was." Yami drops down on the bench next to me. "See, she's my sister, which means she's mine to protect and defend. This is me, protecting and defending."

My glare turns on my former best friend. "Announcing my relationship status to the entire team. That's protecting your sister?"

"Sure as shit is. Because if you do anything stupid to hurt her, all of these guys" — Yami nods to the full locker room — "will know."

"Do you trust me that little?" I ask, my voice dropping lower. For all his bluster and joking, Yami's words sting.

His eyes widen. "Fuck. No, man." He runs a hand over his jaw. "That's not it. I'm just giving you shit. You know we're good."

I raise my eyebrows. "Really? Because I care about Evie. And I'm pretty damn sure she cares about me, too. I don't know what our future is gonna look like, especially after what your sister said to her, but I hope it's got me in it."

"Ah, fuck." Yami's head falls back against the wall behind him. "You know about Viv's freak out."

"Evie told me some of it. I know she's gotta focus on findin' a job, and I won't stand in the way of that."

Yami stares at me for a long minute. "I respect that you can see she's got to focus on herself right now. I know you're a good guy, Darling, I always have. I trust you, and I trust Evie to make her own decisions."

I nod. "Thanks."

Yami holds up a hand, his gaze narrowing. "But. If you do something stupid like think Vivienne is right and you're wrong for Evie, and that makes you push her away, then I *will* have a problem with you."

Well, fuck. I hadn't realized that was what their sister said to Evie. And it hits a little too close for comfort.

But that doesn't stop me from looking Yami square in the eye.

"I swear to you, I only want what's best for Evie. And I trust her to know what that is."

What I don't say is that I wish like hell I knew if a reality existed where *I* was what was best for her.

Don't ask me how I get home after practice without crashing into something — or worse, someone. That's how distracted I am after leaving the stadium.

Yami's announcement in the locker room was annoying, but I can see how it was necessary, too. He got everything out in the open, and I'm relieved I don't have to hide how I feel about Evie.

But realizing how I feel about her is like a train that started out really far away, only to naturally grow closer and closer, until now it's barreling down on me and there's no way I can get off the tracks.

It's too soon to say if it's love, and I still don't know if she's "the one," but what I feel for her is real. It's more than just attraction, it's more than just enjoying spending time with her, wanting to be around her, and not wanting her to move away. It's so much more.

When I turn my truck off in the parking garage under my building, I sit there, staring blankly at the cement wall in front of me.

Evie and I need to talk. She needs to know I'm here for her, that I want to support her. But also that I want to be with her, whatever that looks like. It's time to man up and tell her.

With that resolve, I get out and head inside.

I open the door to my apartment, and Ruthie comes scampering over. Dropping down, I ruffle her ears. "How's my good girl? Did you have a good day?" She leaps up and tries to lick my face, so I stand up. "Thanks, but no thanks. Only kiss I want is from your mama."

"Good luck getting her to stop," Evie says, her voice warmer than it has been since we left Ontario. She walks over to me and wraps her arms around my torso. I pull her in close, savouring the feel of her in my arms. This is what was missing ever since her sister put whatever doubts in her head. The easy affection and connectedness, the peace I feel when she's with me.

I kiss her head, then lean back so she looks up at me and I can kiss her forehead, her nose, and finally, her lips. "Hey, honey."

"Hey," she says softly, kissing me again. "How was practice?"

We release each other, but I take her hand in mine as I kick off my shoes and follow her into the living room. Her computer is on the coffee table, the screen dark. I sink down on the couch and pull her into my lap before I answer.

"Good. Everyone's feeling strong. Your brother outed us to the team, by the way."

Evie pushes on my chest and looks at me, outrage on her cute face, making me smile. "Are you serious? What did he say!"

"Just that the entire team better watch out and make sure I don't fuck up."

"Oh my God." Her eyes roll back and she reaches for her phone, but I squeeze her tightly, pulling her back into my arms.

"Leave it, it's fine. He's your brother and he loves you. That's all."

"Yeah, fine, but still. He needs to mind his own business," she says pertly, and I kiss her lips over and over until they relax under mine.

I know we need to talk, but as she kisses me, all the overwhelm and uncertainty fades into the background. This is what matters. That she's feeling good. That we're happy. Our kiss turns deeper, my tongue plunging into her mouth, chasing hers. My dick is hardening under her, and from how she squirms, I know she can feel it.

"Rhett, wait," she murmurs against my lips, pushing on my chest again.

Reluctantly, I let her sit up but not move out of my lap. "Is it important? Because I haven't had you in almost a week, and I'm dyin' to get you naked and screaming my name." I lean in and kiss the bare skin at the base of her neck.

"It is."

That makes me freeze, my lips still against her. Slowly, I lift my head and take in her serious expression. Guess we're talking now.

"Okay, what's goin' on?"

Evie's tongue darts out to lick her lips, but she looks at me straight on. "I got an interview for my perfect job."

Relief floods me and my smile is instantaneous and genuine. "That's fantastic. I knew it would happen."

Evie's nodding, but she isn't smiling back. Apparently, this isn't all good news. I don't let my smile fall, even though my chest starts to feel tight.

"It's not here. It's over on Vancouver Island, in a town called Dogwood Cove. They…they want me to interview in two days, and the job starts this September."

It's my turn to nod along with what she's saying, even as a chasm appears inside of me. Sure, Vancouver Island isn't that far. But it's not *here*. Still, I hold strong. Her future comes first.

"I'm happy for you, Evie." That much is true. "You deserve your perfect job, and I hear the island is a nice place to live."

"It is, I've always liked it when I've visited." She fidgets on my lap, and even though my emotions are not on board, good luck telling my body that. Even now, as I'm feeling all kinds of fucked, my dick is still hard just from holding her.

"I might not get the job," she hedges, and I shake my head in disagreement.

"Of course, you will. You're amazing, Evie. Smart, and kind, and the best person to do this kind of work. You'll get the job."

I can see a small smile trying to break free on her face, and it dawns on me. She's not letting herself be excited, but she is. Time to put my misgivings aside and make my girl happy.

Nothing can possibly be more important than that.

I reposition my hands to hold her better and stand up with her in my arms.

"What are you doing?" she says, a laugh in her voice.

"Told you, I want to get you naked and screaming. We've got somethin' to celebrate and I can't think of a better way. Can you?"

I'm already walking to the bedroom, kicking the door shut so Ruthie doesn't disturb us, when she answers.

"No, I can't."

Chapter Thirty-Four

Rhett

As soon as the door closes, I immediately grab the hem of her shirt, yanking it over her head. Thank fuck, her need matches mine and we scramble to get each other undressed as fast as humanly possible.

I'm trying to ignore the racing of my heart, the panic in my chest that is asking *what if this is the last time?*

It's not. I know it's not. Even if she takes the job, it's not as if she's moving immediately. We're not done yet.

There's not a fucking chance I'm done with her before I've had a chance to tell her what she means to me.

When we're both naked, we fall onto the bed with me landing on top of her. For just a second, I let myself pause and drink her in. That long black hair is fanned out, those pink lips open and desperate to be kissed. Every inch of her body, mine for the taking.

"Rhett," she whispers, her fingers stroking down my cheek. I turn to kiss her palm, then move my mouth over her soft skin, covering everywhere I can reach with desperate kisses as if I can somehow tell her how I feel without saying it. Without even knowing it myself.

I move down, her legs shifting impatiently beneath me. When I reach the juncture between her thighs, I look up her body to see her biting her lips, eyes closed.

"Eyes on me, honey."

She lifts her head with a small gasp, and I reach my hand up with a command. "Suck."

Her mouth opens, and her tongue darts out to swirl around my fingers before she pulls them into her hot, wet mouth.

"Good girl," I growl when she releases them with a pop. Without giving her any other warning, I plunge those fingers into her sweet pussy, keeping my eyes trained on hers. It's messy, and rough, and frantic, and I can't do a damn thing about that. I need to see her let go on a deep, visceral level. I need to know I can command her body, that I can bring her pleasure like no one else ever has.

And minutes later, she explodes around my hand with a hoarse cry, her fingers gripping my hair as she chants my name. Only then do I lower my head and lap up her sweetness, slowing down the thrusting of my fingers. My eyes close as I savour this moment, when she has surrendered fully to me, to what I do to her.

Fuck.

She's got me in a goddamn chokehold. I can't lose this. Lose her. But if I try to hold her back...I'll lose her anyway.

When she shudders one more time, and I sense her body go limp, I finally lift my mouth from her pussy, licking my lips.

"Mmm, Rhett, that was incredible," she says, a soft, satisfied smile on her face as she stretches her arms overhead. "Best celebration ever."

Right. She thinks we're celebrating her job interview.

"You deserve it." My voice is hoarse as I move up beside her, lying on my side so I can see all of her. I love how comfortable she is around me, fully naked and still flushed from her release.

"Y'know." I start stroking my hand lightly up and down her body, cupping her breast before traveling down again. "I just realized we kinda abandoned your lessons."

Evie's brow furrows. "What lessons?"

I lean in and cover her nipple with my mouth, laving it with my tongue before releasing it. "Your lessons in making damn sure you get all the orgasms you want, every time."

Her laugh comes out a little breathless. "I don't think I need any more lessons, you take care of that easily."

But what about when it's not me you're with? I hold back from saying that, knowing nothing would kill the mood faster. That doesn't stop me from thinking it. I place my lips over her other nipple, giving it the same attention. "Because pleasing you pleases me, honey. That's how it should be."

I grind my hard dick into her hip as proof of what she does to me without even trying.

"Oh," she moans as I lightly drag my fingers up and down her thigh. "Could I...would you want..."

I lift my head with a crooked grin at her nervousness. "Honey, the answer is yes to whatever you're trying to ask. But not right now. Right now, I need to have you." Hopefully, she can't hear the raw need in my voice. But it's the fucking truth. I need her. With a desperation that doesn't make any sense.

She moves in to kiss me, but I gather her hair in my fist and tug her back. "I'll kiss you senseless later. Right now? Get on your hands and knees for me."

Her eyes widen as she freezes for a second before complying, scrambling to turn over. When she curves her body to look back at me, I have to squeeze the base of my dick to stop from blowing all over her.

"Evie." It's all I can growl out, seeing her there, ready for me.

Her smile is full of sexy confidence as she gives her ass a little shake. "Take me, Rhett. I'm yours."

Goddamn.

I grip her hips, leaning down over her back to press kisses along her spine. A small whine escapes her as I get down to the round flesh of her ass. I grin against her skin just before biting down gently and then sucking the reddened skin.

"Are you...did you just leave a hickey on my ass?" Amused outrage colours her words, and I lift my head with an unrepentant grin to see her looking back at me over her shoulder.

"Gotta mark you so everyone in Dogwood Cove knows you're mine."

She rolls her eyes. "I'm going for a job interview. There's absolutely no reason for them to see my ass or know anything about my relationship status."

Right. Because our relationship has nothing to do with her job search.

I swallow down the unpleasant feeling that brings up. "Fine. Maybe it's so you remember me, remember this moment, every time you sit down." To emphasize, I lightly slap her ass, right over the bite mark.

Evie drops her head with a small moan. "God, Rhett."

I grab my dick with one hand and slide it through her wet slit, teasing her clit. "Fuck, you're so ready for me, aren't you?"

"Always."

"I don't know if I can be slow and sweet, honey," I warn her, nudging the tip of my dick at her entrance. "Those rough edges are ridin' me hard."

"Give it all to me. All of you."

I push into her, groaning out her name as I bottom out, my hands holding tightly onto her hips, leaving more marks on her pale skin. "So fucking good. So perfect." I move my hips back and snap them forward, making her whole body move. She drops her head to the pillow, angling her hips up for me. "You're perfect like this, Evie. Such a dirty, sexy, perfect girl."

Her moan is muffled by the pillow, her hair covering her face. I reach forward and brush it away so I can see her. I move my hand to the base of her neck as I start thrusting in and out. Her mouth falls open in a pretty little O.

"You like that? This pussy is mine right now." I grunt, then one word comes out again. This time, a growl of panicked possession.

"Mine."

"Yes." Her hand reaches around blindly, grazing my leg. "Yours."

I can't hold back. But I need this moment to last. Forever, ideally. Because when it's over, she's leaving.

Pulling out, I flip her over like a rag doll, lifting her legs up to rest on my shoulders before slamming back inside of her. She arches her back, those beautiful tits pushing up, begging for me to bite them. So I do.

Fingers rake through my hair, gripping strands so tightly I'm pretty sure I lose a few. I don't fucking care. I need her to want me just as badly as I want her. *Maybe then she'll come back and not want to leave.*

I pause mid-thrust and shake my head slightly. What the hell am I thinking? Fuck, she's scrambling my brain. I can't make her stay. I can't hold her back.

I won't be the reason she gives up her dreams.

My movements falter for a few seconds, but I focus back on the feel of her right here and now. She's with me. Under me. Surrounding me. She's here.

Out of nowhere, my orgasm hits me. No warning, no lead up, just all of a sudden, I'm shouting her name and exploding into her, feeling her body clench and pulse around me in return.

When my body finishes shuddering, I collapse onto her, feeling her hands come to my back. Her heart is racing underneath mine and there's some comfort in that. In knowing I'm not alone in how being with her affects me.

"You're kinda heavy." She giggles, and I immediately roll off her.

"Sorry."

Evie shifts onto her side, lifting up on an elbow before leaning in to kiss me. "Don't apologize. I like it, I just also like breathing."

I chuckle. "Fair enough."

She brings one hand to rest on my chest. "That was..." She trails off, and her lower lip gets caught in her teeth. I reach up and pull it free, smoothing my thumb over it.

"Yeah."

She drags a long breath in and out. "Yeah."

"Want a ride to the ferry terminal tomorrow?"

Her head moves side to side. "No, I'm going to drive. I want to explore the area a bit after my interview."

"Okay." Tension starts to creep back into me, making me feel weighed down, as if an invisible force is pushing me into the bed.

Evie studies me for a second, then another. I don't want to think about what she might see if she looks too hard. Can she see how I feel, when I'm not even sure what that is?

I force a smile and lift my head to kiss her again, threading my fingers through the tangled hair at the back of her head. "You're gonna do great."

I can feel her smile against my lips when I kiss her once more before letting my head fall back on the pillow.

"Thank you for being so supportive," she says, cupping my cheek. "It means a lot to me."

"Of course." I force out a smile. "I've said it before and I'll say it again. You deserve everything you've ever wanted, Evie. This is your dream, how could anyone not want you to get it?"

Something flashes over her face. "I mean, it's not my only dream." Her gaze drops down to where her fingers are lying against my chest. Can she feel my heart pounding?

"But it's one of them. It's a big one."

There it is again. That flash of disappointment. I'm fucking this up somehow, but I'm at a loss as to how. I gather her into my arms, and she comes willingly enough, thank God.

"Everything's gonna work out the way it should."

Her arms tighten around me as I feel her head move in a nod. Then she relaxes and lifts her head to kiss my jaw. "I hope so."

I shift down so I can kiss her lips in return. "I know so. Now you better get some sleep, honey. Tomorrow's a big day."

She gives me a small smile before rolling over and scooting herself back into my body.

Hours later, Evie's sleeping soundly in my arms. I want to hold her tighter, wrap my body around her even closer, if that were possible.

I can't shake the feeling that the ticking clock on our relationship has sped up way faster than I can control. And if I don't figure out what the fuck I'm doing, time is gonna run out, and all of this will be gone.

CHAPTER THIRTY-FIVE

Evie

"Do we need to do some positive affirmations or meditations to help you calm down?" Rhett gives me a small grin as he rubs his hands up and down my arms.

I take a deep breath in and out, exhaling on a shaky laugh. "I mean, maybe?"

I don't know why I'm so nervous about this. I've interviewed for all kinds of things, from jobs to volunteer positions to university and my master's program. But there's something about this job that feels different, that feels like it could be the start of something amazing. Even though it does mean moving away from Kai and Rhett.

But I can't think about that right now. I have to keep my eye on the prize.

"Okay, well, I better go or I'm going to miss my ferry reservation." I give him a tremulous smile and Rhett pulls me in, pressing a sweet kiss to my forehead before a not-so-sweet one to my lips.

"Remember, this is what you want. This is what you've worked so hard for. You've got this."

He backs off slightly, and I study his face. Sure, he's smiling, and on the surface I can see genuine pride and excitement for me. But there was something different about him last night. A desperation, as if he didn't want to let me go and was forcing himself to.

"Alright, I'm going," I say, more firmly this time. Then I drop down into a squat and hug Ruthie's big head to my chest.

"You be a good girl for Rhett, okay? I love you." I kiss the end of her nose and stand up, brushing fur off my pants. "Are you sure you can handle her with your schedule?"

"You betcha. Me and the little lady will be just fine," he says gently, giving me another smile.

Inside, I want to scream at him. How is he so calm? How is he not begging me to stay and wait for a different job? Even if this is only an interview, I'd like to think I'm a good fit and have a solid chance of getting a job offer.

Which means leaving Vancouver. Leaving him.

"Monty's parents are visiting for a few days and agreed to help with checking on her and walking her when I'm at the stadium. We're good here, and you'll be back in a couple of days."

I nod, knowing there's no one I'd trust more to look after my dog.

"I guess this place will feel pretty empty if Ruthie and I move to Vancouver Island," I say lightly, then immediately regret the words. "Sorry. That was silly of me to say." I look down at the floor, but Rhett's hand tilts my chin right back up.

"Damn right, it's gonna feel empty. Hell, even with Ruthie still here, it's not gonna be the same without you. We'll miss you, honey."

Then tell me not to go!

Except, I don't want him to do that. He wouldn't be the man I've fallen for if he wasn't so incredibly supportive, encouraging, and selfless.

I look at him, that easy smile on his face, and commit it all to memory. Our future might be uncertain, but in this moment, I feel lucky to be cared for by a man like him.

And just like that, my emotions threaten to overwhelm me again. Am I crazy for considering a job that will put so much distance between us, even if it is my dream come true?

"Yeah. Okay. I'll talk to you later?" I turn, blinking away the burning in my eyes.

"You bet. Call me tonight, we have an afternoon game, so I'll be home by six." His arms wrap around me from behind, and I can't help but sag into his embrace. "You're gonna knock 'em dead."

More frantic blinking before I spin in his arms, a smile plastered across my face.

"Thanks." I lift up on my toes to kiss him, keeping it short, knowing I can't hold back much longer. Then I walk out the door, down to my car, and start the drive through town that will take me to the ferry terminal and onto a boat to carry me over to Vancouver Island.

And I let the tears fall the entire way.

Several hours later, I'm all cried out and determined not to worry about my relationship and focus only on my interview for the rest of the time I'm here.

I pull into the parking lot of Oceanside Beachfront Resort and climb out of my car. When I breathe in, I inhale nothing but clean, fresh, salty sea air, and the sound of waves hitting the shore, and birds overhead.

"Wow." I take a moment to drink in the picturesque scenery. I haven't had much time to explore since moving out west, and we certainly don't have places this beautiful in Ontario.

When I confirmed the interview and started looking for somewhere to stay, I immediately fell in love with this place online. And now I'm really glad I decided to splurge on one of these adorable cabins right on the oceanfront.

It's the perfect place for a cute couples' getaway, and I can see me and Rhett walking along the beach in his offseason, relaxing with a glass of wine as the sun sets.

If there still *is* a me and Rhett after tomorrow's interview. Things are still so new, we've never discussed our future as a couple, and here I am, throwing a pretty big monkey wrench into it.

But I'm getting ahead of myself. I haven't even met my potential future employers, and I'm panicking about how to keep my relationship going if I get the job.

I take in a deep, cleansing breath of ocean air.

Rhett has been nothing but supportive of me. He's the kind of man women dream about. Heck, I dreamed about him for years, and now he's here, and he's mine. I have to trust that somehow, everything will be okay.

As soon as I'm checked in and somewhat settled, I take a seat out on the small deck that overlooks the ocean. The sight and sound of the waves lulls me into a much more relaxed state.

A few minutes later, my phone, sitting on the small, wrought-iron table beside me, starts to vibrate.

I answer his call, and despite everything, seeing his face makes me feel warm inside.

"Hi, how was the game?"

"Hey, honey. Game was great. Everything go okay on your end? You all settled in?"

I nod and stand up to show him the beach and the cabin. "Yep, this place is so peaceful." I pan the phone around, and he lets out a low whistle.

"Damn, that is gorgeous. I bet Ruthie would love the beach."

I turn the phone back around. "She would."

Settling back down in my chair, I draw my feet up and tuck them under me. On the other end of the line, I see Rhett also shift on his couch, but when he winces, I frown.

"What's wrong?"

This time, his grimace is a mixture of discomfort and embarrassment. "I'm fine, Evie. Seriously. Just tweaked my knee at the game."

He lowers his phone to show me the ice pack strapped to his left knee, and Ruthie's head resting on his lap.

"Ruthie's keeping me company, and the trainers figure I'll sit out tomorrow but then be fine."

"Sounds like more than a tweak if they're not letting you play," I protest.

"Nah, it's nothing. Really. This knee's been buggin' me for a while, and it just didn't like the way I moved today. Don't worry about me, honey." He gives me a reassuring smile, and I settle back into my chair.

"Well, I'm sorry you're in pain and I'm not there to help."

"That's sweet of you, but it's all good. Me and Ruthie got this."

Just as he finishes talking, I let out a big yawn.

"You've got a big day tomorrow. Time for bed?" He gives me a tired smile of his own. "And I'll talk to you tomorrow after you're all done."

"Do you still have to go to the stadium even if you're benched?"

"Yeah, I'm meeting with the trainers first. They'll put me through some rehab movements and see how things are doing. Then I'll watch the game from the dugout. But text me anyway? I want to know how it goes, and I'll call as soon as I can."

I nod. "Okay, sounds good."

"And Evie?" His smile falters slightly, into something endearingly nervous. "There's somethin' for you in the top of your bag. Open it when you're ready for bed?"

My own smile grows wide. "That's going to be absolute torture, you realize that? I want to go and open it now."

Rhett chuckles and shakes his head. "Nah, promise me you'll wait."

"Okay. I promise."

"Night, Evie. Sleep well, and good luck tomorrow."

"Goodnight, Rhett."

I make myself stand up and go inside, grabbing the sandwich I packed to eat as a light dinner, sitting down on a chair that looks out the window. I eat slowly, letting my thoughts drift like the waves against the shore outside.

But my curiosity — and impatience — get the better of me.

When I unzip my bag, telling myself it's because I want to head to bed early and relax, I see a folded piece of paper, but I force myself to set it aside until I finally climb under the covers. I stare at the paper, debating whether I should prepare myself to swoon, or to have my heart ache.

"Stop being an emotional chicken, Evie," I mutter to myself, and unfold the paper, only to have a photograph fall out. It's a print of Rhett holding Ruthie, and I have no idea when he took the picture, much less got it printed. But seeing the two of them makes me miss them both, even though it's only been a handful of hours since I saw them.

The printing on the accompanying note is messy, but I can read it. Still, it makes my heart ache to see the evidence of his dysgraphia and to think about how he must have struggled in school. And now, because I can see how painstakingly hard it must have been for him to write this out, along with the fact that he went to that effort and didn't type it, means more than I can say.

Before I even start reading, tears build in my eyes. This is why I'm here. To find a job that will allow me to help kids flourish, regardless of their abilities.

> *Evie*
> *Today is a speial day. Today you follow your*
> *dreams. Iam prod of you. but I will miss you as*
> *well. Cant wait till we see eachother soon.*
> *Love rhett*

Love.

I stare at that word for a long time.

I love him. I love Rhett Darlington. And in that moment, I can't figure out why the heck I'm here, interviewing for a job that's not close to him. But then Vivienne's words about not holding myself back because of him filter through my mind.

They also mix with my mom's words about following my heart.

And to make things even more complicated is the deep-seated uncertainty swirling in my gut. Because the uncomfortable truth I have to accept is that all the uncertainty I'm feeling is at least partly my own fault.

I've let Viv's words weasel their way into my mind, making me doubt myself and Rhett unfairly. I've held back from telling him how I feel; I haven't told him I want a future with him. And a part of me, the part that was hurt four years ago when he pushed me away, has been so scared of being pushed away again, that I've held back, waiting for him to give me some sort of sign that he wants me as much as I want him.

Except I've been blind to all the signs he *has* been giving.

And this note has ripped away the blindfold, making me see things so much more clearly.

I'm in love with Rhett, and I want a future with him. And that starts with me saying just that. Only then can we try to find a way forward, together, regardless of what happens tomorrow.

With that in my head, and his note on the table beside me, I climb into bed and somehow manage to fall into a deep, dreamless sleep.

Chapter Thirty-Six

Evie

The next morning, I pull into the parking lot of Dogwood Cove Elementary School, a clean and bright building with a big playground, a community garden, and a large playing field. My email said to meet Reid Corser, the principal, outside the main doors, so I lock my car and make my way there just as the door opens and a tall, dark-haired man walks out with an easy smile on his face.

"You must be Evangeline?" he says in a deep voice, stretching out his hand.

I nod, taking his hand in a firm shake. "Yes, but call me Evie. And you're Reid?"

"You bet. Thanks for coming over, we're really excited to meet with you."

"Of course, I was honoured to be asked to interview." I follow him into the quiet school, empty for summer break. Hopefully I sound like a competent professional and not a brand-new graduate interviewing for her first real job. I swallow down my nerves as he leads me to what's obviously the staff room. Two others are waiting there, and Reid makes introductions.

"This is Ranjit Singh, the superintendent for our district, and

Kora Sanchez, the special education teacher over in Westport. We're lucky to have the budget for our own special ed teacher for the two Dogwood Cove schools, but you'll primarily be based here at the elementary school, which is why I'm sitting in on the interview panel," Reid explains as we all take our seats.

Everyone around the table seems warm and welcoming, making me feel at ease. "That's wonderful, so many districts are having to cut back on their supports for children with diverse needs. It's good to hear that's not the case here." I give them a broad smile. "Helping children reach their full potential, regardless of their backgrounds or learning styles, is all I've ever wanted to do."

Over an hour later, Reid walks me back out of the school. My heart is going a mile a minute, and I don't think I could stop grinning if I tried.

"Evie, I have to say, you're perfect for this job."

Inwardly, I'm cheering at Reid's words, but I outwardly maintain my composure. "That's great to hear, thank you."

We reach my car, and Reid puts his hands in his pockets. "I shouldn't say this, but I suspect we'll be in touch very soon with a formal offer. I think you'd be a great addition to Dogwood Cove. We're a small community, but we've got plenty of amenities, and the people here are wonderful. My friend Ethan is the town mayor and owns a bunch of rental properties. I'm sure he could hook you up with an apartment if needed."

I'm still reeling from what he said about a job offer, so much so that I barely hear what else he's saying. All I manage is to nod along.

"Make sure you take some time to check out the town if you

can. The main square has a great bakery that Ethan's sister owns, The Nutty Muffin. Best muffins around, if you ask me."

"That sounds wonderful, I'll make sure to check it out before my ferry."

Just then there's a rumble of thunder overhead. Reid and I look up in surprise to see dark clouds in the distance.

"Huh. Looks like that summer storm they predicted is coming in earlier than expected."

"Does that happen often over here?"

Reid shakes his head. "Not any more than on the mainland. But it shouldn't cause a problem. As long as it doesn't get too windy, the ferries will still run so that you can get home."

A fat raindrop lands on the sidewalk in front of us and Reid chuckles. "Right, better get going. Nice to meet you, Evie. I'm sure we'll be speaking again soon."

We shake hands, and Reid turns to jog back inside just as the rain starts to pick up.

Chapter Thirty-Seven

Rhett

Sleeping in my apartment without Evie feels wrong.

Which is to say, I didn't sleep much at all last night.

Sure, I can also blame it on my knee, which aches like a son of a bitch. But really, it's the fact that my bed still smells like her, even though her side is cold and empty. I even tried to coax Ruthie up, but she's missing her mom as well and spends most of the night whining in her crate even with the door wide open.

I'm grumpy as fuck, tired, and sore. I take Ruthie out, feed her, and mainline a cup of coffee, all in my pajamas, without a care for who might see me.

After I eventually get out of the shower, I pick up my phone to see if there's a message from Evie, but the screen is annoyingly blank. I'm sure she's busy prepping for her interview, but still.

"Fuck."

Did she see my note and the photo I left for her last night? Did she cringe at my painfully messy printing? Or did she see it for what it was — me wanting her to know how much she means to me.

Ruthie yips, then barks louder when there's a knock on my door. Frowning, I limp my way over and look through the peephole before unlocking it in a hurry.

"Mama? What the hell are you doin' here!"

My mom steps inside, leaving her suitcase in the hall, and flings her arms open wide. "Surprise!"

Ruthie barks and bounces at our feet as I pull my mom in for a crushing hug. "What is goin' on?" I say, my face hurting from my smile. I draw back and look down at the woman who raised me. "Damn, it's good to see you, Mama, but why didn't you tell me you were coming? We were on the phone two days ago, you should'a said something!"

"And miss out on surprisin' you? Where's the fun in that. Hold on, what's Evie's dog doin' here?" She crouches down to pet Ruthie, laughing when the puppy manages to land a lick on her chin. "Well, you're adorable, aren't you."

"Her name's Ruthie," I say, scratching my head as she straightens. "Evie left for Vancouver Island yesterday for a job interview, so I've got the puppy."

I don't say that the puppy *and* Evie have actually been staying here for weeks. But a quick glance around the apartment tells me it won't take much for my mother to figure it out. The book she was reading is still sitting on the coffee table, a pair of her shoes are by the front door, and she still has a lot of her stuff in the spare bedroom. Might as well come clean. I never could hide things from my mama.

"Actually, ah, well, Evie and Ruthie," — I gesture to the puppy who's been distracted by her toy in the living room and is whipping it back and forth with her teeth — "they've been staying here this summer. Kai can't have pets in his apartment."

"Evie's been stayin' here?" Mama raises her eyebrows. "You

better be acting like a gentleman, Rhett Darlington."

I step behind her to grab her suitcase, and so she can't see the heat climbing my cheeks. "'Course I have been."

"Good."

Just then, the alarm on my phone goes off. "Shit, I gotta go. I have a session with the trainer for my knee." I gesture down with a grimace. "Tweaked it yesterday. I won't be playing tonight, but if you want to come watch the game, I'll leave a ticket for you."

"No, that's okay, honey. I'm tired from the flight. You go, take care of that knee, and we'll catch up soon." She waves me off just as Ruthie comes bounding back over. "I'll take a quick nap, then spend some time with this beautiful girl."

"Okay, if you're sure." I move to the closet and grab my bag and shoes. "And when I get back, maybe you can tell me what made you decide to come all the way here without tellin' me?"

This time, Mama's the one to blush. "Can't a mother want to see her favourite son?"

"I'm your only son, nice try."

"Fine. I wanted to surprise you and say thank you." She gives me a knowing look. "You know what for."

I smile and pull her in for a hug. "It was nothing, Mama."

"Paying off my darn mortgage is not nothing, and you know it. But go, and when you're back, I'll make us a late dinner and we can talk."

I lean in and kiss her cheek. "It's good to see you, Mama."

She reaches up and pats my cheek in return. "You too, Rhett."

With that, I head out the door, and drive to the stadium. My thoughts drift to Evie, as I realize she'd be in her interview right now. I'm sure it's going well, which brings up all kinds of mixed feelings.

I want her to be happy. And successful.

I also want her to be here. Not there.

And I need her to be here *now*, so I can figure out how to tell her that.

But I want her to be there, getting her dream job.

I want it all. And somehow, we're gonna have it.

Chapter Thirty-Eight

Evie

Instead of heading straight back to my cabin on the beach, I take Reid's suggestion and head to the center of town. As I drive slowly down the main street, I feel as if I've been transported straight into a movie or feel-good sitcom. There's a large green town square with a bright white gazebo in the middle of it, dotted with large trees. And along the streets are businesses with bright awnings and signs.

I see the bakery Reid mentioned, and a café right next door. There's a bookstore, a dance studio, and so much more. It's the type of town I'd love to explore over a lazy weekend, but the rain coming down outside ruins that idea for now.

Besides, if Reid's serious and a job offer is coming, I'll have plenty of opportunities to get to know this adorable town.

By the time I get back to Oceanside and dash inside my cabin, the wind is whipping around outside, making me more than a little concerned based on what Reid said about the ferries. My boat home is scheduled to leave in about two hours, so with some trepidation, I open the website to see if I'll be making it home tonight.

"Damnit," I curse when I see the sailing has been canceled

pre-emptively. Of all days, why today? I don't want to be stuck here alone. I need to be home, so I can talk to Rhett and tell him how I feel. Hopefully, we can figure out our relationship before I get a job offer that could change absolutely everything.

I could call him, but the conversation we need to have isn't one for over the phone. But I will take the time to send him a text about the ferries, even knowing he won't see it until after his game. I don't want him to worry. No sooner have I pressed send on my message does my phone light up with an incoming call from the front office of the resort.

"Hello?"

"Hi, Evie? It's Summer, over at the front desk." The owner's voice is cheerful and warm. "I wanted to check in. I know you were meant to leave today, but did you know the ferries were canceled?"

"Yes, I just found out. I don't suppose I could stay another night?"

"Of course. That's what I was calling to offer. And if you need something to eat, I can send someone over with one of our premade picnic lunches. We got a fresh delivery today."

"That would be amazing, thank you so much."

"No problem. Have a good night."

I breathe a sigh of relief and gratitude for her generosity. With that taken care of, all I can do is wait out the storm.

I curl up on the comfortable chair that faces the large front window looking out over the stormy ocean and call the one person I can count on to help me make sense of everything.

"Hi sweetie, how are you?" My mom's smiling face fills the screen.

"Hey, do you have a minute?" I tug a blanket over my legs.

"For you, always. Where are you right now?" She squints, and I realize she must see the bed in the background of this one-room cabin.

"I had a job interview today." I pause as she makes a surprised sound. "But it's over on Vancouver Island. I rented a cabin last night, but my ferry home got canceled, so I'm staying a second night. There's a crazy storm right now."

"Oh! Well, I'm glad you have somewhere to stay. But tell me more about this job!"

I tell her about the town, about the interview, and about Reid's comment regarding me likely getting an offer soon.

"Honey, it sounds absolutely perfect for you," Mom gushes. "I'm so proud of you."

"Thanks."

Her head tilts to one side, and her brows draw together slightly. "Why don't you seem thrilled about this? Is it Rhett?"

My chin drops to my chest. "Yeah," I say in a small voice before lifting my head. "But also no."

Mom just waits, smiling patiently at me.

"He's been nothing but supportive ever since I found out about the interview. Almost too supportive." I pause, realizing how crazy I sound. "I appreciate it, don't get me wrong. But I guess..."

"You wanted him to ask you to stay in Vancouver."

"Is that stupid of me?"

"No, sweetie. Not at all."

I tug the blanket up higher, my gaze drawn out the window to the dark grey sky, rain splattering against the glass. "I keep remembering what Viv said, about not holding myself back because of him. Or anyone, I guess. But…"

"But you love him."

I turn to look back at my phone. "How did you know?"

"Oh Evie, I've been your mom a very long time." She chuckles. "And I've seen you around Rhett ever since Kai first brought him around. It might have started as a harmless crush, but when you were all here to see Oba-chan, it was obvious things had progressed."

"For me, maybe," I say miserably. "But I don't have the first clue how he feels."

"Well, have you told him how you feel?"

I blow out a loud breath. "Yeah, no. Not exactly."

"It's a universal fact that most men are terrible at sharing their feelings. Especially if there's a chance their fragile hearts might be hurt. You have to be the brave one, Evie."

"But what if he does love me? How can we be together? Am I meant to give up my dream job for him?"

"You don't think you can have the job and Rhett?" Mom looks at me again with that look. The one that says I'm missing something obvious. It's the same look she used to give Kai when he was searching for something that was right in front of him.

"I don't see how that would be possible," I reply honestly.

"Don't you think Rhett deserves the chance to try and figure that out with you? If that's what you both want?"

"I guess so."

"I know so. You can't make decisions for him, nor can you make decisions without having all the facts. You know that."

I'm quiet for a minute, absorbing her words. Then my head

slowly starts to move up and down. "You're right. I can't." I give her a shaky smile. "Thanks, Mom."

"I'm always here for you. And I'm so proud of you. You are an exceptional young woman, and you deserve all the happiness."

After we hang up, I stare out the window for a while longer, turning over everything she said in my head.

Could I really have everything? Can I be with Rhett somehow, and still take this job if it's offered to me?

Can I have all of my dreams come true, or is that just a fantasy?

I won't know until I talk to Rhett, and I can't do that tonight.

But there is one more person I can talk to while I wait it out.

When my sister answers my call, I can tell she's nervous.

"Hello?"

"Hi, Viv." I'm proud of how calm and steady I sound. "How are the boys?"

"They're fine, but they're already in bed. Sorry you missed them."

My heart aches knowing my own sister doesn't think I called to talk to her. Then again, with how we left things in Ontario, maybe I shouldn't be surprised. "I didn't call for them."

"Oh."

"Viv —"

"Evie —"

We both start, then stop and laugh. "You go first," I say.

"Thanks. I really want to apologize for how I was at the hospital. I stand by what I said, but Mom and Kai have both told me my delivery sucked." She lets out a pained laugh. "And I guess they're not wrong."

"Thank you for apologizing. I didn't like hearing what you had to say, and yeah. It hurt. But you should know, you were right. I was holding myself back for Rhett."

I hear her intake of breath, but instead of letting her speak, I push on. "I was — no, I am — so happy with him, I didn't want to let anything come between us, not even my dream job. You helped me see how foolish that would have been."

"Following your heart isn't foolish," she interrupts, and this time I let her. "But you can have both. You deserve a good guy and your dream job. You deserve everything."

I smile, even though she can't see it. "Funny, Mom said almost the same thing."

"Well, you should listen to her. Not me."

We both let out a quiet laugh. "Thank you for always watching out for me, Viv. Just, next time you need to say something, maybe be a little nicer about it?"

"Deal."

We chat for a few minutes longer, and when I hang up, I feel lighter than I have in days.

I know my way forward.

Which means, I need this storm to clear, and fast. Then I can calm the storm inside my heart and head as well.

Chapter Thirty-Nine

The skies are grey when I pull up at the Tridents stadium, and it matches my mood. Stormy and grumpy.

But two hours later, when I finish with the trainers, I take a look outside to see rain pelting down.

"Game's canceled," Monty calls out as he comes strolling down the hallway, Lark by his side. "Coach and Mike just announced it. This storm is only gonna get worse. They're even predicting lightning."

"Shit," I say, glancing down at my phone for the first time since this morning. Sure enough, there's a message from Evie. I press play and hear the electronic voice read out her message telling me her ferry has been canceled.

"Fucking hell."

"Hey, what's wrong?" Monty and Lark come to stop beside me.

I stuff my phone back in my pocket with a frown. "Evie's on the island for an interview and her ferry home got canceled." My teeth grind together. "And my mom decided to show up for a surprise visit."

"I thought you liked your mom," Monty says. "And I'm sure

Evie's fine."

"I love my mama. I just wasn't expecting her to be here. Evie's stayin' where she is, so yeah, she's fine, but I..." I don't finish my thought. Because telling them that I hated sleeping in my own bed without her feels wrong.

"But you miss her." Lark gives me a knowing smile, and I give a brusque nod in return.

"Sure. And I wanna know how the interview went."

Monty still looks bewildered. "So call her."

Lark shoves him gently. "Dan."

"What?" He looks from her to me, shrugging. "If I've learned anything recently, it's to not wait to tell people how you feel. If he misses Evie, he needs to tell her that."

"I mean, that's not terrible advice," Lark says with a laugh, looking back at me. "Go home, visit with your mom. Then call Evie and tell her you miss her."

"Yeah." I stuff my hands in my pockets. "I guess."

They start to walk past, heading toward the parking lot, when Lark calls back at me over her shoulder. "And rest that knee!"

When I get home, I unlock my apartment door, calling out, "Mama? Game got canceled, so I'm home for the evening."

"Wonderful. Maybe you can explain this." Mama walks out of my bedroom holding the tiny pair of sleep shorts Evie uses.

"I figured Evie would be in the spare bedroom, so I went to take a nap in your bed. Imagine my surprise to see two toothbrushes next to the sink, and I'm pretty sure these are not your size." She sets the shorts down on the edge of the couch and puts her hands on her hips. "Seems like Evie might be more than just a roommate."

Oh. Shit.

Chapter Forty

Rhett

Shit, shit, shit, shit, shit.

"Y'see, um. Well." My face is bright fucking red as I look everywhere *but* at my mom. It's not as if she doesn't know I have sex. I'm a grown-ass, red-blooded, American man, for Christ's sake. But she's never once come across evidence like this. And for it to be Evie, someone she's known for years, feels doubly awkward.

Mom breaks the stare, laughing at my obvious discomfort. "Oh Rhett, bless your heart. I'm just teasin'. You and Evie are adults, and I trust that I raised you right and you're being respectful. I ended up napping in the spare room." Mom smirks as she sits down at the end of the couch. Ruthie immediately hops up and drapes her long body over her lap. "Now. Sit down and talk to your mama."

I sink down at the other end, taking a few slow breaths to try and settle my embarrassment. "I'm still sorry you had to figure it out like that. I shoulda been honest from the start."

Mama waves her hand. "It's fine. But tell me, is it serious? It better be, if you're messin' around in the bedroom."

I shift in my seat. "I really do not want to be discussing my bedroom activities with you, Mama. Respectfully."

"Do you love her?"

I freeze.

"Rhett?" Mama leans forward. "Son. What's going through that handsome head of yours?"

I swallow around a suddenly dry throat. The week my dad died, I remember sitting by his bedside, listening to him talk. During one conversation, he told me to never settle for anything less than the love he and Mama had for each other. I was just a stupid, selfish teenager at the time, and love was the last thing on my mind. I just wanted to figure out how to graduate from high school and make it to the big leagues.

Now I find myself wishing I had asked him how the hell I would know if I ever found that kind of love. Maybe then I'd be able to answer Mama's question.

"I don't know."

Mama rears back, surprise on her face. "I must admit, that is not what I thought you'd say. I was very much gettin' the feeling she was the one."

I let my head fall back against the couch as I slump down, staring at the ceiling, one hand going to scratch Ruthie's back. "How the hell would I know?"

"What on earth do you mean?" Mama sounds so legitimately baffled by my question, I turn to look at her.

"How would I know if she was the one? I've never been in love, never had feelings like this for anyone. You always said you and Dad were soulmates, but what does that even mean? How did you figure that out? Everyone says it'll just happen, but how? How am I meant to know if Evie is *the one*?"

"Oh honey." Mama's face falls. "You've been waiting for some big sign, thinking it'll be coming from somewhere other than inside of you." She shakes her head. "Your daddy and I failed you, I guess, if we let you believe falling in love was like that. It isn't, Rhett. It doesn't come from anywhere but your heart. Sometimes, love means wanting nothing more than to see that person happy. It means doing the little things you know will bring a smile to their face. It means nothing feels better than their hugs. It means pushing through the hard times because the good times are worth fightin' for." She lifts Ruthie off her lap and moves next to me, taking my hand in hers.

"Your father and I, we loved each other very much. I knew he was the one for me. But not because there was some magical moment or big, clear sign that we were meant to be together. I knew because he made me feel safe and happy every day. Because my heart, when I really stopped to listen to it, told me there was no one else I wanted to spend my life with."

"Evie makes me feel safe," I say quietly, returning to staring at the ceiling. "She sees me, Mama. She sees past me playing baseball, past me not being able to read. She doesn't just see who I am on the outside. She sees who I am on the inside."

"Then she's a lucky woman. Because you're an amazing man on the inside, and on the outside. And I'm not just sayin' that as your mama."

My hand lifts to brush away a tear. "Fuck." I turn with a wince. "Sorry, Mama."

She waves me off with her free hand. "It's fine. Sometimes big emotional revelations need a curse word or two."

"But how can she be the one if she's gonna leave me for this job?" I quietly voice the fear that's been making my stomach twist for the last twenty-four hours.

"Because if she matters, then you'll find a way to make it work."

"You make it sound so simple."

"It can be, if you let it." Mama pats my hand, then settles back on the couch. "Try listening to your heart instead of your head."

I try to do just that. And for a second, all I hear is the rain coming down outside, hitting the window. Until the voice in my heart finally gets loud enough to be heard over the pounding of my heart.

"I love her, Mama."

As soon as I say it, there's a flash of lightning, followed by a boom of thunder. And then we're plunged into darkness when the power goes out.

"Glad you figured it out, son, but did your *sign* have to be so dramatic?"

The next morning, Mama informs me over coffee that she's going to stay in a hotel for the remainder of her trip. "You and Evie need time to talk, and you don't need your mother hovering. But tell that young lady to come and sit with me at the game tonight, y'hear?"

"Yes, ma'am," I say with a grin, bending down to hug her tightly. "Thank you, Mama."

"I did nothin' except get through your thick skull to make you realize what you already knew. Same thing I had to do with your daddy plenty of times."

I chuckle. "We know where I get my hardheadedness from."

"And your softheartedness." Mama cups my cheek. "You're a good man, and Evie's a lucky lady."

"Thanks." I cover her hand with my own. "Come over for breakfast tomorrow with me and Evie?"

"I'd like that," she says with a smile. "Now you make sure to hit the ball hard for me tonight."

"Straight into the outfield," I promise with a grin.

After she leaves, I tidy up the apartment, including the incriminating sleep shorts that are still on the arm of the couch. Even once that's done and laundry is on, I can't sit still. I'm too tightly wound, and Ruthie is picking up on it, judging by how underfoot she is. "C'mon, let's go for a run, little lady."

Mindful of my knee, I take it slow and easy on a short jog around the neighbourhood to try and get my mind to settle. Evie hasn't been in touch since her message telling me about her ferry being canceled, and I'm reluctant to reach out simply because it would be impossible not to blurt out the fact that I love her.

And she deserves more than just an impulsive text.

Besides, my head keeps spinning, trying to come up with a way to make it work if she gets the job. Which I'm sure she will.

When I get home, I take a quick shower and start gathering things that I'll need later. I'm not due at the stadium for a couple more hours, and I'm not sure how I'll last that long without spontaneous combustion.

It's as if saying the words *I love her* last night released the pressure on a valve I had tightly shut. And now it's exploding out of me, uncontrollable.

I'm on the floor, working through a set of fifty push-ups, when my phone vibrates. I collapse down, stretching my arm up to fumble it off the coffee table.

It's a message.

From Evie.

For once, I don't make my phone read it out to me. I open the message, needing to see her words for myself, even if it takes longer than I want it to, just to read one short message.

> **EVIE: On the ferry now, be home soon. We need to talk.**

My heart fucking sinks. Then she sends another.

> **EVIE: I can't wait to see you.**

There's a heart emoji, and my sinking heart flip-flops and starts to lift. Goddamn. I need time to hurry the hell up. A glance at the clock tells me she should be home before I have to leave.

I don't waste a moment trying to type, instead dictating a quick response.

> **RHETT: Same honey I'll be here waiting**

My brain snags on one word. *Home.* She said she would be home soon. Does that mean Vancouver, or does that mean here with me?

I don't want to read too much into it, but my heart lifts just a little more.

And I drop back down for another round of push-ups.

Chapter Forty-One

Evie

I'm nervous riding up the elevator of Rhett's building. The door opens on his floor, and I step out slowly. Considering how impatient I felt on the ferry ride over from the island, I'm surprised I'm not sprinting down the hall to see him.

But the anticipation I felt over telling him about Dogwood Cove and the job, and about finally telling him how I truly feel about him, has faded into an anxious tension thrumming through my veins.

There's a chance he won't return my feelings. A good chance. He said from the beginning he wasn't the guy for more than just some fun. Was I the one that pushed for more and he simply went along with it? I want to trust my gut that says no, Rhett's so much more than just a man I have ridiculously good sex with. I want to trust him when he says I mean a lot to him.

But I'm still just a girl, hoping the boy she loves will love her back.

And that's kind of scary.

I reach the apartment door, and I can hear Ruthie's claws on the floor inside and the deep rumble of Rhett's voice.

Somehow, those sounds, so familiar and comforting, settle

me.

I insert my key and open the door to see Rhett on the floor, facing away from me.

"C'mon, girl," he says in a frustrated huff, then his head whips around when the door closes behind me. "Evie!"

He stands up quickly, his hands behind his back. But my attention is drawn down to Ruthie who's racing across the floor, a big red bow halfway tied around her neck.

"What's this?" I say, bending down to love on my puppy. Her sloppy kisses make me giggle as her entire body shakes and wriggles with excitement. "Why do you look so fancy?"

I stand up and look at Rhett. He's staring at me, a small smile curling the corners of his lips. "Hi."

"Hey, honey." We stay like that for a second. And then, I don't know who moves first, but we come together in an instant, lips crashing, hands grasping.

"Fuck, I missed you," he growls between kisses. "It was only two days, but it felt like forever."

"You've been gone longer before," I reply as his lips travel down my throat. "But I missed you, too."

His head lifts, and all the frantic desire comes to a standstill. "I have been gone longer. But that was before." He lifts his hands up to cup my face, their span wide enough that his thumbs can rest on my cheeks while the rest of his hands are holding my neck.

"That was before I realized I'm in love with you."

My gasp is swallowed up by his kiss. And as my body starts to melt, he scoops me up in his arms, turns, and sets me down on the dining table. I wrap my legs around his waist and pull him in even closer.

He loves me.

He's in love with me.

"Wait," I try to say, pushing feebly at him. "Wait. Stop." Rhett tears himself away, his breathing ragged, those brown eyes wild.

"I don't care what you're gonna say, honey. I love you. Doesn't matter where you get a job, I'll still love you. Even if you don't love me back yet, that's okay, I'm not goin' anywhere. I'll work hard every goddamn day to deserve you and I'll wait for you to love me, too. Just don't say you don't want me —"

I cut off his frantic rambling with a soft kiss, feeling his shoulders drop away from his ears.

"Stop talking, Rhett Darlington. It's my turn."

His forehead lowers to meet mine as we take in a breath together.

"You are more than enough for me, and you deserve this love, this happiness. And you don't have to do anything to make me love you. I already do. And I have for a long time."

"Thank fuck," he exhales just before his lips land back on mine.

I let him kiss me for a few more seconds before pushing on his chest again. "I'm not done."

He nods, pushing his hair back. "Right. Sorry. I just... You..."

"I know. But let me finish. The interview was amazing. That town, the job, it's perfect. I loved it." I watch him draw in a breath and hold it. And I know he's waiting for the hammer to fall. "But I'm not going to take it. Because it's missing some-thing. *You.*"

His breath falls out of him in a loud groan. "No, honey, you've got it all wrong."

I lean back, my brows drawing together. "What?"

"You have to take the job." He takes my hands in his, squeezing them tightly. "You said it, it's perfect. You loved it. And I love you. So take the job. We'll make it work. I don't know how, just yet, but we'll figure it out. Because that's what you do when you love someone. You do whatever is necessary to make them happy and help them see their dreams come true. Vancouver Island isn't all that far. We can do this."

"But..." I start to say, then stop, studying his earnest face. "Really? You mean it?"

He nods emphatically. "I do, honey. I'm not goin' anywhere. Move to the island, hell, move across the country. I'll follow you as soon as I can. But no matter where you go, I'm not losing you, Evangeline Yamaki. Not when I finally have you." He kisses my hands that he's still holding on to.

A smile starts to break free on my face as I let myself consider the impossible. Having both the job of my dreams and the man of my dreams.

Then an alarm goes off on Rhett's phone.

"Fuck." He leans in and kisses me swiftly. "I know I said I'm not going anywhere, but I actually do *have* to go. To the stadium. Or I'll be late. But take the job, Evie." He kisses me again. "And then come to the game and watch it with my mama."

"Wait, she's here?" I look around the apartment, but there's no sign of his mother.

Rhett laughs. "She was. She got a room at a hotel for the rest of her surprise visit after finding your pajamas in my bedroom."

"Oh my God." My face flames red as I pull my hands free to cover it. "That's mortifying."

Rhett gently lowers my hands. "Nah. She's happy for us. She's the one who got through my thick head and helped me realize just how desperately in love with you I am."

That makes me melt.

"So come to the game and you can thank her in person." He winks and steps away, just barely moving out of reach of my hand as I try to swat him.

He picks up his bag and moves to the door before pausing. "Oh, and Evie?"

"Yeah?" I hop off the table and move over to him, reaching up for one more kiss.

"There's somethin' in the bedroom for you. Wear it later, okay?"

I'm still floating on cloud nine a few hours later when I walk in the special entrance for family and friends of the players at the Tridents stadium.

Wearing a jersey, not with Yamaki on the back, but with Darlington.

"Evie!"

I turn at the sound of my name and see Willow Lawson walking toward me. Dressed in a Tridents green blouse, dress pants, and low heels, she's the perfect balance of professional and chic. As she should be as the head of media relations. I don't know her well, but Rhett and Kai like her.

When she pulls me in for a brief hug, I'm initially taken aback, but quickly give her a squeeze in return.

"I'm happy to run into you," she says brightly, gesturing down the hall. I fall in step beside her as she continues. "I wanted to make sure you knew that if you need anything, just ask. Now that your relationship with Darling is out there, it's only a matter of time before the media catches wind. If anything feels uncomfortable, just come to me and we'll help, okay?"

All I can do is nod, my brain still processing that. Somehow, I hadn't thought about the public side of dating a professional athlete. Being Kai's sister has never put me in the limelight, but being Rhett's girlfriend? That might be different.

"Thanks, Willow," I manage to say just as someone calls her name. She glances over her shoulder in the direction of the voice and raises her finger.

"Great. And hey, you should come out for drinks with me and the girls soon. I'll text you!"

She's gone with a wave, and I turn to find my way to the seat marked on the ticket Rhett left for me. I know I'm about to see his mom, who I haven't seen in a couple of years. And while he claims she's happy for us, I'm still nervous.

But as soon as I find her, a few rows back from the dugout, that nervousness disappears.

With a wide smile so similar to her son's, Jolene stands up and pulls me in for a tight hug. "Evie, it's so good to see you again." She holds me by my shoulders, looking me up and down. "Love suits you."

I blush as we take our seats. "Thanks." She pats my leg and leans into my side.

"Now, don't blush on my account. I'm thrilled you and my son have found your way to each other. He needs a good woman to give all that love he has in his heart."

I relax. "He's a wonderful man."

"Yes, he is."

The top half of the first inning passes by quickly, with our opponents only getting one run in. When the teams switch over, Rhett is second up to bat. And as I watch him take some swings in the warm-up circle, my phone vibrates in my lap. I chance a quick look down and see it's an email.

From the superintendent of the school district in Dogwood Cove.

With the subject line *Formal offer of employment.*

My palms instantly feel sweaty. I know what Rhett said, that we'd make it work. But that was before I even knew if I'd get an offer, no matter how confident Reid was that I would.

"Everythin' okay, Evie?" Jolene asks. I nod without even looking her way.

"Rhett's up to bat," she says, and my head shoots to the big screen as I watch him walk up to the plate. He turns to look in our direction, and right there on the jumbotron, I see him smile. Then he points his bat down, resting the tip in the dirt, and slowly writes something in the middle of the box.

R+E.

It's clear as anything on the giant screen, and the entire stadium goes wild, even more so when he looks back at me and winks.

"Oh my," his mom murmurs as I blink back tears. "He's got it bad."

Around us, people are talking excitedly. It's not hard to figure out that the girl with tears on her face, wearing Rhett's name, might be the girl he just dedicated his swing to.

And when the bat connects and the ball goes flying straight to center field, we all cheer on his home run.

But no one cheers as loudly as I do.

Chapter Forty-Two

Evie

Jolene tells me to say goodbye to Rhett for her and that she'll be over for brunch tomorrow before giving me a hug and heading back to her hotel.

I make my way down to the hall outside the locker room to wait for Rhett, nervously bouncing on my feet as I reread the email from the superintendent.

> Evie,
>
> I'm pleased to extend a formal offer of employment to you for the position of Special Education Teacher at the Dogwood Cove schools.
>
> You impressed everyone at your interview, and we feel confident you'll be a perfect fit for our team and the kids of Dogwood Cove.
>
> Please be in touch at your earliest convenience to go over particulars, including a small stipend available to offset the cost of moving to town. If you'd like to be connected with someone to assist with finding housing, just ask.

We're all looking forward to working with you.

Best,

Ranjit Singh

"What's got you so excited?"

I glance up from my phone to see three women approaching. Willow, a redhead I'm pretty sure is dating another player, and Lark, with one hand on her very pregnant belly.

"The boys won, isn't that reason enough?" the redhead says, smiling in my direction. "Hi, I'm Sadie, not sure we've officially met. You're Kai's sister, right?"

I nod, but before I can explain my other connection to the team, Willow beats me to it.

"And she's dating Rhett," she says, raising her eyebrows.

"Oooh, dating the brother's best friend! I love it," Lark says, clapping her hands.

"Lark's a new convert to reading romance," Sadie comments.

"Blame Willow's best friend. Have you read her latest?" Lark turns to me excitedly. "Her bestie is Starla Barrows. Her books are so freaking hot." She fans herself.

My mouth falls open at the casual drop of a very popular author's name. Turning to Willow, I stumble over my words. "Really? Starla Barrows is your friend?"

Willow shrugs. "I mean, I call her Tori, but yeah. She lives in Dogwood Cove over on the island with her son and boyfriend."

Wait. That means, if I take the job, I'll be living in the same town as one of my favourite authors. As if that offer could get any better.

The door to the locker room opens then, and the guys start

spilling out. The volume and energy are high as they're all celebrating their win. I smile at a few of them before Kai reaches my side.

"Hey Gigi, did you see that fourth inning? Damn, my arm was on fire." He actually lifts his bicep up to kiss it before hugging me, and I roll my eyes.

"Yeah, yeah, you were great." I hug him back, only for him to push me away, an insulted look on his face.

"Evangeline. What are you wearing?" He spins me around forcibly and gasps. "How dare you!"

"Settle your ass down, Yami." Rhett's slow drawl reaches me at the same time his arm snakes around my waist, pulling me from Kai's grasp. "She looks better wearin' my number anyway." With his free hand, he tips my chin up to kiss me softly.

"She's a Yamaki, she should be wearing my name," Kai protests, but his eyes betray him, showing he's not that upset.

"I'll wear whichever dang jersey I want to, thank you very much," I reply, shoving my brother's shoulder. "But good game, Kai."

I let him pull me in for another quick hug. "Thanks, sis. See you kids later, be good!" With a wave and a bro hug for Rhett, he jogs down the hall after a couple of the other guys, no doubt heading out for some fun since they have the day off tomorrow.

"You ready to go?" Rhett asks, his voice low. "Do some celebrating of our own?"

I look up at him. "Yes." I take a deep breath and continue. "Because we can also celebrate me getting the official job offer."

Rhett lets out a whoop before sweeping me off my feet and spinning me around. Laughing, I swat at him. "Put me down."

He does, only to lean in and kiss me deeply. And without a hint of hesitation or anything other than pure joy, he says, "I'm so damn happy for you, honey."

We move to the exit, Rhett's arm draped over my shoulders. He says goodbye to everyone we pass, players, staff, even janitorial staff. Rhett's got an easy smile for everyone.

Once we're in his truck and headed home, he turns to me at a red light, squeezing my thigh. "So when do you start?"

"I haven't said yes yet. But if I do, they'll want me there before the beginning of the school year." To my shock, Rhett doesn't reply, but he does immediately put on his turn signal and pull his truck over to the side of the road before putting it in park and turning in his seat to face me.

"What the hell do you mean, you haven't said yes?"

He actually sounds shocked, which has me leaning back in surprise. "I only got the offer earlier, during the game, and I need to think about it. We need to talk about it."

"Evie, there's nothing to talk about. That job is exactly what you want and I told you we'd figure it out. Didn't you believe me? Because I sure as shit meant it. Take the job. I'm not goin' anywhere."

I unbuckle my seat belt and climb over the middle console to squish myself onto his lap, kissing every inch of skin I can find. "I love you," I mumble in between kisses.

He kisses me back just as frantically for several seconds before holding my face and leaning back slightly. "And I love you. So damn much. Trust that, and trust in us. Okay? We'll be fine, even if you're not in my bed every night."

Tears well up in my eyes, and he kisses each one as they spill down my cheeks. What did I do to deserve all of this? To deserve him?

"I might not be there every night, but tonight I will be. Take me home."

When we get back to the apartment, anticipation crackles between us. But instead of ripping at my clothes or tossing me over his shoulder like I kind of want him to, Rhett gives me a gentle smile and a kiss on my forehead.

"I'll take Ruthie out."

All I can do is blink at him as he clips on her leash and disappears out the door. It only takes me a minute to realize I've got an opportunity to surprise him.

Rushing down the hall, I head straight to the bathroom for a quick clean up and to brush my teeth. I stare in the mirror, fluffing my hair. "Why bother?" I laugh to myself, knowing that not only will the straight black strands never fluff, but also, they'll just get messed up when Rhett's back.

At least, I hope they will.

Oh, who am I kidding. They totally will.

In the spare bedroom, I dig through one of the boxes I haven't unpacked since moving in here and unearth a couple of candles. I set them out in Rhett's room and light them. The flames flicker across the walls as I start to feel even more excited.

We've had sex many times. But tonight, we'll make love.

He won't be gone long, so I quickly strip off all my clothes — except for his jersey and climb onto the bed. My timing couldn't be any more perfect, as I've no sooner settled back against the headboard when I hear the front door open and close. I can make out the sound of Rhett getting Ruthie settled back in her crate, and while I can't make out what he says, his warm, low murmurs of affection toward her just make me love him even more.

Then he's here, one hand on the upper frame of the doorway, leaning against it and looking far too sexy as his hooded eyes take me in.

"Damn, honey." His voice is like caramel running over gravel, a perfect combination of sweet, sexy, rough, and ready. I'm speechless, and a little bit breathless, as he prowls over to the bed, slowly peeling off his own clothes until he's down to just his tight black boxer briefs. Then he climbs onto the end of the bed, lowers his head, and begins to kiss me, starting with my feet, then moving up my legs, alternating from side to side.

It's slow, sensuous torture, trying to stay still and not pull him up to where I want him. When he finally reaches my upper thighs, I can't hold back anymore. My hands go from clutching the duvet beside me to his muscular shoulders.

"Rhett."

He lifts his head at my whine and gives me a devilish smirk. "I'm takin' my time and you can't rush me."

His southern drawl is somehow even more pronounced, and I swallow back a whimper as his big hands slowly push his jersey up, baring me to him.

"You're a fucking goddess, Evie. And I plan on worshipping you all night."

He kisses my belly button, and I suck in a breath as I feel his tongue drag up my stomach. Then suddenly, he's looming over me, those brown eyes burning into me, lit up from the flames of the candles. "I love you."

I reach up for him and pull him down to my lips, kissing him. "I love *you*."

His body settles over me, not in a crushing way, but more like a comforting weighted blanket. A very *heavy* weighted blanket, with a rigid part pushing into me, the annoying fabric of his underwear not doing anything to hide the heat pulsing from him.

"I want to take my time, but —" His voice is ragged, and my lips turn up in a smile.

"We've got forever for that. I need you now."

Silently thanking the grappling techniques learned from years of practicing Aikido, I manage to get my feet up around his waist and hook my toes into the waistband of his underwear. He lets out a startled laugh when I push them down, freeing his cock at last.

"Now that's a party trick."

With a smug smile, I decide to show him another one. It's easy enough to hook my legs around him and push on his chest. Of course, this isn't strictly from Aikido, and if Rhett wanted to, he could prevent me from flipping him. But this benefits us both, and he goes easily enough until I'm straddling his hips, the jersey settling back down.

"As much as I love seeing my name on you, this has to go." Rhett lifts the offending garment up and over my head before chucking it to the floor and bringing his hands to my hips. "That's better. Now get on up here and gimme a taste."

"What?" I sputter in confusion as he pushes on my ass.

His hand lands on my ass in a swift slap. "I need to feast on that sweet pussy of yours. So. Get. Up. Here."

Oh. Well, then.

I must take too long to respond, because suddenly Rhett's strong arms are lifting me and forcibly moving me up his body. I grab the headboard to stabilize myself, but then he's tugging me down, and his tongue is on my pussy, and every other thought in my head disappears.

He dips in and out of me, teasing along my slit. My hips rock back and forth across the rough stubble of his face. I become aware of a keening sound and it takes a second to realize it's me. I'm making that sound, lost to the pleasure Rhett is wringing from my body.

"Fuck, Evie. You're drowning me in your sweetness." His words are a rumble that I feel more than hear against my sensitive skin, and it's almost — *almost* — too much to handle. But just as I'm about to push his mouth away, Rhett lets his teeth graze across my clit before he sucks it between his lips and hums, and I explode.

I hope to God I never meet his neighbours because I can't hold back. I'm desperately clutching at his head, my legs are shaking, and I'm shouting his name as wave after wave crashes through me. And Rhett's strong hands are there the entire time, holding me, easing me through the most intense orgasm of my life.

When I start to crumple down on him, he tugs my body down, so that instead of collapsing on his head, I do so on his strong, hot chest.

"My God, I think I just died," I mumble into his pec.

His laughter vibrates underneath me. "Hope not, because I'm nowhere near done with you."

Chapter Forty-Three

Rhett

Evie's eyes are closed, her pink lips turned up in a deliciously satisfied smile as I roll us over so that I'm over top of her again.

I look down her body, this gorgeous, perfect woman who's all mine, noting the reddened skin between her legs from my stubble with a primal, possessive smile.

I wanna mark her all over.

She's mine. Forever. Wherever. No matter what.

I lean down and kiss her, knowing full well that she can taste herself on my lips, seeing as her juices are all over my face.

"Mmm. Taste how sweet you are." I push my tongue into her mouth when she opens under me. For a woman who started out feeling so unsure about herself, about sex and pleasure, she certainly has turned into a bold, sexy, dirty girl. And I fucking love that it's all for me.

I rub my jaw along hers, noting how her skin turns dark in the candlelight. *Mine.* I want to be mad at myself for taking so damn long to get to this point. To realizing that all along, she's been right here in front me. The one woman for me. My soul mate, my partner, my love. But the energy it would take to be mad is better spent loving her.

Lifting one of her legs up, I encourage her to wrap it around my waist before taking my cock and lining it up with her plump pussy. "I'm never gonna want to stop lovin' you, Evie. Never."

"Good," she whispers back, her eyes shining with pure, unfiltered love.

I push into her slowly, but without stopping, until my hips meet hers. All I can do is stare at her, at this woman I love.

I fucking *love* her.

Her body pulses around my dick, squeezing it tightly, as if to say she'll never let me go.

Good.

I pull back slightly, then push back in. Then again, farther this time, in a longer thrust that has Evie's head going back, her chest arching up and her hand bracing against the headboard.

My mind chants three words in time with the rhythmic thrust of my hips.

I. Love. Her.

And when I can't hold back any longer, that mental chant comes out of me, and I find myself lowering down to whisper it over and over in her ear as I pulse inside of her, feeling her walls clench in response as she, too, loses herself.

When my body stops shuddering, I roll us to the side, staying inside of her even as my dick starts to soften. I'm not ready to lose this connection yet. Evie snuggles into my arms with a contented hum, and for a moment, I close my eyes and thank God, the universe, anything and everything for giving me this.

"That was incredible." Evie's voice is more than a little breathless.

"Sure was. Every time with you gets better and better," I say, kissing the top of her head.

She squirms a little in my arms and looks up at me. "I think I need to clean up, though."

"Right. Just…" I squeeze her in tight again. "In a minute?"

Her soft sigh is all the permission I need.

Eventually, we get out of bed, only to get right back in a few moments later. I lie on my back and Evie cuddles into my side. "So, I should say yes to the job?" she asks in a small voice.

"You absolutely should." There's no hesitation in my response. I know it'll hurt, having her move away, but this is what's meant to be. I know that.

I gesture at her to pass me her phone. She does, and I find the email from the school in Dogwood Cove. Turning to her, I raise my eyebrow. "Just don't go fallin' for some small-town guy over there. Got it?"

She giggles, shaking her head. "I already fell for a small-town boy. A southern charmer. And I happen to love him."

"Good answer." I kiss the tip of her nose, then I turn back to the email. It takes a while, but for once, I don't feel embarrassed at how slowly I type as I write out what I hope is an appropriate response, accepting the job. When I'm done, I hand the phone to her. "Here, you better edit it." I give her a wry smile. "Words aren't my strength. But you're takin' that job, so you can help other kids do better than me."

She lifts one hand and places it on my cheek. I turn and kiss her palm as she says, "You do just fine with your words, Rhett Darlington."

A moment or two later, she presses send and puts the phone down. "Done." She turns her big eyes up to face me. "I have a job."

I roll on top of her and stroke her hair away from her face. "Hell yeah, you do, honey. Congratulations."

Then I spend the next hour showing her exactly how proud of her I am, and how much I love her.

The next two weeks go by far too fucking fast, and then it's time for Evie to move.

"Where do you want these?" I ask, holding the stack of T-shirts I just finished folding. Evie looks up from the floor where she's zipping a suitcase shut and sighs.

"I forgot about those."

I glance down at them, then at her. "Yeah, sorry, they were in the laundry with my stuff."

She stands up and comes over to take them from me before setting them on the bed and then tucking herself in for a hug. "Don't apologize. I'm going to miss having my laundry mixed in with yours." A pained laugh escapes her. "God, that sounds pathetic."

I kiss the top of her head, letting my lips rest there for a second. "No, it doesn't. I'm gonna miss the little things, too. Your hair clogging my drain, Ruthie's toys everywhere, your — *ooof*."

Her smack on my stomach reassures me I've managed to turn the moment of sadness around. Even if I do mean every word.

"You know, you could leave some stuff here." I've been waiting for the right moment to suggest this. "A toothbrush, some clothes, whatever. For when you come to visit."

Evie steps back, keeping her hands on my hips, and looks at me with a wobbly smile. "Yeah? I could, I guess."

I nod firmly. "You *should*. Maybe even leave some of your favourite things so you're motivated to come back a lot."

This time, her laugh is a lot more genuine but still tinged with sadness as she throws herself back into my arms. Her words are muffled against my chest. "Don't you realize I *am* leaving my favourite thing here? Unless you can fit in my suitcase."

"Ah fuck, Evie," I mutter as I tip her chin up and kiss her deeply. She has to leave for the ferry in an hour, and I can't even go with her since the team is shipping out shortly after for an away series. And this time when I get home, she won't be here waiting for me. She'll be in Dogwood Cove.

We don't have time for me to make love to her again, no matter how much I want to. But there is time for me to give her one thing.

Reluctantly, I pull away, but only so far as to grab my phone off the dresser. I open the calendar app and tap a few buttons. Seconds later, Evie's phone vibrates with a notification.

"What's that?" she asks, leaning down to pick it up off the floor.

"Take a look," I say, not filled with nerves, but anticipation. Hopefully, she's excited, and hopefully, she sees this for what it is. My effort to prove to her that we'll make this work.

"Rhett..." Her mouth falls open, and her eyes start to glisten. "These are float plane bookings."

"Every weekend I'm in town, I'm flying you back Friday night to be here. And whenever I have more than a day off, I'm heading over to you. If you get a longer period off, I'll fly you to wherever I am. But these here, these are booked and paid for. We won't have more than a few weeks between seeing each other at the most, honey. And when the season's over, I'll come stay with you." I pause and swallow. "If that's what you want."

She looks up at me and tosses the phone on the bed before leaping into my arms. Thank God for my reflexes. I catch her and turn us around so I can sit on the bed as she peppers my face with kisses. "Of course, it's what I want, you silly man. I want you as often as I can have you. This is amazing. Thank you."

We kiss for several minutes. Needy, desperate ones. I know I'm not alone in wanting to commit every second with her to memory to help get me through the times when we're not together. But the alarm I set to make sure we didn't get distracted and make her miss her ferry goes off, and we have to pull apart.

I reach over with one hand to turn off the alarm before turning on my side and tucking her back into my body.

"I don't know if I can do this," she whispers.

"'Course you can. You're so strong, and brave, and this is everything you've been working toward. You can do this, because you're not doin' it alone. I'm right here with you."

I feel her take a deep breath and exhale it slowly.

"I love you so much." Her hands tighten around me. "And I'm going to miss you." Her voice cracks on the last word, and then I feel the moisture seeping into my shirt from her tears.

"I'm gonna miss you, too, honey. You've got my heart now. Take care of it, okay?"

Her head moves in a jerky nod, and I tip her chin up so I can kiss away her tears before placing one last soft one on her lips.

"I love you, Evangeline Yamaki. A little bit of distance won't change that."

Chapter Forty-Four

Evie

I reread Rhett's message for the thousandth time. The typos tell me he took the time to type it out himself instead of dictating, and that just makes it so much more meaningful. Every day, he somehow manages to make me feel beyond loved, beyond cherished, in the littlest of ways that are no less significant than some grand gesture would be.

From voice memos and selfies to a surprise flower bouquet waiting for me when I arrived at my rental two days ago, he's making sure I know how much he loves me.

It doesn't make me miss him any less, however. Even Ruthie has taken to pacing the small furnished apartment we're staying in, whining as she obviously wonders where he is. She slept on the bed beside me last night, and while there was some comfort in having her next to me, I wish it was Rhett.

But today is the first day of my new job. And the halls of Dogwood Cove elementary are full of the sounds of children laughing and chattering, teachers greeting students, and all the happy, noisy chaos of an elementary school full of bright minds.

My schedule today is light. All I have to do is pop into the classrooms to introduce myself and lay eyes on the children that will make up the bulk of my caseload for the year. There's a staff meeting after school, and then I'm free for the evening.

"Hey Evie." Reid sticks his head into my office just as I'm finishing hanging a string of lights on the wall.

"Hi."

He leans against the door frame and looks at what I've done to the space. "This is awesome, very welcoming." He gives me a grin. "Wanted to check in, see how you're doing, but also see if you had a chance to touch base with Jackson?"

Right, the town veterinarian, one of Reid's friends. I swear, it seems everyone knows everyone around here. "I've got an appointment with him next week for Ruthie's checkup. Thanks for the recommendation."

"Of course." He pushes off the door and turns to give a high five to a kid who's walking past. "See what he thinks about Ruthie becoming a therapy dog. He's a good judge of animals, and I think the kids would love having her around."

My mouth falls open in shock. "Really? You'd be open to that?" When I brought up the idea of a therapy dog as a future resource in my interview, I hadn't been thinking of Ruthie specifically. She's still so young and rambunctious. To say nothing of the fact that I figured I'd have to prove myself as a professional before attempting to add that in.

"Yeah, definitely. It's a solid idea. But we need Jackson's approval, and she'd have to go through training, I'm guessing.

Keep me posted, okay?"

I nod eagerly. "I will. Thank you."

Reid leaves and I sink into my office chair. How does this job keep getting better? The only thing missing is a six-foot-something baseball player with soft brown hair who gives the best hugs in the world.

Glancing at the clock, I see I have a few minutes before I'm due in the kindergarten class for the next round of students that are coming in for their gradual entry. Picking up my phone, I send a text to Rhett.

> **EVIE: Guess what! The school wants me to see if Ruthie would make a good therapy dog. That means she could come to school with me and help support the kids!**

I'm not expecting a reply, since if I remember the schedule correctly, he's got practice today and a game tomorrow night. But to my surprise, he replies almost immediately.

> **RHETT: She'd be awesome at that can't talk right now love you**

> **EVIE: Love you too!!!!**

I set my phone down, my cheeks hurting from the wide smile on my face. Hopefully he doesn't get in trouble for dictating a quick message at practice.

The rest of my first day flies by, and before I know it, I'm saying goodbye to my new coworkers after our staff meeting.

I've just closed my office door when I overhear two voices

from down the hall.

"You know who that is, right?"

"He's from the Tridents, isn't he?"

No way.

I pick up my pace until I'm almost running toward the front doors. I push them open and there he is, casually leaning against his truck, holding an enormous bouquet of flowers. There's a massive smile on his face as he opens his arms wide just in time for me to crash into him.

"You're here? How are you here!" I say, hugging his neck tightly, breathing him in. "Oh my God, you're here!"

"Of course I am. I couldn't miss my girl's first day." His voice is thick with emotion as he holds me, my feet dangling off the ground.

Eventually, he sets me down, only to take his free hand and cup my chin, bending to kiss me.

A throat clearing behind us makes me step back, and it's then I realize I was basically mauling my boyfriend in the school parking lot.

Crap.

"All the students are gone, but still, we need to keep things professional at work, Evie." Thankfully, Reid's voice is more amused than condemning.

I'm red with embarrassment when I turn around, but then Rhett reaches one hand out from behind me. "Sorry 'bout that. Won't happen again, promise. Just wanted to surprise Evie. I'm Rhett."

"Reid. And I know who you are. Good game last night." Reid shakes his hand then looks back at me. "Have a good evening,

Evie. Rhett, nice to meet you."

Once he's gone, I turn back to Rhett and drop my forehead to his chest. "Oh my God. That was mortifying."

Rhett's deep chuckle is comforting, as is the hand he runs up and down my back. "Sorry. Couldn't help myself."

My head lifts. "Don't apologize, I was just as much to blame. I still can't believe you're here. Don't you have practice?"

He presses a swift kiss on my forehead. "Coach let me skip it to be here today. I gotta go back for the game tomorrow, though." Holding the door to his truck open, he gestures at me to get in. "I'll bring you back for your car tomorrow on my way to the ferry."

I can't stop staring at him as he pulls out of the parking lot. He's really here. For me. He skipped practice for me. "I love you," I blurt out. "Like, so much."

Rhett glances at me with a soft smile, his hand coming to rest on my thigh. "I love you, too."

I point out where to turn, but instead of listening, Rhett drives straight. "No, you have to turn back there," I protest, only getting a squeeze of my thigh in response. Then he turns in the opposite direction from where my apartment is at the next intersection. "Where are we going?"

"You'll see."

A couple of minutes later, we pull up in front of an adorable little house with an honest-to-God white picket fence. The house itself is pale blue, with darker blue shutters, a tidy yard with a flower bed, and a wreath on the front door.

Most importantly, there's a "For Sale" sign out front.

Rhett parks right next to the sign and turns off his truck.

"What are we doing here?" I ask, my head bouncing back and forth between looking at him and looking at the house. "Rhett?"

"Do you wanna take a look inside?"

"I want you to tell me why we're here."

He just laughs. "Isn't it obvious?"

Maybe it is, but I'm scared to say it. What if I'm wrong, and the ridiculously happy kernel of hope bouncing around in my chest is crushed.

Rhett reaches over and runs his thumb over my lips, freeing the bottom one I hadn't realized I was chewing on. "I was thinkin', if you like this place, you could stay here, not in that rental. That way, Ruthie gets a yard to play in, and there's space for family to come visit."

"I can't afford to buy a house," I whisper, still not daring to let myself believe this is happening.

"But I can." He smiles softly. "And I want to."

"Here?"

"If this is where you are, then yes. I know I've got to finish my contract with the Tridents, but maybe then, I don't try to sign another. There's more to my life than just baseball now. There's you. And I want a future with you. A home, a family, all of it."

Love, happiness, joy, it all slams into me in waves that have me laughing and crying and scrambling to undo my seat belt so I can hug him.

"Oh my God. Oh my God! Rhett!" I kiss him over and over as he pulls me into his lap right there in front of our future home.

Eventually, he pulls his head back, his eyes dancing with excitement. "So that's a yes to takin' a look inside?"

"That's a yes to everything. To a future, to a home, a family, everything, as long as it's with you."

"There's no one else for me, Evie. You're my girl. Forever." He leans back in for another kiss.

"Forever sounds good to me."

Epilogue

Rhett

Two Years Later

I drop my hands onto Monty's shoulders with a whoop. "How 'bout that, Monty! Champions!"

Moving between him and Lark, I drape my arms over their backs.

"That last run, Darling, that was amazing," Lark says, hugging my side. I'm only sorta paying attention to her, my gaze scanning the crowd, looking for the one person I really want to celebrate this win with.

I spot Evie with Yami and their parents, standing with my mom just as her gaze finds me.

"Yeah, thanks, Lark."

My friends are forgotten as I push through the crowd to my girl. I scoop her up and spin her around. "We did it, honey."

"That was incredible, Rhett." She's hugging me so tightly, and this right here might feel even better than winning the championship. Being in her arms is where I want to spend the rest of my life.

And that starts now.

I set Evie down and turn to my mom. "Hey Mama," I say,

taking in the tears on her face. "Don't cry." I pull her in for a hug.

"Your daddy would be so proud of you."

Well, shit, here come my own tears. I can feel Evie's hand on my back as Mama and I rock back and forth, equal parts celebrating and grieving. Eventually, she pulls away and wipes her eyes. "I'm so proud of you, son."

"Thanks, Mama."

Kenji and Helen are next, congratulating me on the win. Then Kenji pulls me to one side and in for another quick hug. He slaps my back lightly and says, "Welcome to the family, Rhett," he whispers and I stiffen slightly.

"I haven't asked her yet," I say quietly as we separate, but he gives me a knowing smile.

"She'll say yes." He subtly passes me the ring box he's kept safe this week.

Having his confidence in me, and his blessing over me and Evie, means a lot. No one could ever replace my own father, but knowing I'll be the lucky guy who gets to call him father-in-law is pretty damn great.

I find Evie again and pull her through the thinning crowd until we come to a stop just past third base. Out in left field, the position that defined my entire professional career.

"Any regrets about announcing your retirement?" Evie asks, twining her arms around my neck.

I glance down at the grass, then back at her. "None at all." I lean in and kiss her before reaching up and unclasping her hands. I draw them in front of me, pressing them to my chest. "Baseball is my past and I'm lookin' at my future."

All the sounds and chaos around us fade away as she takes in a sharp breath, watching me drop to one knee right there in the grass.

"Oh my God," she says, her eyes shining with unshed tears.

"Evie, for two years, you've had my heart. And I've never felt safer or more loved than with you. I don't know how I lived life without you or how I didn't realize you were my everything right from the start. Because being with you has made my entire life, my entire self, better in every possible way. All I ever want is to be the man you deserve. And that alone makes me work to be a better man, every single day. Our journey started the day you moved into my apartment with the puppy you found on the side of the road. And I want our forever to start today. Will you spend your future with me as my wife?"

She's already nodding, those tears now free-falling down her cheeks. "Of course, I will. A thousand times yes. Yes, yes, yes!"

I pop up and swoop her back in my arms again, both of us laughing and crying. Then I hear the cheers of our friends and family surrounding us. Ignoring all of them, I set Evie down, and with shaky hands, pull the ring free from its box and slide it onto her finger.

"Guess it's official, then?" Yami comes up and hugs us both. "I'm losing my teammate but gaining a brother?"

"Guess so." I laugh, hugging him back.

"Those Little Leaguers don't know how lucky they are."

I slap his shoulder affectionately. "Thanks, man." I'm excited to start working as the head of player development for the Mid-Island Little League next spring, helping the next generation of baseball players grow and develop their skills. Who knows, maybe one day, one of them will be standing here, on a field, having won the championship.

They still won't be as fucking lucky as I am, to be surrounded by the best teammates a guy could ask for, his family, and the love of his life.

Evie's been swept up by our moms, and I move over to stand behind her, wrapping my arms around her and pulling her back into my chest.

She lifts her hand up and admires her ring before twisting her head to look up at me. "Is this real life?"

I lower my head to kiss her forehead. "It better be, because it's everythin' I never knew I could dream of."

Someone shouts that it's time to get off the field, but I ignore them, turning Evie in my arms so I can kiss her again.

Hell, I never want to stop kissing her. And now that the season's over, I can move into our house in Dogwood Cove, we can start our life together, and I can kiss her good morning every day, and make love to her in our bed every night.

Yeah, this future, our future, is better than any dream could be. And it's time to start living.

Our southern charmer and his best friend's little sister get up to some spicy shenanigans at the ball field in their extended epilogue. Get it now by signing up for my newsletter by scanning this QR code.

ACKNOWLEDGEMENTS

I've been looking forward to writing this book for months. Rhett stole my heart when he first walked onto the page, and I couldn't wait to share his story. I like to draw inspiration from real life, and Rhett is no exception.

One of my kids has dyslexia, ADHD, and anxiety. He is so very smart, creative, sweet, courageous, and funny. He has so much to offer the world, just as Rhett does. Loving someone with neurodiversity is incredibly rewarding. Watching them when they struggle, can be painful, but when they overcome their struggle? It's an honour to watch them shine. If you have someone in your life who is neurospicy, or like me and my kid you are yourself, you are amazing and the world deserves to know you.

However, capturing Rhett's essence as an adult with dyslexia was not always easy. I have ten years of parenting a child with dyslexia but I knew it would be different for someone like Rhett. I have to thank my dear friend Carly for helping make him authentic, from writing his text messages the way she would herself, to using her training as a therapist to me understand his emotions. And of course, since I'm the farthest thing from a southerner you could possibly be, his accent and linguistic mannerisms were made possible by the very talented and true southern girl Kait.

Thank you as always to my team, Carolina, Erica, Kelly, and of course editor Chris. To Kari and Jane for creating the perfect covers. To Roxie and Theresa for keeping me sane. To Chelle for making sure I didn't mess up the baseball aspect. And to my family, for being by my side this entire time.

ALSO BY JULIA JARRETT

<u>Dogwood Cove</u>

Always and Forever

Rumours and Romance

Work and Play

Truth and Temptation

Then and Now

Passion and Promises – A Collection of Dogwood Cove Novel-
las

<u>The Donnellys of Dogwood Cove</u>

Dare To Kiss You

Hate To Want You

Pretend To Love You

Promise To Marry You

Dare To Marry You- A Donnellys of Dogwood Cove Holiday Novella

One Night To Win You

The Vancouver Tridents

Break The Rules

Fake The Game

Catch Her Heart

Steal A Kiss
Curve Into Forever

About Julia Jarrett

Julia Jarrett is a busy mother of two boys, a happy wife to her real-life book boyfriend and the owner of two rescue dogs, one from Guatemala and another one from Taiwan. She lives on the West Coast of Canada and when she isn't writing contemporary romance novels full of relatable heroines and swoon-worthy heroes, she's probably drinking tea (or wine) and reading.

For a complete listing of Julia Jarrett books please visit www.authorjuliajarrett.com/books

<u>Follow Julia:</u>
Instagram @juliajarrettauthor
Facebook Reader Group: Julia Jarrett's Nutty Muffins
TikTok @julia.jarrett.author